WINNERS

a novel by Eric B. Martin

WINNERS

a novel by Eric B. Martin

MacAdam/Cage

MacAdam/Cage
155 Sansome Street, Suite 550
San Francisco, CA 94104
www.macadamcage.com
Copyright © 2004 by Eric B. Martin
ALL RIGHTS RESERVED.

Library of Congress Cataloging-in-Publication Data

Martin, Eric, 1969–
    Winners / by Eric B. Martin.
      p. cm.
    ISBN 1-931561-92-3 (alk. paper)
    1. Title

    PS3563.A7236W56 2005
    813'.6—dc22

                                        2004014852
Manufactured in the United States of America.
10 9 8 7 6 5 4 3 2 1

Book and jacket design by Dorothy Carico Smith.

for Meredith

1

H E WAKES QUICKLY, reaching for her as the world collapses. The room is creaking in its wise, wooden joints, and the bed shivers and bucks beneath them. He holds her, wraps her small naked body in his arms like a soldier covering grenades. A jolt of consciousness rips through her as she awakes.

"What!" she blurts out, "what what?" She jerks upright, terrified, pushing his hands away. Her body coiled to fight and flee at once.

"It's okay," he says. He sits up and puts one hand against the wall, making sure that's true. He touches her shoulder to calm her, he hopes.

"I thought," she says. She pulls the blanket up to cover herself. "Someone's in the house," she whispers.

"No." Shane listens. The apartment is absolutely still and quiet. Through the open windows, he hears nothing outside in the unusual warm night. No sirens, no footsteps, no barking or crying in their neighborhood of thin infants and chubby dogs. "An earthquake," he says.

"Oh." She lets out an enormous breath. "Jesus, you scared me to death. Feel my heart. It's not a big one?"

"No. Just a little baby."

"I always miss everything." Her breath should be appalling but it's not. She slides back down into the belly of the bed, nuzzles into his arms. He kisses her hair, her forehead, the corner of her eye. "An earthquake," she whispers, taking his wrists and pressing his hands against her body. "How romantic. Are there songs? What time is it? I have to sleep."

"I don't know."

"I was having five dreams at once."

He rolls on top of her, holds his body up so she can barely feel his weight. She doesn't move much, wrapping one limp arm over his back, humming with mild pleasure and fatigue. He doesn't last long. It's been a while. He lies back flat staring into blackness while she drapes her body across his side, breathing slow and deep.

"Five dreams," he says. But she's already gone. He wonders if she'll remember. He lies there feeling her breathe and waiting for a sudden movement: a twitch of sleep, an earthly shiver, an aftershock. Shake, he thinks. Why not open your mouth and swallow us all up.

At 6:45 he's in the van, headed for an unpromising address. The radio sings chipper rise and shine, a look at traffic and weather coming up, no mention of the quake.

He's driving through a no-man's land between Hunter's Point and China Basin and the Mission. The streets lose their names in here, split by old railroad tracks, confused by loading docks and staging areas and grimy fencing. A place subject to antique directions: turn right at the car wash, left at the broken camper van. Every year he visits one or two of these guys, oddballs dug into the last unregulated cracks of the city, with only a wood- or coal-burning stove for heat. They open a phone book (probably old and yellow and out of date). They find his father's original ad (a quarter page, in green and black). There are other ads, but a particular kind of person sees this one and must respond. In the ad, for thirty years, a jolly looking man with broom and tall hat has been dancing atop the roofs of the hilly city. Green flames belch from a chorus line of chimneys behind him. These people take one look at jolly-man and call him up. They tell him where they live and ask if he can clean their chimney.

"Sure," Shane tells them. "Seven o'clock all right with you."

"In the morning?"

"I've got a slot."

"Shit. You got an early-bird discount or something?"

"We'll work something out."

His dirty-chimney early bird lives in a land of trucks, an ugly, functional part of town that houses grunt support for the dazzling prime time city. Disposal, storage, delivery, repair. His wife never comes here: no restaurants, no stores, no meetings, no parties. No startups.

This side of town still spits and bleeds, eats fast food, wolf whistles. But its time will come. China Basin, South of Market, Dogpatch, the east edge of the Mission—all these places were once garages and workshops and parts stores, peppered with broken windows and empty lots. Ruled by contractors, craftsmen, Mexicans, mechanics. Import. Export. In his not-so-distant youth those were true blank spaces off the map, where the winds puffed their cheeks and blew and big serpents floated nasty in the squiggly sea. Now every ugly-duckling inch of it has turned valuable, active, pending. Even in this neighborhood without a name, he looks around and wonders: how much longer will this go untouched?

The homey directions lead him to a sliding, chain-link gate in front of a concrete lot of motorcycle carcasses. To the north, one of the city's great hills rises steeply into the morning light, although this is not an angle he's paid attention to before. Potrero Hill. He stares at the slope of pastel rectangles, the barracks-style housing projects spaced up and down in little boy blue, princess pink, mint Disney green. Their surprising orange roofs set the hill on fire—orange, of all things, a brief morning dream of Spanish tile and Mediterranean show. He doesn't know yet that Sam's home is up there. He doesn't know that he will be walking beneath those orange roofs tomorrow.

He shakes the gate gently. "Hello?"

A large dog rounds the corner briskly to investigate. The dog has rottweiler in him, shepherd, maybe a little

Lab, some lethal combination that belongs behind a chain fence in a neighborhood without a name. It fixes a bead on him, accelerates, and smashes its muzzle against the fence, howling through large and fulvous teeth. He stands back and waits as the owner early bird appears, limping heavily.

"Shut up, Roach," Early says. "That's my doorbell." He glances past Shane to the van: Ford Econoline 250, 1977. Shane's dad bought it used in '79. Old but the body's good, very little rust, and there's a new engine, transmission, seats, struts. Tires, bumper, paint. There have been many reasons and opportunities to buy something newer, but the van has history now and Shane understands it and has always liked its shape. It is, he believes, the kind of van everyone secretly hopes will arrive when they call a chimney sweep.

"D'you go to Washington?" Early says, suddenly.

"Yeah." Shane tries to recognize him.

"The basketball player, right? My little brother was on the team," Early explains. He says the name and a face leaps up from the past, a tall boy with bad skin picking his ear at the end of the bench.

"How's he doing?"

"Ah, he's alright," Early says. He shrugs and opens the gate, content to leave it at that. The dog watches and waits, ready.

"Gonna tear me up?"

"Nah. Just let him sniff you, no problem."

Shane holds still while the dog trots up and nudges

its nose jauntily against his crotch, flipping his balls from side to side.

"That's a lot of faith," Shane says. "That he isn't going to bite my dick off."

"He don't like dick. Roach never ate anyone I didn't want him to."

Inside, the warehouse is filled with motorcycle guts. Hoses, wiring, engines, handlebars, clutch plates, gas tanks, exhaust pipes. At the back a living area opens up, the makeshift plumbing exposed in clear tubing low along the walls. A wooden ladder climbs to a small makeshift sleeping loft. It's how Shane imagines his brother Jimmy would like to live.

"You want some coffee?"

Shane shakes his head, eyeing the cast-iron stove that sits at the end of the room in the wide bowlegged stance of a pit bull. The L-shaped stovepipe plugs into an industrial-sized chimney that juts out from the wall. This was a factory once. Chances are, the chimney is original.

"So uh. How'd you end up doing this?"

"Family business." Shane shrugs, smiles, lets Early know it seems a little strange to him too.

"Seem like a good gig, though. All those chimneys. Working for yourself, that's the only way to go."

"Definitely."

Shane pops the pipe out of the wall, trying to work some grip into his hands and shake off that familiar morning weakness. Inside the dark hole, he can see the undersized bricks. Original, then: no one's built with them since the twenties. Early stands too close behind him, peering over his shoulder. Most of Shane's clients have never looked inside their chimney before. They don't think of it as possible but once he shows them otherwise they can't seem to get enough. They realize that's where secrets live, in the trunk of the house, where you can count the rings and read history aloud. If you speak chimney. If you know what chimneys mean.

The brick is old but it looks good. Years of burning wood in here, dirtier than coal but less acidic, easier on brick. Big fires. Not a warehouse—something happened here, once upon a time, something needed to stay warm. Shane reaches in and touches the creosote, collected like coral in a thick double helix as far as he can see. He gives it a pinch. Rock candy.

"How long you been in this place."

"A while."

"Used to be a factory?"

"Got me."

"Great space."

"Yeah."

"Is it yours?"

"Own it? Fuck." Early shakes his shaggy head. "Just waiting for that knock on the door. Some dot-com dildo, you know: 'What are you still doing here?' I'll just be like, 'Yeah I know asshole—I been expecting you.' Game over." Early raises his eyebrows, turns his palms up to say, *You know what I mean.* Shane does, although his wife confuses things. Maybe we'll be rich, she says. It's happening to people like them, to companies like his wife's. Across town, up the hill, she's starting to stir right now, stretching her arms out wide, clinging to the bed like she's climbing a cliff. Does she remember? Maybe she'll remember suddenly, midmorning, at the office. Maybe she'll come home early tonight.

"You feel that quake this morning?" Shane says. Even a five point could be good for him, a city of cracks, his own little boom. The chimney is a fault line.

"Nah. Was there?" His former teammate's brother is stooping down to get a better look inside his filthy chimney. "Pretty bad in there, huh?"

"Hasn't been cleaned in a long long time."

"I tried to light a fire a couple days ago."

Shane reaches up inside to crack off a tiny stalactite of creosote.

"Shit," Early says.

"They call this third-degree buildup." He can barely stand the sound of his own voice sometimes. *What am I, a dental hygienist?*

"Sounds expensive."

"Not really. Just dangerous." Shane gives the man an estimate, shaving a percentage off for old times' sake. Early chews his substantial lip, as if he thought it might be free.

"That's the deal, huh."

"Washington special." *The cheap bastards. Burn the world down, see if I care.* As he leaves to get his stuff, Shane can hear Early there behind him, reaching up into the chimney and scraping away with a knife.

***

He works two more jobs nearby and then drives back across town through what seems like an entire city at leisure: everyone strolling down the busy, commercial streets and packing the cafés and butchers and shoe stores. Shorts, cutoffs, tank tops. Shirts unbuttoned halfway down. Skirts, sandals. Brand new restaurants open their doors and windows to the outside air as the waiters set tables, rolling back their wrinkled sleeves. Record stores blare music to the curb and beef scents the streets from Mexican griddles everywhere. A beautiful day, bright and still. The cold summer has ended and the fall is beginning its old and simple trick, dismantling the fog and sharpening the edges of the sun to give them rare hot days and near warm nights. Earthquake weather. Days so nice that even the earth has to shimmy and shake.

He passes Mission Dolores park where the southwest slope is filling up like an amphitheater, the gay boys and a few straight stragglers stripping down and aligning themselves on blankets in the sun. Beneath them the center of the city on its sunken stage: the line of palm trees on Dolores Ave., the colonial palace of Mission High. The Catholic mission itself, the oldest building in the city, built in a once-idyllic plain of orchards and fields. The diagonal slash of Market Street disappearing into the towers of downtown. The bridge. The bay. The famous views are changing. The city is on steroids, swollen with people, cars, companies. Fairy-tale buildings have erupted overnight, pulled full grown through the ground by great cranes. Up close, the new people and their liquid money are pouring into every concrete crack, straightening and renovating, blistering up in glass and steel. There are new live/work spaces and office buildings and old Victorians scrubbed and powdered and coiffed. His city has never been a place of stasis, but in his more than thirty years he's never seen anything else like this. No one has.

At the bottom of the hill Shane crosses an invisible column of sudden verdant cool, and then it's warm again. The tennis courts across from Mission High are almost full. There are two basketball courts down there, too, one in front of the High School, one behind. He's played on both of them with kids and drunks and decent players too, but only on the weekends. He happens to know the schedule for every regular outdoor basketball game in town, just as he happens to know that the best game in town during the week is at the Firehouse court. His court.

The feeling is always the same when he hits the next intersection and signals for the left up towards Market Street. His body knows. A tiny bird flaps its wings somewhere between his chest and throat. It is completely irresponsible of him to pass up jobs in his busiest season, September. The light stays red. He already feels the ball spinning in his hand. A wrinkled dollar bill quivers on the dash. He doesn't care about money but he hates not doing his part. They made $1,000 a day for 100 days in '89, his dad and him, a run like that would be something. A quake like that today and you could charge these new

people triple, too, you had to, because it still meant nothing to them. $3,000, then. No basketball. What would she
make of that? He wonders if she's remembered yet and
slips the cell phone off his belt.

Fourteen months ago, on the asphalt court they call the
Firehouse, he broke his right foot playing basketball. One
clean crack, base of the fifth metatarsal, known as a Jones
fracture. Beware an injury with a proper name. After a
month he sawed off his cast with a bread knife, ran the
hills for a week, and hurried back to the Firehouse to
break his foot again, immediately. Three months later he
broke it a third time. Thus passed a lost long year on and
off crutches—casted, prone, showering with a garbage
bag tied around his lower leg. Long days in the house,
softening and hopping, moping, acting like a pathetic
jerk. He laid off the two guys he'd just hired, his first-ever
employees after six years working alone. His business
went on hold, his sex life turned to shit, his wife began to
hate him, his brother Jimmy stopped talking to him, his
mother called him every night and cried.

    He spent most of that empty year sitting in the front
room, staring out the windows like a cooped-up hunting
dog. A man encased in wax. He slept late, hopped down
the stairs to collect the morning paper, threw it up to the
landing, crawled back on hands and knees and filthy yellow cast. Sprawled across the couch, taking painkillers for
no particular reason, he started at the upper left-hand
corner of the paper and consumed it comprehensively,

finishing each story, following the jump pages inside and then circling back. The gay guy was taking on the black guy for mayor, the Nasdaq hit 5,000, the opera tried the Ring Cycle but critics were mixed. Oracle was hiring and hiring and hiring. No one was firing. Some dude already wanted to sell his green '99 Outback and Carl Deed, eighty-five, died at home, survived by a younger brother. When he'd finished every word he turned on the television and watched sports. One channel showed old games, classics, where slim Pickney danced through Georgetown's monsters, Bednarik flattened Gifford, Valenzuela slouched heavy from the mound, again and again.

He slept and ate constantly, making extravagant lists for his wife of needed food. He fried potatoes several times a week, cooking them twice to perfect the crunch, filling the house with the rich tang of oil. He ate too much cheese. He'd always been healthy, pretty naturally: you worked with your body, cooked at home, you hooped six days a week and got to be a decent specimen. Stunned by inactivity, the specimen decayed slowly, waiting to walk again, to run, expecting to snap out of it and return to the old body as if arriving home after a brief, disastrous vacation. His own scent turned stale, then sour. By the time foot break number three rolled around he really really really didn't give a shit. He sank down into the couch with a sense of permanence and ate and watched TV and eyed the busy city with all its filthy chimneys and all its busy, pleased prosperity.

His wife, Lou, meanwhile worked like crazy and

managed and provided and paid the bills. She was seldom home. He missed her but they both wordlessly agreed she might as well take advantage of his shittiness by taking care of business. She left him alone. She went on business trips. She went to conferences. It seemed possible that at one of them she might have kissed someone. She must have thought about it at least. This damaged Shane was not a man she recognized, but they both thought they could wait it out. During her absence and his hibernation Lou continued to operate the house by computer remote control. A cleaning woman appeared once a week. Clothes, books, movies, meals, curtains, light bulbs, electronics arrived at their front door. Brightly colored bins and boxes came and went in the bulky arms of young men made cheerful by stock options. Doing him the favor, they'd carry everything up the stairs, biceps bulging out of tight knit neo-corporate-branded shirts, asking what'd ya do, how d'ya do it, aw dude bummer, nodding respectfully at his curt response. They left him there with the goods and the receipts and he spent the afternoon examining the artifacts, balancing on one foot as he put them away.

After eight months of hardly working, he'd finally climbed back into the van in April, resurrecting the business, although to his wife's dismay he didn't hire anyone to help. For days he called old clients, reminding them he was alive, invoking his father, strolling down memory lane. He was quickly busy again. He went to physical therapy in the evenings and an obscure gym at night. Not his wife's luxurious Paragon, not his b-ball buddies' well-equipped Koret, not the spanking Y downtown. A cramped and dank low-ceilinged thing on outer Mission where no one known could possibly arrive. He hired a cheap, enormous man named Craig to be his personal trainer and grappled with machines as Craig bullied him to greater weight, one more, one more. Craig yelled at him and he fantasized about dropping enormous bar-bells on the giant's toes and neck.

But slowly his old calves and thighs emerged. His stomach hardened again. A recognizable shape returned. His clothes shrank tight around his shoulders, neck, arms, thighs. It was as if someone had challenged him to construct a body that could never break again. He began to run miles and miles through the summer wind and fog, striding out through the avenues in outrageous orthopedic shoes, touching the ocean sand and then hus-tling back. He stretched in the morning after waking up and at night before going to sleep. He exercised his foot and ankle for hours, rotating and flexing against the resistance of blood red Therabands.

It was August before he could play again, after a secret month of practicing alone at the middle school down the hill from their house. In the hours between the gym and Lou's coming home he'd jog down to the empty court to run sprints, shoot, dribble, jump. Shuffled side to side, changed direction quickly. Threw hard chest passes to the concrete walls. Afterwards he'd go home and sit on the stairs and feel his foot, stick his finger against the exact point of the healed break. Press until it hurt. Bend the foot up and down, side to side. There were days when it still felt sore, and his doctor told him the healing process would not be final, continuing for years.

"You're very stubborn," his doctor said. "You should take up golf."

"Like Jordan."

"They say it's an excellent game."

"Sure." He was almost a friend by now, this doctor, another local who grew up in the Richmond and had sports sins of his own.

"What about surfing."

"What about basketball."

"What will you do when you break your foot again?"

"Jump off the Golden Gate. Little hang time before I go."

"Well. Keep hitting the gym."

"I hate the gym."

"Strength is everything. Flexibility is everything."

"I'm strong. I'm flexible. I never went to the gym in my life."

"Well you do now," his doctor said. "I seen guys like you, work with their hands for a living, think they're fit, never been hurt in their lives. And then wham-bam. Your body will make you listen to it, eventually."

But in the end his doctor gave him his blessing and glucosamine and calcium and sent him on his way.

The shocking thing was that the world survived. It didn't absolutely need him, it turned out, it didn't depend on his good health or character or contributions and found a way to function smoothly in his absence. But when he returned quietly to the land of the living, nothing was the same. It was as if he'd lost his seat and he couldn't find it again and couldn't find another one either. So he stood, kept moving, he worked, he paid bills, he put money in Ma's account, he spoke sternly to his delinquent brother, he cheered on his busy wife and sometimes begged for children, he fixed the van and painted the bedroom and cooked dinner and did all the things he did before and nothing was the same because for a little while there he plain gave up. He gave up, he fucked up, he knew it, and he swore he'd never do it again.

The cell phone rings through and she answers on the first ring. "It's me," he says.

"Hey. It's my favorite *Homo sapiens.* I was just thinking about you."

"Between meetings."

"Between meetings. During meetings." She drops her voice to her open-office whisper, a tone she has developed to create privacy where there's none. Her voice like that has a distorted sound, the muffled echo of holding a hand over her mouth. "Was there an earthquake? Did you molest me this morning?"

"Yes. And yes."

"Oh goodie. I didn't see anything online so I thought I made it all up."

"Do you remember your five dreams?"

"No. I don't dream. I gave it up. Something had to go."

He hears the staccato of a keyboard. "Are you multi-tasking me?"

"Sorry. It's nuts here today. Our server's possessed. And I'm waiting for the Wallet to call."

"I'll let you go. ETA tonight?"

"Decent."

He turns onto his favorite street, the street that leads to the court.

"I've got nothing much to say except I love you."

"Oh my. Say that again."

"You heard me, lady."

"I love you too. I'll call later."

"Okay."

The phone winks once and falls gently into his lap. I'll work late, he thinks. Lou. Then his body remembers what's about to happen, and he guns it up the steep street, parking quickly and jogging up the stairs to the court.

2

THE FIREHOUSE should be packed. Noon is the unofficial starting time but most hot September Fridays have guys showing up by 11:35. Everyone wants to be first, no one wants to wait. Shane arrives late but somehow he has beat the rush and jumps on right away with Alex and Dragon and Finesse. And Jimmy.

"I got some information," his brother says as they walk out to the court, his enormous feet flapping like clown shoes. Rex likes to call him Sasquatch, although everyone else just sticks with Jimmy.

"Save it," Shane says. "Let's get these guys."

Shane hits the first shot of the game, brushing his defender off an excellent pick from his brother. He slips past Jimmy's shoulder and the pass from Finesse is waiting for him at the rendezvous. The orange ball comes spinning into his hands, the knees bend and the toes flex and in one easy gentle wave the body ripples up, the right hand firm behind the ball, the left relaxed as guide. The elbow straightens, the ball goes off, the wrist flops like the Palmolive lady dipping her fingers in a regenerative salve. Spinning backwards, the ball slices through the still air, and Shane lands on the ground with his wrist still flopped and takes a step forward, moving toward the hoop to follow his shot. But the shot is going in. He knows it, he watches the ball hit the back of the rim and the backspin sends it down, buh-chu, dropping briskly into the net like someone stepping through a door for an appointment. He starts backpedaling for defense, arms loose, jaw relaxed, and Jimmy is there beside him, not looking but putting his fist out for a bump. Bump bump.

"All day," Jimmy says quietly, and slides off to guard his own man.

A dynasty. Some of the big-time players are missing today—Mac, Skeletor, D-One—and Alex owns the boards, Dragon and Finesse are hitting, there's no one to stop them from winning five straight games except maybe the heat. The heat almost gets them, too, dropping their hands to hips and knees, forcing them to breathe conscientiously and complain. Goddamn. Finally they slump smugly to the pavement, slick with sweat, congratulating one another on all those whuppings in a row. Shane stares at his shoe, exhausted, his face stretched out in a smile by some happy pressure in his head. The fibers of his shoelace seem distinct and visible.

"Wife cooked my peas last night," Finesse is saying. They laugh. They all use frozen peas to ice their parts:

ankles, knees, elbows.

"How that ankle?"

"Ah, you know, for shit. Every time I sprain it I think, time to hang it up."

"Nah."

"I don't know, it gets so I'm afraid to go home. I walk in that door with a limp? and my wife starts yelling at me so loud she has to put her hands on her own ears. The neighbors must think I'm beating her silly."

"The neighbors don't hoop."

"They never do, do they?"

Shane closes his eyes, his sweat-soaked shirt balled up beside him, bare skin roasting in the sun. On these rare hot days, there's nowhere to hide. The guys have talked about planting a tree up here to get some shade. A tree: like they'll all keep coming up here long enough to wait for a goddamn tree. It cracks them up. It's one of their favorite conversations. What tree and when, irrigation, growing cycles. Live oak versus hybrid laurel.

He finds his cell phone and glances at the time. He's already late for his afternoon appointment. Afternoons after ball, he is always late.

"So you want the news or what," Jimmy says.

"What's that, you got a job?" Some of the other guys are getting up, reluctantly, collecting their stuff, moving on.

"Me? Now what would I do with a job."

"I don't know. Stick it up your ass."

"Oh yeah, in da butt, Bob, definitely. In da butt."

"What."

"Sam," Jimmy says, nodding slowly. "Rex says he still goes over that gym where they all used to go."

"Which?"

"You know, that people's gym went over the dark side? Where all these dudes went. Over in Potrero."

They turn east and for the second time that day Shane finds himself looking at the tall ridge running between Sixteenth and Twenty-sixth Streets. Beyond it, the far thigh of the San Francisco Bay. From this direction the orange-roofed projects are invisible but he can make out a white bulbous water tower on top of the hill, a patch of green that looks like a miniature park. His brother's talking about a place on the downtown side, nestled into the South of Market fringe. His wife's gym, the hippest in the city.

"No shit." Shane looks around for Rex but the big guy's already gone. "Hey," Shane calls out to the rest, "any of you still go over to Paragon?"

"Naw. Not since it was Mike's, man. We all over at Koret."

"That's what I thought."

"Hell yeah. They don't even got a court no more over there."

"Just all that dot-com step kick spinning Tae Bo shit."

"Pretty boys and yoga bitches."

"Whoa, dude, yoga works."

"Mike's though, Mike's was the shit, bunch a fucking boneheads, free weights, sick little runs over there, that little half court? Shay, you never came down there, huh?"

"Nope," Shane says.

"Yeah, you the outside purist natural man."

"Working on his savage tan."

"Parole officers, remember that, they come in to Mike's looking for their runners. Remember that?"

"You wouldn't even recognize that place now."

"I know, I seen it."

"What's Sam doing there?"

"No idea."

"We used to get him in on guest pass," Finesse says, "trying to bulk that kid up."

"That was fuck long ago. He still there?"

"Sam, huh. Y'all still looking for him?"

"Yeah," Jimmy says.

Sam was fifteen when they first played ball with him, pure arms and legs with a tiny little head on top. Five years ago, been up there ever since. An ugly cute kid, oddly colored, Sam's always struggled to grow into a body that seems to be assembled from quality spare parts. Skin half-baked between white and black, freckles on the inside of his arms, short almost-brown hair that's always trying to become huge and shrubby. Big full Crayola lips, thin pointy nose, small dark eyes too close together. No body hair except for one small patch shaped like Nevada behind the right shoulder. He's one of those guys you look at and want to ask: what are you? Shane doubts Sam's physical self has ever served him well except when it comes to playing basketball.

Basketball, though—basketball transforms him absolutely. Shane's seen it happen when Sam pulls within earshot of the bouncing ball. His walk changes, he starts the strut: chest out, shoulders back, arms bowed out lightly, a looseness in the forward hips. His shiny red sweatpants swinging loose around his legs, flaring out around his ankles like some seventies pimp royalty. He looks cocky. He plays young. Sam glides and bounces, floats and lopes. There are better shooters and passers and defenders and ball handlers but the way Sam moves through space still makes them stare. Sam has youth, and the rest of them have started to lose it. The whites of the kid's eyes are whiter, the skin on his arms tighter, his smell more vegetable, less animal. A smoothness in his cheek and scalp. They aren't friends, none of them up there are really friends, they have this zealot thing they do together and that's it. All right maybe some of them hit the gym together, or meet up to watch a big game now and then. Not Shane. Never. The pure thing to do, he believes, is to keep everything on the court. But even Shane feels something extra for Sam, with his freckles and his big hair, they all do, they all feel something for the kid growing up before their eyes. For five years they've cheered him, given him shit, teased him about his flashy sneakers, complained about the gold chain and ratty watch he refuses to take off. Even Lou has heard about him: the kid, she'll say sometimes, how's the kid?

They've taught him things, too. The way Sam spins

he got from Anthony; that little jump hook Bindo taught him; Ray's one-two dribble behind the back. And every time Sam sets a down pick at the foul line, Shane remembers the morning years ago, between games, showing him what that simple trick could do. No glory—just a teammate wide open to the hoop. For glory, Sam had the dunk.

Sam had been playing with them for a few years by then. He was eighteen, he was growing, he was jumping in disturbing ways. The guys had started taking him to Mike's Muscle, trying to bulk him up. Or sometimes instead he'd kick around with Skeletor, a true leaper, who was showing him the footwork, the brute mechanics of dunking a basketball. Sam could get up there just fine, high enough to use two hands, but something wasn't adding up. Maybe there were secret sessions, because the first time any of them saw Sam do it was in a game. A game was ten times harder. They all remembered: Sam picking off the bad pass at midcourt and tossing the ball out in front of him. The ball bounced out alone as Sam staggered toward it like the fastest drunk man in the world, and when he caught up he grabbed it with one hand, stretched out his legs in one long stride, and leapt to leave the earth for good. A bright day with the sun baking the amphitheater of the court. Sam took off and the rest of them stopped, waiting for the collision of boy and rim. Two hands, Sam flying, reaching for the rim like the edge of a thousand-foot cliff. He dunked. The ball went flying through and Sam hung on to the iron for his life, swinging two long full seconds like a lusty chimp, dropping to the ground crouched and ready, arms extended to wrestle or Kung fu.

Skeletor was the first, turning away from all of them, stretching his arms out to the city. "Gahd-damn!" he roared, and then all of them were swearing and whooping, slapping one another. "I think I have a hard-on," Jimmy said.

Shane laughed and Jimmy laughed and when Sam looked over their laughs had settled to great dimpling smiles meant for him. They must have seemed to Sam like two creatures as different from himself as plankton or giraffes: full-grown, full-white, Irish-looking lads, right proportioned and even handsome, relaxing comfortable in their bodies. Wide shoulders, good chins, thick sandy hair, long light lashes, blue eyes. Catholic schools and college educations stowed behind their excellent teeth. Sam caught them smiling at him the way brothers smile at each other and in that instant of inclusion they watched him fight it for a second before the hard knot in his jaw relaxed. It was the kind of smile that bunched up in the middle of the face instead of spreading side to side, the lips almost puckering, the face contracted. The smile trying not to smile. They came rarely but Shane still got to see those smiles a good couple times over the years.

Sam is missing.

For five years, the kid's been out there every week. He

never misses. If not on Tuesday, Thursday; if not on Thursday, Friday. It's rare that he's absent any of those days. Shane knows because he never misses either, broken feet aside.

The last time Sam showed was a month ago. They've been speculating: he moved, got hurt, arrested, married, a job, a kid. These are all known causes for guys' disappearances in the past. There are players Shane remembers from ten years ago who stopped showing up forever; there are others who wink out for a while and then return with some explanation why.

It happens, but the game goes on. A chimney sweep breaks his foot. A twenty-year-old kid vanishes. A sportswriter buys a house in Marin or Stockton, a physical therapist takes on one too many clients, the record store dude opens a second shop, the bartender gets a desk job. The cook moves to Texas, the painter lands a big fat contract with the city. There are babies born, shapes lost. Surgeries. Businesses are born and die, love is consummated and dissolved.

Shane used to think that their game was in grave danger of ending any time. They don't know each other, after all, not in the way people know people: addresses, educations, spouses, lineage, religion, income, backgrounds, beliefs. Last names. Phone numbers. Addresses, emails. They don't know any of that. Two or three bad weeks of weather or no-shows might be all it takes. One guy loses faith, stops coming, then another guy, and before they know it the game's over. Yet in all the years he's been coming to the Firehouse, those two or three bad weeks have simply never happened. The noon time comes and the guys show up. The game goes on.

Chances are that Sam is coming back. But when? The kid's duffel bag has been sitting in Shane's van since the last day Sam came up to play. A good day on the court, for Sam, and the kid made Shane look terrible. It happens sometimes. If Sam is really on his game, things can get difficult fast. The kid's trademark move starts on the right side, he crouches down a little bit with some phantom stomach cramp while his gold chain sways slightly in a hypnotizing side to side, and then he explodes like a piece of popcorn, flying either straight to baseline or across your face into the middle. The crossover is the worst. He's on your left and then he's on your right, an electric current jumping the gap. Ducks his head, tucks the ball into his chest and takes the two long strides and jumps. Let's say you've managed to stay with him but now it's the jump that kills you, he's just rising and rising, cruising around like some Broadway Peter Pan. Sometimes Shane feels as if there are secret mini-trampolines hidden around the court and only Sam knows where they are.

It worked out that Shane had to cover him three times that day, and on a day like that Shane hated covering him. The kid was kid no longer, the gym made sure of that. Sam and Shane, grunting against machines— they both want something, they both want bigger and better. And although Shane the grizzled all-around working man can still usually win the wrestling matches under the basket, on Sam's good days it doesn't matter. Those days make Shane a bad person. He feels like grandpa out there, grabbing the kid's shirt and poking him in the ribs and hooking him and holding him and trying to tire him out. He did all the tricks that day, but it didn't matter. Sam kept scoring, pulling fantastic rebounds, reaching over everyone's head and snatching the ball from the air like a spinning coin. Smacked his hand against the backboard to leave it vibrating in his wake.

Shane couldn't say anything to him during the game, getting worked like that made him so fucking mad. But that was just on the court. It never takes long afterwards for the murder in his head to stop. He remembers hissing every evil word he knows and then taking the deep breath, putting out a fist for the congratulatory bump.

"You got me, Sam. Day like today, I can't hold you."

"Yeah." Sam frowned, mildly embarrassed. "Ai-ight."

"My turn next time." I just got back here, after all, he thought, I been hurt, although he didn't say it. As if time were going to make anything better instead of worse.

"Yeah." Sam nodded, looked down at his watch. Time was waiting for him too, and Shane watched Sam's shoulders drop and sag, the soul of basketball leaving his body. "I gotta run." He turned quickly and jogged off the court, disappearing down the stairs into the world below.

"Good riddance," Jimmy said, as they watched him go. "Man, he ate your ass *up*. Mmmm. Yummy yummy ass."

"I'll let you check him next time."

"Someone better. He made you his bitch."

Everyone was gone except for Dragon. The three of them lingered on the sideline: Shane stretching and pretending, Jimmy worn-out dissatisfied, Dragon smoking his occasional little victory lap of dope.

"You want?" Dragon said, holding out the pipe.

"Naw, thanks."

Jimmy reached out for it and took a big semi-professional hit, passed it back, frowning, thinking, still in the game. They talked for a little bit about all the things they did wrong and then reluctantly got up, starting off their separate ways. At the edge of the fence Dragon called out.

"Hey Shane." Shane turned expecting some brief final salutation, a strange Dragon word of wisdom, but instead the Dragon was pointing to a small green gym bag on the sideline, left behind. "Whose that?"

It wasn't unusual. At game time, most days, the sidelines become a jumble of belongings: spare shirts and sweats and keys and water bottles and phones and pagers. Things get left behind. There's an animal state of mind that comes when hard play drives the real and practical from everyone's mind. You forget if your rent is due, if your parents are alive or dead, you forget your nice or lousy yesterday as well as who or what you came with: a brother, a basketball, a small green gym bag. You forget to think. You can try to remember, but the game starts and the inside of your head gets damp with sweat and nothing will stick. Thought after thought unpeels itself and teeters in the sprinting wind and falls away, until all that's left is action and reaction. And sometimes when the game ends and the guys leave right away, they walk back out into the world still stripped down, animal, feeling nothing, slack-jawed, comfortably numb.

So they forget the things they come with, but they never lose them. There's always that last someone to leave who grabs the orphaned ball or shirt or brother or hat. There's always Shane.

"Not mine," he told the Dragon, jogging back to get it. From the bag's open mouth flashed the familiar pair of red sweatpants with the white reflective stripes down the side. He tossed Sam's bag in the back of his van where it sat through Wednesday Thursday Friday and then a week and then another until they finally took a peek inside, wondering where the hell the kid had got to.

Paragon, Jimmy says. Paragon's a start.

Shane has always believed that the court is separate, a universe in itself. Church and state. He expects people to respect the clean white lines, to keep their wives and weekends and business to themselves. He doesn't want to ring their doorbells. He doesn't want to look for Sam. But Jimmy is another story.

His brother doesn't work, doesn't do much of anything, fancies himself a writer, still lives at home with Ma. His brother has time and believes in a different universe and different rules. Ever since the day they opened up Sam's bag and found too much, Jimmy's come to life. Sam's trademark sweats; a tight-rolled plain gray T-shirt that smelled like soap; short clean white socks; a pale blue spiral notebook; a brown canvas toiletries bag, stuffed; silver CD Walkman; mini plastic sleeve with four discs; black cell phone. A couple hundred dollars. Neither of them said a word. It was not the kind of bag you breezily leave behind.

If he's not back by Tuesday, I'll find him, Jimmy'd said.

Tuesday is gone. His brother has sifted through the details for an address, a phone number, a convincing piece of evidence, but the notebook's filled with scribbles and the cell phone has no charge. Now Jimmy sits there grinning, giddy with success.

"Paragon," he says again.

"I have to work," Shane says.

"Yeah well you don't give a shit I'll go alone."

"Tomorrow?"

"Then pick me up," his brother says. "Tomorrow."

3

HE DROPS JIMMY OFF at Ma's house, cleans two chimneys in the Haight, and heads home to wait for his wife.

Lou is five feet tall, with straight black hair, green eyes, Spanish lips, good skin. Big breasts, no butt, no hips—I tend to flip on curves, she says. She talks a lot, fierce in her pursuit of conversation, willing to attack herself and others for sport. A small woman aware of all the obstacles. A reader, once: her undergraduate thesis involved urban planning and the nineteenth-century novel. She was an English major when he met her. She still smokes cigarettes sometimes when she's drunk. As a child she lived in Connecticut, where her parents are messily divorced. She brushes her teeth too many times a day despite the dentist's complaints. Everyone remembers her laugh.

On weekdays, Lou wakes up around seven o'clock, maybe nine or even ten on Saturday. She doesn't do well in the mornings, and takes her showers very hot and very,

very long. She does not share Shane's childhood training of the California drought years, when lawns faded to wispy gold and the toilet had its old-wives' cautionary refrain: if it's yellow let it mellow, if it's brown flush it down. As a hygienic girl from the wet and verdant East, Lou knows that's disgusting and she'll have none of it. Well poached, she races naked from the bathroom to the bedroom to play her frantic morning round of outfit roulette, opening drawers, rattling hangers to the floor, emptying half her closet until she hits some voodoo winning combination and sweeps through the kitchen for the coffee Shane's left brewing there. Seldom eats. She hops in her brand-new car and drives down through brutal traffic to Menlo Park where she drops cleanly off his radar.

In the evenings Shane gets home first and reconstructs the morning from the evidence: the stained and empty coffee pot, the kitchen lights left on, the dresser drawers ajar and crumpled clean-clothes rejects on the bed. He likes taking care of her, maybe that's a little wussy of him but he always has. He doesn't mind coming home to clutter he can quickly tidy up. He rinses dishes, makes piles. It might be hours before she gets home. During his broken-footed days she developed the habit of going straight to the gym in the evenings after work. She doesn't like it. Exercising is a chore, but you have to do your chores. Fat would be a disaster. The gym is part of the job. By now her schedule seems powerful, supreme, and permanent: work, gym, sleep, with Shane sprinkled in between. Her company has devoured weekends too. The company's taking off, everyone says so, but Shane pictures a bloated cargo plane trolling down a desert runway, not some lithe and silver rocket.

Sometimes in the mornings he invents a thin excuse to linger, shadowing her around the house as she gets ready. They have a cup of coffee and sit at the little table looking out across the city. She's mildly unhappy when she's tired and it makes her like him more. She kisses him on the lips and puts her head against his chest and moans sadly with fatigue. She takes his hands and loops his arms around her and asks him if he loves her.

"Yes."

"You're sure?"

"Pretty sure."

"I can't imagine why."

"You're lovable. You crack me up."

"No."

"Because you're cute?"

"Am I? That must be it, then."

Or they sit quietly drinking coffee, skimming the morning paper until both their clocks strike something and they kiss and run.

Shane is amazed at how hard she works now. He tries to work hard too. He tries to get home later than she does every now and then but he can rarely manage it. There's always one more thing she can do there at the office, but he has to go home eventually. The people he works for want their houses back. They kick him out, send him home to cook dinner. He usually makes something simple, but he also loves that moment when she comes walking in the door to a minor feast and sips wine barefoot in the kitchen while he finishes up. Other nights he fills with sport: watching it on TV, going to the gym, bundling up for a night game out at Candlestick. He visits his Ma and brother or has a drink with high school friends. Occasionally he reads. The days seem temporary, caught between. Behind them hang their effortless beginnings and in the distance up ahead loom children and a continuing decent chance that they'll be rich.

Let's have kids now, he says.

Hold your horses, grandpa, she says. This part of life is when you work.

You can work and have kids.

She laughs. Most people never even get one shot, she says. Rich. I'm serious. It could happen.

He parks at home and walks down to his local grocery store in the vein of shops and restaurants that run through the valley, west to east. There's everything you could want down there if you have the money. They pretend they do. The people who live up there with them among the Escher-tilted streets certainly do. Slightly stinky in his dirty clothes, he browses beside fit mothers and natty fathers picking out plump tomatoes and fresh halibut and entry-level pinot noir. Lou still doesn't eat much but has fast recovered from a bout of vegetarianism, and he's been having a good time making up for lost meat: poking pork chops, squeezing chickens, massaging marbled beef.

On his way home she drives past him, angling up the street in her sleek new car. She's talking sternly to herself or holding one last communiqué via hands-free phone. The car is particularly shiny tonight, recently washed and buffed like a leather evening shoe. She doesn't see him. He stares after her and watches her pull in ahead of him and park on the ridiculous hill. She steps out of the car and he hides behind a tree like a comic book villain. She marches toward the door with her red leather bag and laptop, her hair perfect, sunglasses giving away nothing, her face serious. She looks like a real person. She looks like the word *mature*. She pins her possessions against the door with thighs as she unlocks and disappears inside. His pulse syncopates. He doesn't move. He is stalking his wife. He watches their living room window up above and pictures her first strides through the house alone, sunglasses coming off, her face relaxing. In the kitchen she attacks the refrigerator with niggling, fasting hunger; moves to the bedroom to pry herself free of shoes and hose; hits the living room and cranks the stereo to blast her way back to their other life. He waits. There's the music, not Bach or Mozart but good ol' rock 'n' roll. He lingers, hoping to see the glass doors slide open and his wife step out onto the little porch with a glass of cold white wine. After a few minutes he goes inside.

Lou is sitting on the couch, staring at silent images on TV while listening to her own soundtrack of three-chord din. She never watches television. She's still in her work clothes but everything is untucked and unbuttoned, her edges flapping loose as she comes undone. She looks better now, an adult halfway defrocked.

He leans over to kiss her head and she recoils slightly, like a suspicious cat. She's in a work coma, work has reared back its wooden bat and beaten her half to death.

"I get you anything?"

"No."

"Drink? Heroin?"

"No."

He comes back with two beers and puts one in front of her and the other to his lips. She leaves hers frosting smoke.

"It's Friday."

"Is it?" She tries to sigh but yawns instead, covering her face with her hands.

He takes a long pull on his beer. It's cold and perfect, the best thing he's ever tasted in his life. "Did you eat?" This is his solution. "You didn't eat."

"You know, I just got home, give me a couple minutes, all right?"

He leaves her there and shucks his clothes and takes his beer with him to shower and blast the day into the drain. He decides not to masturbate and shaves instead, nicking himself twice on the hinge between his throat and chin where he always nicks himself. He waits without hurry for the blood to stop, watching it seep and bead, blotting it dry. She likes him better when he's bloody and smooth. He changes into light cotton pants and a pale blue shirt and finds her where he left her but more upright, doing the crossword puzzle, pen flicking across the page.

"Look at you," she says. She sounds improved.

"Here I am." He tries again and this time gets her, an entirely good kiss. "I was gonna figure something out, foodwise. You must be hungry."

"No way can I be hungry. I have like lunch three times a day."

"Something light."

"All I do is lunch. God, I feel so gross. Like I'm wearing a fat suit."

"You're not wearing a fat suit."

"Maybe I'll go to the gym."

Paragon, he thinks. Sam. Stay on target. "You gym. I'll make us something."

"No. I loathe the gym. When I die, they'll send me to the gym for all eternity." She flops back against the sofa. "Man, I am such a bitch. Don't you just want to slap me? *I* want to slap me. I want to slap me silly." She tilts her head back and laughs wickedly, the low throaty staccato bursting out of her like ground birds startled from a bush.

"Come on." He has her by the arm, pulls gently. "Let's go out to dinner." If he can get her out in public she will change, correct herself. She always does.

"No. Gym. Plastic surgeon."

"Come on." He holds her there, half suspended off the sofa, her eyes still glued to the television, until slowly,

slowly, he feels her body giving in. He lifts her to her feet and puts his arms around her and finally she looks up steeply at him.

"You like me, don't you."

"Yep. But I'll slap you if you really want."

"I would not blame you. I would not blame you at all." She puts both hands to her face and smears phantom tears back across her cheeks. "All right. I'll be out in a sec."

They end up in their neighborhood at a little restaurant where Dragon is a cook. It's not far from home but he's never eaten there before. There has always been a reason not to, and one of those reasons is he doesn't want the magic Dragon turned mundane, chopping onions and busting butt, grinding out a living. He wants to keep his b-ball buddies suspended in a jobless state, free from death and taxes and mortgage rates. Maybe that's stupid. Maybe it's too late. Already he's thinking about Sam, Sam rolling down a sidewalk in the Mission, checking out new kicks at Footlocker. Dragon has a job, big fat deal. D-One writes about the Warriors, for chrissake, Alex teaches elementary, Skeletor's in grad school. What's the big deal. Why not eat at Dragon's place, now and then.

They stand in the doorway, Lou suddenly alert as he knew she would be. She looks around quickly at the people in the restaurant, deciding something. Across the room, behind the counter, Dragon appears, grinning as he catches sight of Shane, giving him an excellent nod before bending to his work. It's going to be all right. The hostess seats them at a table near the back, places small manila menus in their hands. The menu says sea bass, rolled beef loin, something involving quail. He orders a bottle of pinot grigio, Lou's wine of choice.

"My guy's here," he tells her. "Lemme go say hi."

He catches Dragon putting the finishing touches on a dish, flecking moist basil and thyme from his fingers and setting the plate on the loading deck with a little spin. He looks handsome in his bloodied white smock, his blue eyes and the small goatee making his face look dark. The Dragon pantomimes a handshake in the air, the whole thing, the court shake: slap, clench, snap, fist, bump. As an exclamation point he grabs the heel end of an unfamiliar-looking root, turns, fires for a trash can.

"Still got it," Shane tells him.

"Always."

"Smells great in here."

"*Smells* is an odd sounding word, isn't it," Dragon says. "Smells." It's a relief to know that Dragon in the restaurant is not a bit different from Dragon on the court. "Smells," he says again, and laughs.

"Like a beef-flavored cologne," Shane says.

"So my prep man says we should go with the Chinese Flame Tree." He nods at a small guy chopping things, who nods back in support.

"For the court?"

"Yeah. Grows fast. Says maybe we'll get some shade before we die." Dragon's eyes skip sideways back to his grill. Their time's up.

"What should we have?"

"What's this we, white man?"

"My wife."

He goes up on toes to examine her. "Ooh la la fi fi," he says. "For a lovely young couple like yourselves, I would suggest whatever I feel like making. You guys like fish, right, scallops?"

"We like it all. I gotta warn you, though, she eats like a bug, you can go on the small side. And if you can make it *look* low-fat and healthy? Big points for me."

"All need big points. I got you."

Lou is sipping her wine when he gets back to the table. "My man's going to hook us up, unless you have something special in mind."

"Your man."

"That's right. I'm connected." The waitress swoops by the table, smiles at them approvingly, whisks away their menus. "Your day got crappy?" he says.

"Crappy! And you?"

He tells her about his morning, slowly, trying to get the specifics right. She's not listening completely but she's trying. He describes the gimpy guy in flannel and his big brick chimney and the motorcycle carcasses and the black dog that let him keep his balls.

"You're making that up," she says, trying not to smile.

"I swear."

"You forget names of people you've met five times but you remember what this guy was wearing. You've always got the details. Sometimes I'll be down there in some awful meeting and I'll think, what would Shane do right now, what would he notice? What would be the story he'd tell me later. Kinda like what would Jesus do, only super California Zen Master Flash style. Or maybe you make it all up. Like that earthquake this morning."

"I made that up?"

"Didn't see anything online."

"Hmm. Good move on my part, though."

She smiles. "But who's to say you're not inventing all these weird characters you meet at work?"

"I'll take you with me sometime."

"Oh I'd make a great chimney sweep assistant."

"You might even fit."

"*Are* there any women in the chimney industry?"

"No. Not one in the whole entire world."

"Why is that?"

"No idea."

"Mmm, all that pumping and plunging. Plumbers, miners, oilmen. Basketball. Men are so excellent at shoving things in holes."

"Isn't that what holes are for?"

"Did you play today?"

"Yes." She nods to tell him she's just asking. He won't say anything else unless she pries.

"Any women on the court?"

"No. Not lately." There's one woman who used to play with them, sometimes, the tiny sister of one of the guys. Good shooter. Lou tries to be interested in Shane's rhapsodies on basketball but she's truly fascinated by this woman who dares to come up and play with him and his large and sweaty friends. She pours herself another glass of wine.

"You know what I wish? I wish there was something *you* liked to do that only women did. And that they kicked your ass at it every single time."

"That's a sweet wish. What would this thing be?"

"Well that's the problem. If there *was* something like that, men simply wouldn't want to do it. They wouldn't just not do it—they'd will themselves to stop even caring about it. And then, then they'd convince the whole world that it wasn't even an interesting thing to do in the first place."

"Wow. Men are smart."

The waitress arrives with two delicate-looking salads, uncommon leaves arranged like flower petals on faded yellow plates. "I just want you to imagine," Lou is saying, as the waitress grinds fresh pepper, waiting for a sign. "You wake up tomorrow and discover that you're the only guy who plays basketball, and every woman is better than you. Bummed out when you're on their team. Won't pass you the ball. Wish you'd just go away."

The waitress listens with interest, but he waits until she's gone before he answers. "And that would make me some better kind of person."

"Not you in particular. Men." Lou picks through her salad as if looking for something valuable or gross. "The world would be a ten times better place. Every time you went up for a shot—blocked! Every time you got the ball—steal! Whatever. But you loved the game, right? so you kept playing with women even though they absolutely and always kicked your ass. That would be so good for you."

"But not me in particular." He pictures her at the gym astride a step master, angrily grunting, with Sam bench pressing twice her body weight nearby. All of us.

"Just for this male bluster and confidence in general."

"You're confident. You're ambitious. You bluster."

"It's not the same thing." She toys with a pale green sprig of arugula, finally hefting it to mouth and chewing comprehensively. "Women pay dearly for our sins. Look over there."

He follows her glance to the table where a younger couple chats amiably, conducting conversation with waving forks. They're twenty-three, twenty-four, they're the age he was when he first met Lou. The girl has short blond hair, slightly spiked, very white smooth skin, dressed in a boyish vest. The boy is delicate, thin, with retro-chic glasses, short cropped hair, simple matte zipper jacket over a bright-colored T-shirt.

Lou leans in, drops her voice. "Take those two. She thinks it's all possibility. They're these equals, right, both gotten everything they want so far. Make good money, great money, work with friends, options, Foosball tables in the office, everyone goes bowling Thursday lunch."

"Rope course retreats. Catamarans in the bay."

"Right, the whole deal. Now, she's at level one, but level one is high these days, you can see the top from there. They go public next week and wham! Or if she gets unhappy, if he gets fed up, fine—they'll just go and start their own damn company. Make their own fortunes." She snaps her fingers, pinches an invisible fly in midair. "The top is right there, and she's going to make it, if she wants, she knows it. Because this is not the old world. This is the new world. Now, is it my duty to go over there and tell her she don't know squat?"

"I'm going to go with 'no' on this one."

"See they're going to pay, because they all believe this shit." The salads disappear. "The old boys' club just got a whole lot younger, you know, they don't pinch butts so much anymore, maybe they don't do deals over moose hunts. But it's still, really, the same old same old. There's *so much* money to be made right now, but guess who's making it? I spent about a million hours on this conference call this morning, a circus, and when we all get on the line of course it's me and eleven dudes. Which means you either get completely ignored, you put up with the little jokes or you have to go hard-ass kung fu on the world. Either way, they've got you. You're a quiet smart nice little cookie or a pushy big-mouth bitch."

"That was your bad day? A conference call?"

"Oh no." She shrugs. "I also had the pleasure of talking to the Wallet. Then Spermy called."

"What did the Wallet say?" He wants to stay away from Spermy if he can.

"He's still talking a ten million mezzanine with a fourteen-month ramp. I think it's stupid, we're ready to go bigger and sooner than that. But now he's got Sloan, too. Jesus. And no joke, five minutes later, Spermy calls. Trying to tell me about his latest book, trouble in paradise with his whore." Her father is a well-known academic in New England who left Lou's mom for one of his students. Lou and her father were big pals until high school when she used to smell their perfume in the car, these girls her father was fucking. Girlfriends closer to Lou's age than her father's. "I got out of there. God knows who was gonna call next."

He nods carefully, keeps his eyes on her. In the wake of these conversations with Spermy, Shane is always very careful not to get caught looking at other humans, some of whom may be female. She's gotten much better—it's almost disappointing—but his wife's reserves of jealously still run deep.

From the netherworld beyond, dinner descends: seared sea bass with a dollop of risotto, a beautiful crepe with a scallop and tomato garnish hinting at its insides.

"You know what this whole day was about?" Lou says, barely looking at the food. "Men simply can't treat women as equals. No matter how enlightened they think they are, no matter if they're gay or straight or old or young, no matter where in the world they're from. For now, at least, men simply don't have it in them."

They eat. She chews so slowly he thinks she's going to spit something out.

"What do you think?"

"What do I think."

"We're just talking."

"You can't have it both ways. That moment in history stuff, oh these are special times, I have to give it everything I've got 'cause you know was my mother part of a revolution when she was twenty-something, was my grandmother? Opportunity of the millennium, all that. That's what I think."

"Yeah. Well. I'm in a shitty mood, I warned you. You should have left me on the couch and put police tape across the door."

"Maybe I should have."

"What can I say?" She prods the back of her hand with her fork. "I hate myself. I wish you'd hate me too."

"Don't worry, honey. I hate you sometimes."

She smiles. "Aw, sweetie. I hate you sometimes too."

He's not even hungry but he eats anyway. He will destroy their meal alone if he has to and get them out of there.

"I'm turning into a grumpy old man," she says. "We're living in the most cheerful times imaginable and I still get like this. It's fatigue. It's too much work."

"I know."

"Can we pretend? Pretend we just got here. We just sat down." She reaches across the table to halt his progress on the crepe.

"Okay."

"Friday night."

"We just got here."

"Just sat down." She smiles at him, finally, a real smile, and he takes another bite. "So how was your day?"

"Okay," he says. "Dog tried to bite my dick off."

4

I N THE MORNING he leaves Lou in bed, pulls on his white mesh shorts and dull gray tee, and drives across the city to collect Jimmy and find Sam.

Shane's mother and malfunctioning youngest brother still live in the pale yellow house of Shane's childhood, out in the Sunset on a quiet uneventful street. Growing up out there, there were a bunch of Irish, and also Chinese, Koreans, Russians. "The Irish and other enemies of the state," his dad used to say. The Asians have increased their share, but physically the Sunset hasn't changed wildly over the years. More Stop signs. No more intersection Sunset Roulette. But this part of the city is still crowded with houses he knows, inside and out. Childhood and cleaning chimneys and parties and friends made and lost over time. The street corners have retained old meanings, spots where they stalked the skirted girls from Sacred Heart or annihilated time on skateboards, scooters, bikes. Trees he puked on. A thousand wistful vulgar sites, thickening as he closes on home.

The sky is blinding blue and still. It's going to be that one day, that one day a year. Drawn out by the warm morning, a few people are walking the streets already, and he examines them as he drives past. He recognizes no one. This is the new sensation of this city, more than anything, this mass extinction of familiar faces. There was a time not very long ago when he couldn't step out of the house without finding a thick parade of living ghosts.

He finds his mother in the kitchen, kneading meatloaf into a bread tin. Always shorter, plumper than he expects. She extends hands coated with grounds of beef and ketchup and crumbs, pantomiming a hug. Her face has turned so soft and sagging that he wants to reach out and mold it back into place. Only her eyes haven't changed: blue and bright and clear under the long blond lazy lashes.

"Getting it out of the way," she says. She knows it's ridiculous to be prepping for dinner at nine in the morning, but she's not taking any guff about it.

"It's gonna be hot today, Ma. You sure you wanna use the oven?"

She shrugs. "You coming?"

"Not tonight. Maybe tomorrow."

She shakes her head, betrayed, as if tomorrow is the worst idea in the world. "There's some things from the bank, I put on the little table in the TV room."

"Okay. I'll have a look."

The insect whine of the television, its sound turned down, hits him in the hallway as he passes the photographs of their McCarthy tribe. A few of Ma's Breens thrown in, for good measure. Grandchildren, nephews, nieces. And then there they are: Shane, Brendan, Tommy, Jimmy. His father and mother are accounted for, but mostly this hall is ruled by four brothers. Shot after shot of costumed freckled boys documents the small and faddish passing of time. Four babies and toddlers, four lads in orange brown striped shirts, four school boys in white button-downs and thin ties, four ripped and sloppy teens. From him to Jimmy is a total distance of six years. They were packed in tight. He passes picture after picture of the four of them, a timeline tilting to adulthood, until one by one they begin to splinter off into wedding photos, first homes, children. Until at the end of the wall only Jimmy stands alone, squinting impish handsome by himself, looking mildly unhappy that they've left him there behind.

He finds the real live Jimmy still in bed, in the room Shane and Brendan used to share. Beside the bed Jimmy has pinned up his own favorite family photo with flat red thumbtacks. Ma and Dad are about Shane's age, both looking young and strong and beautiful, and the boys all dressed up in their Christmas best and smiling big, flashing excellent teeth. Who took the picture? Jimmy is a plump and jolly three on daddy's lap, cracking up at his own private toddler's joke. His feet already look huge.

Outside a throaty classic car starts up, demanding

loyalty and repair. Jimmy sighs in sleep. The car revs down low once and disappears. The young brothers on the wall listen carefully, holding their places, waiting for a sign. Dad squints out at Shane, about to break the silence.

He died on Shane's twenty-fourth birthday, when Shane was still in college across the bay in Berkeley with the golden bears and boys and girls of California, starting his sixth and final year. Shane would end up graduating the following summer, despite abandoning school for the fall semester and dismal performances on most of his exams. Dad had fallen very sick, very quickly, with cancer of the colon that had been developing for a long time. The cancer was old to his body but new to Dad and family—it had only been discovered that summer, the day after the Fourth of July. Dad was a big, strong, energetic man and his weakness made him furious.

"I've got death up my ass," he told Shane. "How the fuck you think I feel?"

He did have death up his ass and it made short work of him. The colon came out but by then the cancer had metastasized to his liver and his lungs. Ma called Shane on his birthday morning. It could have been a happy birthday call but she said the three words that told him he was no longer a son who had birthdays but something else.

"I'm coming," he told her. "I'm leaving right now." But she kept talking about his father, about a smile the night before and a fight with the nurse last week.

It was beautiful outside Shane's window, a bright

Berkeley day filled with gardeners' promises. They'd had the first wet year in a long time, and the hills above the campus were exploding with thick, wild green. All the students and tourists and freaks crowded out on the warm busy streets, packing the parks and benches, riding bikes along the smooth, protected paths. Lou was out there somewhere. Shane was about to meet her for the first time, soon. They would meet and date and move in together and romp around San Francisco and get married on the bluff above the Cliff House looking out over the ocean. They would get their first apartment together, buy furniture and plants, throw a wild New Year's party where Jimmy's friend jumped off the fire escape but nobody got hurt. He pressed the phone against his ear, staring out the window, watching the neighbors' cat making its way along the top of a wooden fence, the loose feline belly swinging as it went. Something was out there, something good, he would go and find it. His mother stopped talking and they stayed on the line in silence, the new widow and her oldest prince, called from his days of pleasure to take his rightful place on the sad, abandoned throne.

"I'm coming," he said again. And went.

He moved home for a few months, and after that spent weekends and sometimes nights there during the week, and then after he graduated he just plain went home. He took over the business and paid the bills and drove across the bay to see Lou as often as he could. Money was a problem. After they buried his father and

Shane sought out the balance books for business and family alike, he found nothing there. There were no books. No life insurance. No bank statements. The ones he finally wrestled from the bank told him very little except that there wasn't any money. How could that be? How could there be nothing? For the next few years, he'd find himself up on a roof or sticking his head into a crusty fireplace and think: what did Daddy do with our money? There'd always been plenty of business, a good reputation, a quarter-page ad in the yellow pages. Shane kept expecting that somewhere he'd find a sign of secret waste. Their father had worked six days a week, and their mother's house seemed to run on vapors, on true voodoo economics. She was one of the most frugal creatures on the planet, a heroic clipper of coupons, roller of pennies. She recycled, restored, made do. She did not spend. He doubted she had bought herself a new article of clothing in twenty years. But still there was no money.

Everywhere he looked in their family's financial history, Shane had the feeling that something was missing, and he wanted a concrete suspect, a sin, a crime even, to explain the situation. Drinking, gambling, drugs, whores. Secrets. He demanded a reason that they were in debt, and he didn't want the reason to be Jimmy, Tommy, Brendy, and him. Sneakers, underwear, tuition, meat. The endless mortgage on the house. He looked and looked but he could never find anything else.

Once he thought he might be on to something, the best of possible explanations. A guy called up a year after

Dad died, and seemed shocked by the news. The guy called himself an old friend of the family. Shane ended up going over there to clean his chimney. The man was strange, quiet, nervous, a drunk probably in the bargain. He lived alone. Nothing in his house looked like it had changed since the late fifties. He didn't say a word to Shane until the job was finished, when the guy repeated that he was an old friend of the family, he was short right now, could he settle up in a month or two. Even when Shane sent him the follow-up bill, he knew the old guy was never going to pay. Maybe, he thought, maybe it was charity, maybe there were a host of these gnomes throughout the city on the dole from his father, year after year. Maybe Dad even used to give them money, buddy loans never to be repaid. He clung to this idea, waiting for the other calls, the other mysterious old friends expecting services for free. He aired his theory to Lou, his brothers, his mother: Christian charity, that's why. But gnome number one was the only one. The other calls never came, and he realized that even he didn't believe it. The gnome didn't call again.

The explanation that he has settled on, finally, is that there is no explanation. Or that maybe their father never understood how money worked, and maybe Shane doesn't either.

In the bed, Jimmy's body. A spare arm dangles over the edge, a hairy leg splays out on top of the covers. He is always relieved to find his brother in some absolutely normal state. A part of him always half expects to open the door and find gore or shame. Disaster.

"Get up."

"What time is it." The body doesn't move but one eye opens. "Am I dead? Is this heaven?"

"The other place."

"Again."

"Your breath stinks."

His brother farts and rolls away from him in a bundle of flesh and sheet. "Ah man. I had the most fucked-up dream."

"Yeah, tell me in the van."

"Okay. But really," Jimmy says, not moving an inch. "Michael Jordan was the devil but nobody believed me."

"Doubted even in your dreams."

"Especially."

"Get up."

"Okay, okay." He sits, kneading his head gently with both hands as if checking a tropical fruit for ripeness.

Paragon dominates a wide intersection at the downtown edge of Potrero Hill. Once this was the middle of nowhere, but things are hopping now. A new neighborhood has been decided. They slog through traffic behind new bulbous Bugs and hulking SUVs and sporty Outback wagons with bikes and surfboards lashed on top. They pass three extensive construction projects: one beginning, one middle, one end. An entire city block sits empty, gouged three stories into the ground, poised for something more massive than them all. The old ware-house buildings that started it have been cleaned and burnished to hold design firms, game coms, software companies. Mild bustle lines the street, young men and women looking purposeful with coffee. Bike racks. Juice bar. Deli, salads, wraps. Starbucks. The gym. It's a big one, filling a healthy portion of the block. Shane hasn't been over here in a long time, but he has a dim memory of a dim place in the emptiness: Mike's Muscle, without even a sign outside. Now the whole front of the building has morphed into glass, flashing shiny steel girders within. Upstairs, a row of exercisers is bobbing on machines.

Jimmy catches his eye as they cruise for parking.

"What the hell is this?" Jimmy says.

"Yeah, yeah. I know."

They loop around the block and stop behind another line of traffic. Up ahead of them, Shane can make out part of the problem: two delivery trucks backing into a loading dock. He recognizes the trucks, which are painted beige and green. They have a small, almost pseudo-European shape, these trucks that used to park their tilted way at his front door in his convalescent days, when Lou would order their groceries online.

"Holy shit!" Jimmy says, spotting the van. "So this is where they live." Online groceries, Shane knows, stand for much that Jimmy believes is wrong in the world. He watches his brother roll down the window. Jimmy leans out and bellows cheerfully, "Hey…Webvan!" One of the drivers turns his head, finds Jimmy smiling at him out the window. The guy nods back, smiles. "Yeah, fuck you, Webvan!" Jimmy yells. "Damn you to hell!" Jimmy is almost completely out of the window now, shaking his fist in a lavish show of rage.

The guy stares, briefly stunned, then shrugs and ignores them as they pass. "He's probably not allowed to give me the finger," Jimmy says.

"But I am." A part of Shane could drive around and shoot the shit with Jimmy all day long.

They park and enter the gym, where Lou has two guest passes waiting for them. She has offered a million times, but they both know they never really want to see the other at the gym. That way lies the end of love. It's still brute and dirty maintenance, even if Paragon is six hundred times as nice as the place Shane goes. The floors are polished concrete, the stairs are shiny steel, the glass ubiquitous and spotless, the whole place shimmers like a space station. The woman at the desk smiles and hands them each two small white towels and calls for Carlos to show them around.

"We were referred by a guy," Jimmy tells Carlos. "Guy we play ball with."

"Basketball."

"Yeah. Young guy named Sam." Carlos shakes his head. "I'm sure you know him. Kind of light-skinned black guy, bushy hair, freckles, long arms. Wears shiny red sweats, stripes."

If this perp talk surprises him, Carlos doesn't let on. "There so many people come through here, man? I bet

I'd recognize him, though. But when you join, we'll be sure he gets a credit. We're all about referrals. That's how we stay we, you know?"

"Sure," Jimmy says, winking at Shane with unusual restraint.

Carlos leads them upstairs to tour the thermoclimed incubation room for heated yoga; a dance studio where salsa hopscotch kickboxing is transformed into aerobics; a big room with eternal stair climbers, quadraceptors, bikes with Internet screens attached, treadmills with private televisions; an interior cellblock with closed doors and no windows for imaginary bike rides, where an unseen instructor is screaming at her stationary cycling cult. A thick-scented pollen of sweat wafts out under the door. Shane looks around carefully, not seeing Sam but feeling something familiar.

"This used to be a basketball court up here, huh."

Carlos frowns. "Yeah," he admits. "The place was a dump, they tell me."

"My buddies used to come here, back when it was Mike's."

"That so." Carlos looks unhappy. Carlos knows this isn't working out. He takes them downstairs, points them in the right direction, and lets them go.

Downstairs is better, a huge open space with machines and free weights, ample room for stretching. Light streams in from all sides. Despite the prettiness of it all, there are some big guys here, too, lording over the workday rabble, men staring at their blood-engorged muscles in the mirror, their mouths slack, examining their own thighs with a kind of exhausted, bovine lust. The music pumps in steadily overhead, a huge bass and beat with a single piece of high-pitched chorus looped a thousand times.

They tour slowly, looking for something Sam. Jimmy shrugs and settles down on a bench press, lying flat while Shane sets up the bar for him. It's a very reasonable weight but his brother lifts it up and down just four times before his arms begin to shake. Shane leans forward, ready to spot if necessary. Jimmy glares at him, clanks the bar unevenly back to rest.

"I am a little pussy boy," he says. "I'm such a little bitch."

"Jimmy."

"Take some weight off." Jimmy jabs a finger at the weights above him. "I don't have those muscles, I mean, what's the point of them anyway?" He bangs on his chest, punching his failed pecs. "Is it just cosmetic? I mean, it's like, am I ever going to be in a prone situation where suddenly I have to lift a heavy object up and down? Ten times. With just my arms. For what, for earthquakes, when you're trapped under a large chunk of ceiling?"

"You could end up with a really fat chick."

"That's a good point," Jimmy says. "There must be practical applications for all these weird machines." He looks around thoughtfully. "But what the hell was Sam doing here?"

"Getting big."

"Yeah, but here? With the Narcissus boys and the

richie rich? You see the dues on this place? You either gotta have bank or be here every day to make it worth it."

"Maybe Rex is wrong."

"Maybe." Jimmy sits up. "One way to find out."

Jimmy heads off to talk to management with some cock-amamie story while Shane lingers near the entrance to watch who comes and goes. Across town, at the Firehouse, the first game is getting under way. Maybe Sam is over there, just arriving, calling winners. That's where Shane should be, for sure.

Someone says his name and he shakes off visions of the open J to find Super Mario standing in front of him. Super Mario: an old lapsed regular from the game.

"Hey there," Shane says. He puts out his hand and they do the slap and bump. "I thought you died and went to Oakland."

"No, worse. I got a job."

"I'm sorry."

"Yeah. No more Tuesday Friday for me."

"Well you know where we are."

"Yeah and it kills me." Mario's a pure shooter, with short fast legs and an unorthodox quick release.

"This your gym?"

Mario nods, sneering as if he's caught a noxious scent. "Last man standing. I was here when it was Mike's and then my new job is right around the corner. So here I am today. With the other digerati."

"Some big dudes here too."

"Yeah." Mario leans in. "Weird place," he hisses. "Geeks, hulks, and fags, with a few gangsters thrown in. Came out the other night and the car next to mine, Frank's giving Frank the business."

"You could still come up Saturdays."

"Don't talk to me about Saturdays."

"Yeah, huh."

They're blocking the throughway and have to step aside for a very well-dressed man with a huge watch sparkling on his wrist. The guy smells expensive and seems to spend an extra second taking in Shane and company, but when Shane frowns at him the expensive guy just smiles and nods pleasantly, slipping past them. The problem with these people is that they're mostly too damn nice.

"You here a lot?" Shane says.

"Some."

"So you ever see Sam? The kid?"

Mario smiles. "Yeah, I see him all the time. Bunch of the guys used to come here, but him and me the only ones left."

Bingo. Shane looks around for Jimmy, but his brother's nowhere to be seen.

"We're looking for him," Shane says. He's about to explain but stops himself, leaves it at that. Mario nods, as if looking for Sam is an acceptable something to do.

"Usually he's here a ton, one of those gym rats." Mario's thinking. "But not lately. I haven't seen him for a while."

"We'll get his number from the gym."

Mario shrugs, as if he doubts it. "The thing is," Mario says, "I'm pretty sure he lives around here. Told me about this game one time, somewhere close. It's funny, I see him all the time but the kid never talks. We talk, it's usually me asking him about you guys, what's going on at the Firehouse."

"Sure," Shane says. "That other game he talked about, you remember where it was?"

"Oh yeah." Mario smiles, happy to be of help. "Rec Center. Potrero Hill."

5

THEY DRIVE OUT of Multimedia Gulch and stop at a metal-grated corner store to ask directions. On the other side of the street, a few doors down, four young Latinos are hanging out in trouble wear, leaning against one another, moving in small concentric circles. The store blares opera music from a speaker mounted above the door, a loud fuzzy tenor bellowing Italian through the streets for his lost or slutty love. Inside, behind the speaker, the store is relatively quiet as Shane buys a sweet iced tea and Jimmy makes tiny conversation with the Asian man behind the counter.

"Potrero Hill Rec Center," Jimmy repeats. The man shakes his head. "Rhode Island Street." The man shrugs. All the streets up here are named after states, and something about that makes it impossible to remember the order. What's the difference between Wisconsin, Connecticut, Arkansas, Rhode Island?

Jimmy taps the counter, studies the man to see if he's lying. "Big opera fan, huh?"

"Ah, you know, these guys out there?" The storekeep points one finger past them to the street. "They no good. Used to hang out in front the store all day. Block the door, bad business." He gives a yellow smile. "But they hate this fucking music. Now they stay away." He bobs his big head and laughs.

Shane picks a direction and sticks with it, passing a line of brand new construction, flimsy live/work lofts for sale at something unspeakable. Shane has never been on this street before. It winds and gently curves, the pavement growing wild with potholes and turning quickly rough and darker, deep-stained with Rorschach oil blots. The van bucks and jolts like a frightened horse. Stop sign. On the corner in front of them, a group of black guys in skull caps and puffy jackets examine the van together. Behind them, the tiered slope of buildings climbs the hill in amphitheater rows, the orange roofs burning in the morning sun.

"Yeah," Jimmy says. "Da projects." He rolls down his window.

They turn left, skirting the development while the corner guys track them like prey or an entertainment sent to help break up the day. Shane doesn't look at them. It seems like eye contact might make something here ignite. Jimmy stares though with unmasked curiosity and one of the guys calls out to him, menace or invitation, it's hard to tell. Shane leans into the gas pedal and the van leaves the guys but not the projects there behind. The projects don't end easily. The place is enormous at close range, concrete building after building creeping up the hill, wrapping around the corner, continuing unchecked out of sight. The street that navigates the projects' edge seems extra wide, a moat to keep castle folk inside.

At the crest of the hill appears a liquor store with its own collection of guys standing outside. "Stop here dude," Jimmy says. "I'm gonna ask."

"Yeah right." Shane rolls through a stop sign but Jimmy is already leaning out the window, calling out to everyone's surprise. "Yo, what's up," Jimmy says.

The two nearest guys stare him down. Shane has stopped the van's forward motion but he is not happy about it. He whispers his brother's name.

"There a Rec Center up here?" Jimmy says. The guys don't answer. "Rec Center," Jimmy repeats, totally uncowed. "Somewhere around here they play ball."

The two guys laugh, not kindly. "Shit motherfucker play ball," one says to the other.

"Mary Poppins motherfucker play ball," the other says, laughing hard.

"In that Chitty-Chitty hoopdi, nigga, don't play no ball."

Jimmy's about to say something else but Shane hits the gas and they're out of there. In the sideview he sees the two figures step out onto the street and gesture after them in obscene and happy triumph.

Then, suddenly, the projects disappear. A line of noble old Victorians stand up tall on the left, and an enormous baseball field spreads out to the right, separated from the projects below by a planted row of eucalyptus and twenty-foot-high chain-link fence. In the green expanse of this mountain fortress, clusters of white people are standing in the grass, watching dogs run madly around the infield and chase each other toward deep left. That's where the Rec Center sits, a half cylinder like an aircraft hangar, decorated with sports figures painted in a child's hand. A football player, number 32, stands front and center, looking small in his tight-fit jersey with the telltale football tucked in to run.

"Who's 32?" Jimmy says, as they park.

"O.J. Simpson."

"Local hero."

The small door to the gym is propped ajar. They hear the pounding of a ball before they enter, but inside there's just one little kid shooting around by himself. Good gym: six glass backboards, elevated spectator stands to one side, springy new wood floor. A scorer's clock sits low against the wall, and directly opposite, competing for attention, blares a television set aimed at the empty stands. That nervous adolescent smell of gym: dust and damp cotton and rubber. Near the entrance hang pictures of league teams and famous visitors.

"Hey, they got Jason Kidd up here," Jimmy says. "Gary Payton."

Shane strolls over to check it out. Both the big-time

hometown NBA stars are there indeed, Kidd smiling, Payton scowling, wearing the loose jerseys of a summer league.

"Who knew."

"Someone."

They strip down out of their sweats and start shooting around. The little boy has been watching them and moves closer now, holding the ball with both hands.

"Hey," Jimmy says to the boy, "what's up, little man?"

"You here all by yourself?" Shane asks.

The boy scowls and hugs the ball tight as if daring them to take it from him. The ball seems about twice as big as his head.

"We gonna run today or what?" Jimmy asks.

"Yeah," the boy says. He dribbles the ball with maximum concentration, then looks back at Jimmy for approval.

"Damn," Jimmy says, very seriously. "Little man's got game, huh. How about the big boys, they gonna come up here today?"

The boy nods, his eyes bouncing slowly back and forth between them. "They mostly black people up here," he explains finally. "But they let you play."

Shane smiles and tries not to laugh but Jimmy loses it, tilting his head back and practically hooting. "Oh yeah?" Jimmy says. "That's good. I'm glad, 'cause we like to play with all kinds of people." He leaps forward suddenly and swats the ball out of the boy's hand and the two of them go running down the court, Jimmy high-stepping with the stolen ball, the boy shouting in delighted hot pursuit.

***

The first guy to show is tall and skinny. He scuffs his shoes on the floors and ignores them, retreating back outside to wait for someone legitimate to show. He returns a few minutes later with a threesome, one short and two big, with weight rooms and tattoo parlors in their arms, all of them half shouting at one another. They glance at Shane and Jimmy sitting in the stands, watching baseball on TV. Shane nods, trying to play it cool. Wait for while, see if Sam shows, strike up a conversation when things get under way. But Jimmy has his own ideas, walking straight down to the court to talk.

"You wanna start some threes?" Jimmy says. They shake their head, ignore him. "Wait for full, huh," he says. "That's cool." He bounces around them on his big feet like a puppy, a little frisky yellow puppy yelping among laid-back Labradors. "Yeah," Jimmy presses on, "friend told us about this run up here, said we should come up." The four of them have still not spoken a word to him, but they're looking at him carefully now.

"Sam," Jimmy says. "You know him? About twenty years old, six foot one, light-skinned guy, freckles, big hair, long arms? He lives over here somewhere, pretty good player. Friend of mine."

"Goddamn," one of the guys says. He shakes his head in disgust, takes a shot that skittles off the rim.

"Five-oh, five-oh," his buddy says, stepping back.

"Shit's deep undercover," the other says, laughing and shaking his head. "Shit nigga talk about light-skin dark-skin motherfucker."

"Chocolate thunder or cafe au lait."

"Sam-bo, right, he be looking for his Sambo."

"No," Jimmy says. "Hey." He keeps talking but Shane can't watch anymore, staring at the television, keeping the Jimmy shape in the corner of his eye only, hoping he doesn't have to come to anyone's rescue. Rescue—scrape his brother off the floor, more like it.

Jimmy shuts up but stays down there with them, grabbing the ball when he can, shooting around. Shane watches his brother keep an eye on the numbers as more guys trickle in. He knows Jimmy isn't thinking about Sam anymore. He's thinking about getting in the first game. The first game matters. They've both been in this position before, alone and separately, and know that when you're the only white guys waiting, and no one knows you—forget it. No one wants to play with the white guy any more than they want to play with a billy goat or that little kid who's shooting around. Shane knows that when you're unknown and white they don't want you unless you look like you might be able to bench press a dump truck or stand about eight feet tall or just hit twenty-five straight jump shots warming up. The gym looks at Shane and Jimmy and sees one white guy who talks too much and another who might be scared or turn to stone when he hears the chorus of intimidation sure to be tossed his way. Shane sees himself and his brother through their eyes, and thinks: these dudes could go either way. Do their part or mess your whole team right up.

Jimmy makes it happen. He waves Shane down to the court and Shane walks out there slowly, arms hanging loose, nodding at their reluctant teammates, sizing up the competition. No pressure—just if they don't win, they don't shine out there, no way anyone's going to talk to them. No way they are going to get to play again.

"Check ball."

The guy who is covering Shane stands about the same height, a little thinner in the shoulders and legs and arms, younger by at least ten years. Brand-new Reeboks, bright red shirt. He stares at Shane with open disdain. Yeah, you ain't gonna do shit. Shane doesn't stare back. He cuts through the middle, sets a pick across but no one seems to notice. Red Shirt follows him at a brisk walk, barely interested in his whereabouts. The ball swings over to Shane on the wing, and Shane catches it, squares to the basket, gives a quick fake. Red Shirt doesn't move, standing with his back straight and face bored, looking through him as if checking out a mildly pretty girl in the empty stands. Shane passes it back out, and his defender smiles: I told you. But the next time the ball comes Shane's way, Shane doesn't hesitate, he snaps the ball and immediately turns to shoot. At the last minute the guy ducks and stomps in Shane's direction like a rhino, trying to startle him, but all Shane sees is the back of the rim as he flops his wrist and watches the ball go cleanly through. He makes three shots like that, misses one, and Red Shirt just lets it happen as if defense is beneath him. Shane tries not to enjoy himself too much, knowing that someone out there is bound to notice. White boy hits a couple open shots, someone's gonna decide to shut him down.

Jimmy has a harder time of it. They've played so long in their pale game that now his brother relies too much on quickness. Now the force of gravity has changed. There are guys plenty quicker than him here. He has the ball stolen a few times, his shot blocked. Shane can see him playing nervous, rattled. This is when Jimmy's temper flares, when he is a danger to himself and others. Shane can't worry about that right now. Red Shirt gives him one more open shot from the elbow, Shane drains it, and just like that, they win.

The next team gathers like a storm cloud at one end of the court. Shane's teammates decide the white boys rate an introduction.

"Darius."

"Kev."

"Jo Jo." The natural team leader is Shane's age, maybe, his height, more muscular. "These next guys got a squad," Jo Jo says. "We take them, we run all day."

"All right."

Jo Jo shakes his head to make sure Shane's listening. "We gotta push it, get out and run. They ain't gonna give you that J. "

"I bet," Shane says. "Let's run."

The next squad is big and quick and mad. He's forgotten games like that, when you can't call a foul near the basket unless someone attacks you with a chair. Jimmy tries it and everyone starts yelling at him at once. Not here: the name of the game is you're gonna get hit. Shane's man stays close this time, breath like a damp dishtowel brushing against his face. Pushes him. Grabs him. For the first few minutes Shane doesn't touch the ball. He acts tired and cowed, lulling his man to sleep. Then he busts back, hits a medium range shot, then slow again. Slow slow quick. He gets free again and hits one way back, two full steps past the three-point line. Fuck yes. He's stronger than he was the last time he played indoors, and this distance seems fine and manageable. It still surprises him, sometimes, what his new body can do.

"Ooh, like Hornacek and shit," someone yells from the sideline. "He killing you Vee."

Vee swears, shakes his head. Bullshit.

Things get tough. Vee wants the ball down low and gets it. He puts his shoulder against Shane's and spins him like a revolving door, lays it in. "Stop fouling, bitch," Vee says. After that the man is everywhere, pushing Shane, roughing him, daring him to look him in the eye or say a single word. When Shane finally gets the ball, Vee reaches out and rips it out of his hands. A cry of disgust goes up from Shane's teammates. He's not exactly scared, but for the first time in a long time, he feels like things on the court are out of his control.

You can't let the Vees of the world do this to you, Shane thinks. He looks at his enemy. The guy has a mother and father, a girlfriend or a wife, a kid or a dog. The guy is just another guy. The next time Vee tries to post him up, Shane keeps shifting, giving the man nothing to push on, nudging him off balance. Vee keeps trying but can't get good position.

They steal the ball from Jimmy, picking off a lazy pass, and pound it back inside to their big man. Shane's teammate Darius lets the guy back him down, lets the guy put up the shot—and then launches himself to get it, one greedy hand stretched up suddenly above the rim. He's so high that he has time to aim and swat the ball in a clean line into Shane's hands, who tosses it out perfect, the ball bouncing and floating for sprinting Jo Jo to catch up. He lays it in, slaps the backboard with a solid thump. "Game time!"

"Dunk that shit, nigga." The sideline chips in. Shane's heart is galloping, stampeding against his chest. He looks over at Jimmy and sees it in his brother's eyes as well. This is fucking basketball. Who have they been kidding all this time? They cross paths, Jimmy and Shane, slapping hands softly at half court.

"You good?"

"Yeah." The gym has gotten loud: sneakers, balls, voices, television. Shane can feel his heart still pounding. He tries to think of someplace he'd rather be.

"Let's keep it going."

"Do our thing."

The next team comes on and Shane catches Jimmy's eye, slides over to set a pick and is run over immediately. The aggressor stands tall victorious lording over his fallen body for a moment. Jimmy steps quickly to him, reaching down to hoist him up.

"What the hell is that?" Shane says.

"Better get outta my way," the guy says, and Shane figures something has to happen until Jo Jo steps in, waves everyone away.

"Come on, come on, play ball y'all. Fuck this shit, come on." He pulls Jimmy and Shane aside. "Don't worry about Rashon. That boy's crazy." He shakes his head at Shane. "And don't set no picks, that shit don't play out here."

"All right." Shane looks at his shoes and at the ceiling, anywhere but at the guy he wants to kill, wants to stick a shard of glass through his throat. Jo Jo's still got him by the arm and releases only when he gives him the nod that says he gets it. You're not going to win that one, Jo Jo's eyes are telling him, you're never ever going to win that one up here, white boy. They're gonna knock you down and get in your head and everything. All you got is your game, 'cause the minute you open your mouth, you lose.

"Okay. I'm cool," Shane says, quietly.

"Let's put 'em away." Jo Jo slaps him on the ass, nods. "Check ball," Jo Jo says.

After Rashon and company, the sailing is fairly smooth, and when they eventually lose after five games it's from absolute fatigue. Jo Jo takes it hard, though, swearing to himself, looking annoyed. Shane sits down next to him on a bench at the end of the court.

"Man," Shane says. Jo Jo shrugs, puts out a fist and they do the up-down bump.

"Yeah," Jo Jo says. "I can't believe we even let those

chumps score basket one. After all that." He calls out to one of the other players passing nearby. "That right, I'm talking 'bout you, nigga, you're weak, bitch, you are weak."

"Beat your fat ass, nigga."

"Beh put your diary, mothafucker, wait 'til leap year."

"That's why you sittin'."

"Talk to me you run five straight." The other guy laughs, struts on back to the court. "Shit," Jo Jo says, watching him go.

"You run like this every Saturday?" Shane says.

"This ain't shit, man. They got butchers and America's Most Wanted here today." Jo Jo turns to him, shaking off the game. "There always something though." He watches Jo Jo hesitate, then decide to grant Shane a conversation. "Most of the time, these thugs don't run." He points out on the court. "Lex, Cliff, Dare, Show, they all gentlemen, we don't need that shit, we just come up to play. During the week, it's pretty civilized. But I can't come during the week no more, working nights, so I up here most Saturdays, if I can. When the once and future convicts come on out."

"I never played up here before."

"Yeah, huh. Where you play at?"

"I'm usually outside, but I'm trying to get back indoors. Concrete'll beat you up after a while."

"Yeah, I don't even mess around with that."

They sit in silence for a second, watching the next game in progress.

"My brother and me, this guy we play with told us about up here," Shane says, finally. "I think he plays here all the time."

"Who's that?"

"This guy Sam. Kind of skinny, tall, pretty good hops. Likes to takes it to the hole, not really a shooter. Long arms. Shot blocker."

"Huh."

"Kind of half white, I dunno, funny looking, almost like freckles all over. Like brown hair."

"You talking about this dude Sauce," Jo Jo says, nodding to himself now, satisfied. "Yeah, I know who you talking about. But he don't really play up here. I mean he shoot around, you know, but he don't play with nobody."

"He doesn't play?"

"Nah. He in here all the time, but he just shoot around."

"I thought he played. I thought I'd see him up here."

"I ain't seen him for a while."

"Me neither. He used to come up and play over my other game, like three times a week. He stopped coming, though. He left a bag up there, too, with a cell phone and stuff. Just been sitting in my van, waiting for him to come back."

"Yeah, I don't know. I haven't seen him."

"You think anyone knows where he lives, like?" Shane says, his heart beating a little fast like he's doing something wrong.

Jo Jo hesitates. "I don't stay down there no more. I

know his momma's up in there, F-3 I think."

"Where's that."

"That's the projects, man. Right over here."

"Maybe I'll go down there."

Jo Jo laughs. "You go, but it ain't recommended."

"I bet. I just want to get his shit back to the man."

Jo Jo nods, thinking. "I don't stay there no more," he repeats.

"Yeah, I understand. I guess I could leave the bag up here, it's just, I don't know, it's got like some valuable stuff, you know."

"Naw, don't leave it here." Jo Jo stands up. "I know what you're saying, that's old school, take care of your boys."

"He'd do the same for me."

Jo Jo nods. "Yeah. Well I'll show you, you want."

6

SHANE AND JIMMY catch up to Jo Jo and a friend on the sidewalk where the pavement meets the grass of the baseball diamond. Jo Jo doesn't say anything as they drop into step, just keeps walking, four abreast now down the third-base line. No baseball today. The infield's dry and overrun by dogs, while out in the wide expanse of right center field a coed soccer game is under way. White men and women kick the ball north then south then north again.

Jo Jo heads for the chain-link behind home plate, where the fence gaps and gives way to a dirt trail through grass and trash, crashing down between the buildings below. Trash everywhere: tiny crushed Bacardi Lemon bottles, impacted plastic forks and cups, cigarette and Cheetos wrappers, digging hard into the hill like ticks. Shane can see the roofs up close now, checkerboards of Spanish tile holding the concrete barracks together, glowing in the afternoon light like a distorted dream of Stanford or Seville. He counts the metal vent spouts by habit. City contract. Even the projects have their cheap little chimneys. He wonders who does the work up here.

"All right now," Jo Jo says, implying something serious.

They follow him into the dark crease between two buildings, ducking under long clotheslines where a few white sheets dry slowly in the shade, hanging abandoned like old surrender flags. The path dumps them into a parking lot that looks like it's been bombed. The parked cars are furniture, their hoods weighed down with girls hanging out in the sun, weaving each others' hair. But it's not the girls he's watching. There are some scary-looking motherfuckers here, their shirts off, pants low, acres of black torso mock beating the crap out of one other. This is somebody's worst nightmare, and suddenly Shane feels like that somebody might be him. Guys suspend their beer cans in mid-drink and halt their bitch-slap fists of fury to stare. Shane tries not to look at anyone. He looks at the cars instead: shiny blue sports cars with bumper bras, rusted pieces of crap held together by silver duct tape. A black SUV shines out across the asphalt like a gun dropped in the sand.

Something jumps at him. Shane flinches, trying to get his hands up, but there's no collision, just two kids whipping by him chasing a third at cataclysmic speed, shouting and laughing and almost falling down. Two older women sit on concrete patios in plastic folding chairs, shaking their heads at Shane. He pictures a jagged bottle thrown from a window, sinking its green triangle teeth into the firm white meat of his thigh.

"S'up nigga, where y'at!"

"G.I. Jo Jo!"

The calls come out from three guys sitting on a stoop, two big silent types and a skinny talker, his thin arms poking out of the cavernous sleeves of a pale blue football jersey, number 27. Tennessee Titans. Shane can't tell how old he is, older than fifteen, less than twenty-five. The quick, intelligent big brown eyes flick quickly between Shane and Jimmy, doing arithmetic, picking apart this passing puzzle fallen in his lap. Jo Jo is shaking hands now, explaining something but not quite stopping forward motion, and Shane and Jimmy follow as close as they can. Shane can feel those eyes still rubbing curious against his spine as they leave the busy lot behind.

They round the corner of another building and Jo Jo stops. Shane stands close against the wall, feels the heat coming off the concrete onto his cheek.

"His momma stay in there," Jo Jo says. He tilts his head at the nearest door.

"All right," Shane says. "Hey, thanks for bringing us down." He doesn't know what else to say. "See you on the court." He hopes he sounds calm. He hopes he sounds like he knows what he's doing.

Jo Jo points at the door. "Watch your ass," Jo Jo calls out as he steps away. Then Shane and Jimmy are alone.

"Damn-it-feels-good-to-be-a-gangster," Jimmy sings playfully, smiling at Shane.

Shane steps towards the door.

"This one," Shane whispers.

"Cool."

"I really hope someone's home."

The walls around the door are marked by barebones graffiti: no bubble letters, no pictures, no colors, only cryptic symbols, statements, and brief proclamations in simple black on gray. Niggas be acting like bitches. God help us all. He can hear his own breath pushing quickly through his nose. His mouth, he realizes, is clenched shut as if he's trying not to speak. This feels like a place where if horrible things haven't happened yet, they're definitely about to.

Jimmy and he both lean forward to knock, then Shane withdraws his fist, which stays balled tight, hanging like a big rock against his side. His brother knocks twice, softly, the true stranger's knock that never brings good news.

Inside, beyond the door, voices, first high then low.

"Who's at?" Deep down but a young voice, right against the door. A boy trying to sound like something else. Talking to them.

Shane leans in near the door. "It's Shane," he says, as if that explains something. "Friend of Sam's," he adds. "We got something belongs to him." He stops for a moment, listens. Nothing. From somewhere on the other side of the building comes a loud solid sound, like a plank of wood dropping onto concrete from a height. Sam's bag feels heavy in his hands. Jimmy stands quietly beside him, staring calmly at the door as if he knows it's about to open and reveal friendly faces awaiting them inside. Invite them in for a spot of tea.

"What you got?" A woman's voice, now, flat and factual, calibrated to penetrate the wood.

Jimmy leans in toward the door. "Yeah, this guy we know, Sam? left his duffel bag up on the basketball court? Where we play? It's got a butt-load of stuff, cell phone, buncha stuff. They told us he lived here, me and my brother. Green, it's a green bag."

"You can leave it right there."

"He lives here, right?"

"Leave it there," the voice says.

"Listen," Jimmy says, "I don't wanna, you know, I mean, I just want to get the thing back to him, you know." Jimmy takes a breath, gets ready for the next long meaningless sentence when the door clicks sharply and swings open into the room.

The woman is tall, five eight or nine or maybe ten. Her face is smooth as a glazed pot, not a wrinkle in sight. Late twenties, Shane thinks. Wide brown eyes looking out from brilliant whites. Long lashes, painted, light silver eye shadow, eyebrows carefully directed in thin arched lines. Her deep brown flesh flows from tight jet-black short shorts, the legs well scarred above one knee. Thin arms lost in an oversized red T-shirt. Her short crinkled hair is molded back tight against her head, frozen into tiny waves.

She glances quickly at their hands and then their

faces and then all up and down. A tall young boy stands at her hip, killing them with his eyes. Ten years old, maybe more. At the window beyond, a younger boy and a little girl look on with absolute curiosity.

Jimmy glances at Shane and she follows his lead, both of them waiting for an answer.

"We're friends of Sam's," Shane says.

"Friends," she says, exhaling, half laughing at them. "Sam." The older boy shakes his head, scowls.

"This is his duffel bag, isn't it?" She looks at the bag as if it's the carcass of a skunk. "Left it up there at the court."

"Court what," she says, and then shakes her head as he opens his mouth again, waves her hand in dismissal. "All right, all right, come on in here a minute." She opens the door one notch wider and steps back aside, and they slip into the new and welcome space.

"Thank you," Shane says, as she closes the door behind them, quickly, and locks it.

The house smells like old carpet and artificial cheese. The ceilings seem low enough to reach up and touch, and light trickles into the main room ahead of them through thick dark blue shades. She points and they walk ahead of her, the boy slipping around to let them pass. The younger kids stay against the window, holding to the sill as if they're keeping it in place.

"Well, sit down," she says, motioning to a couch of no particular color on one side of the room. "Demetrius, go watch your sister. Go on."

The oldest boy grabs his little sister's hand and hauls

her off to another room, while the younger boy, seven or eight, stands like a statue of curiosity, staring at them with his mouth slightly ajar.

She crosses to an armchair as they sit. The springs of the couch are shot, and they sink so low into the cushions it makes Shane feel like a little kid. The rag fabric is slightly rough like rashed skin. From their sunken vantage on the couch, she lords over them, leaning back in her chair, her legs crossed at eye level. The effect is disconcerting, the two of them slumped like couch potatoes, necks craned back, trying not to look at thighs.

"So you all mister and mister who?"

"Shane and Jimmy McCarthy."

"Which one which."

"Shane."

"Jimmy."

"We're brothers. We both play with Sam up at his regular court, over at the Firehouse."

"No one call him Sam," she says, examining her nails which are long and smooth and painted red.

"That's not his name?"

"Naw. The kids up here they call him Sauce if they call him but his Christian name Samson. Yeah," she says, watching their eyes. "Samson."

"He always said his name was Sam."

"I ain't surprised." The younger boy moves over to her, stands next to her with his fingers resting delicately on the arm of the chair. Something about the way the boy's hand rests there, the way he stands both protecting and protected, tells Shane that she is not a sister or a cousin or anyone except for a mother. She is the boss of this boy and this house and anyone else who lives here. This is Sam's mother. Shane stares, as he estimates her age and does the calculations. Late twenties is impossible. She is older than she looks.

"He ain't here," she continues, staring back. "When he leave that bag?"

"A month ago," Shane says. They all look at the bag together, sitting there on the coffee table between them.

"It's all in there," Jimmy says. "Cell phone, CD, you know, he's got some stuff in there he must be missing."

"So you just go through it."

"Sure," Jimmy says. "I mean, wouldn't you?"

"We were looking for an address or something." Shane tries to pull her stare away from Jimmy, but they're deep in some eyeball contest now. "We just wanted to get it back to him. We just wanted to be sure he's all right."

She snorts at Jimmy and Jimmy smiles as she turns her sights on Shane. "Okay? I don't like people in my business." Her eyes are dark and angry and he should look away. "You hear me? That's the first and end of story, so I stay out of yours I appreciate you stay on out of mine."

"Give me a break," Jimmy says. "We're just trying to help."

She keeps her eyes on Shane. What does she see sitting here? What is he, anyway? "I'm sorry," he says. "I understand. We just wanted him to get his stuff." He struggles to get up out of the black hole of the couch.

"What I give a fuck about his stuff," she says.

"Hey," Jimmy says, "now why you mad at us? Don't shoot the messenger."

"Jimmy."

"He's not here. He gone."

"Gone?" Jimmy says.

"Is he all right?"

"I don't know. You tell me, if you a messenger, what's the message." She stands suddenly, steps forward, and collects the bag off of the table and disappears into the next room, the boy jerking along behind her as if attached by rope. They hear the zipper open, objects clinking against a counter. There's a small human noise and then a moment of silence.

"All right now," her voice calls out from the next room in a new key. "Don't go nowhere. Lemme get y'all a drink."

"Shit," Jimmy whispers. "What the hell's going on?"

"We don't know," Shane says quietly. "We don't know anything."

"She knows something."

"Come on. Let's just go."

"No, sit tight."

In the next room, now, she is chatting with her kids. Someone giggles, someone laughs. She returns alone a minute later with brown-tinted dimpled glasses, a chlorine-scented lemonade with a few ice cubes clinking around inside. She smiles. She looks like a different person. "Okay. Never did win a Miss Hospitality, huh."

"Thank you."

"Y'all all right, though. I, you know, I just." She sighs. She sits back in her seat, crosses her legs again, smiles as if they're two new neighbors she's invited in for a spot of pie. "So where y'all stay at?" From behind her, the older boy appears at the doorway, watching them again.

"We grew up in the city, over in the Sunset. I live up in Noe Valley now, Jimmy still lives over there with our Ma."

"That right."

"Did you grow up in the city?" Jimmy says.

She frowns at him, shakes her head. "So you say Samson run witch y'all."

"With me and Jimmy and like twenty other guys I guess, all different ages, Sam's always the youngest. Samson. Sorry." The name feels strange on his tongue.

"Uh huh. Where this at?"

"We've been playing at the same court, outdoors, over above Duboce Triangle, years now. I think he came up, what was it Jimmy, maybe first time five years ago?"

"I don't know," Jimmy says. "I'd have to check my day planner."

"There ever since. He's a really great kid, everyone out there really likes him and respects him. You know how it goes, he's like, one of the guys."

"You all play basketball," she says, as if that's the only detail in all that worth talking about. "And Samson come down wherever to play ball witch y'all. When?"

"He never talks about it?" Jimmy says. "Or you two just don't talk much." She ignores him, keeps her eyes on Shane.

"Tuesday, Thursday, Friday, right around noon." Shane speaks slowly, watching her face for a flicker of recognition. "Saturday morning, ten o'clock or so. Sam doesn't really come out Saturday." She nods, her face revealing nothing. They sit there for a while, sipping lemonade made from mix.

"You got me figured out, huh," she says, finally. She's talking to Shane. He feels like for a split second the two of them are sitting on a sandy dune at sunset, alone.

"I don't know about that," Shane says. "No. I don't think so."

"We don't even know your name," Jimmy says. "We don't even know who you are."

"Mmm," she says, as if trying to decide what to go with. "Debra. Debra Marks. Now tell me something. You saw him a month, or was it less?"

"About a month."

She nods. A decision has been made. "Y'all got a car?"

"Up at the Rec Center."

She frowns. "You do me a favor."

"Be happy to."

"Get your car and come back here." She sucks in her bottom lip, calculating something, a math equation she hasn't puzzled out for a long time. "I send Demetrius with you, he show you the way. Demetrius!" Her voice packs sudden power, and they hear feet pounding down the stairs. She crooks a finger and the boy goes quickly to her, bending his head next to her for whispered council. When he raises his wide eyes to them he gulps slightly, trying to see what his mother trusts in them.

"Come on," he says.

7

SHE'S WAITING FOR THEM in the parking lot when they return. Changed: sweat suit in dark blue, a little crinkly and mildly shiny, as if made from the skin of some modern, urban reptile; white high-tops right off the shelf with bubble heel; thin gold chain and cross dangling loose around her neck; bright white Nike baseball cap wedged on tight. She looks young, a little brash and nervous at the same time.

Silent Demetrius all but leaps from the van, mission accomplished. He hasn't said a word to them yet, doesn't like what's going on. He doesn't like it when Debra tells him, "Y'all staying at Mimi's, all right?" The boy purses his lips and stomps one foot gently before running down the building and around the corner, out of sight. She watches him go and when he disappears she doesn't have kids anymore. She leans back, reading the side of the van.

"Chimney what?" She shakes her head. "Get the hell

out of here." The van continues to amuse her as she climbs inside. She takes in the chaotic innards, her eyes skipping quickly across the tools of his trade: wire brushes, extending rods, vacuum, carbide saw, cordless drill, palm sander. Goggles, knee pads, surgeon dust masks. Black vinyl gloves. A big reddish toolbox with wrenches, screwdrivers, pliers, hammers. A carpenter's handsaw. It must seem like too much stuff to her. It does to most people.

"You really clean those chimneys?" she says.

"I really do."

"You a story." She shakes her head. "And you what Santa's little helper?"

Jimmy grins. "Nah."

"I didn't think so. Uhn-uh. All right, go right out the lot, I'll show you." She sits pressed back against the front seat, her cap pulled tight over her eyes, calling out directions as her sweat suit snaps in the miles per hour breeze. They drop down the back side of the projects with the high cliff above them and the brilliantine bay to the right, turning on her mark until suddenly they're on the clean, quiet streets of Potrero Hill, where pale faces talk calmly in the sun in front of a deli clutching clean brown paper bags with seeded baguette tops protruding like periscopes. A small phalanx of joggers trots by, chatting breathy as they stride, their slim albino legs slicing through the late afternoon. Shane smells yeast, a brewery brewing somewhere close.

"Here," Debra says, leaning across him to jab a thin,

sure finger at a large pastel-colored shopping center. Her shoulder hits Shane's and she pulls back, leaving a scent behind her: glue, leather, plastic, tangerine, soil. She shoots him a look like he's reached out and pinched her nipple, but before he can say sorry she pouts up her lips and smiles at him as if to say, Well you little dirty dog. He gives the road in front of him his full and undivided attention.

They park underground, follow her from the shadows to the stores above and into the stocked fluorescent aisles of the UrbaMart where she pilots a cart through the store as if shopping for an invisible family of eight. He and Jimmy trail behind, silently watching her gather: toothbrush, toothpaste, cough syrup, aspirin, soap, detergent, sponges, aluminum foil, ketchup, mustard, canned beans, tuna, boxes of flavored quickie rice, a bag of potatoes, multipacks of chicken thighs and pork chops, sausage, soda, cheese, chips. The store is huge—it's been a while since Shane has been in a supermarket like this, far from Noe Valley. Jimmy watches Debra, transfixed as she evaluates every purchase, comparing the prices with a knowing finger aimed at cost-per-ounce breakdown. At first she pays neither of them any mind. Then she starts asking Shane the occasional question: has he ever tried this cereal they have on sale? Which kind of ant traps work best? Why are those light bulbs so expensive? He doesn't know much but she listens to his best shot as if he's written treatise on the matter. She has Jimmy push the cart.

At the register she removes a wrinkled blank check and a book of food stamps from her pocket, glaring at the price screen as if she has memorized the true cost of every item and stands poised to cry foul at the smallest misprint or mistake. The three of them watch the numbers. Without quite realizing, Shane is holding his own wallet, pressing it flat in his hand like a courtroom bible. When the clerk turns to announce the total, Debra puts her head down and begins her calculations, tilting open the corner edge of the food stamp book to count, but maybe now she's also watching him out of the top of her eyes as he slides his bank card through the reader. She stops counting as he punches in his passcode, OKs the total, no cash back. The register rattles it home.

"Thank you Mr. McCarthy," their thin clerk says, reading his name off the receipt and handing it to him without a glance.

She doesn't say a word as they head back to the car, Shane and Debra walking side by side as Jimmy madly kicks and wheels the cart ahead like a kid. When they've loaded the last bag into the van she makes a thoughtful noise, as if a brilliant idea has just occurred to her.

"Y'all mind I stop into the Fit Right," she says. She seems about to explain more but instead waits for them to nod. "While I'm here. Y'all come along you want. You need you some new kicks." They all examine Shane's b-ball shoes together.

"These still got life in them."

"Yeah. " She disagrees. "Well they having a sale."

The sale at Fit Right is in full swing, and the clothing racks look like they've been ransacked by angry Huns or Mongols unable to find their size. She starts in shoes, drilling in on a simple pair of black flats and some silver spaghetti-strap medium heels designed for a party on a hot and distant planet. When she heads into the bra section, Jimmy follows but Shane wanders away with propriety. Lou would never shop here, would she? He didn't know where she shopped, but not here, ever. He stands in front of a dress rack, fingering clothes his wife would never wear.

By the time he finds Debra and his brother again, their cart is filling up: the shoes, the bras, sweaters, a blouse, a pair of pants, a small collection of assorted items for her kids. A man's jacket made out of some light phosphorescent skin.

"That's for your brother," she says, catching him. "You get some kicks?"

"No."

"Come on now, you didn't even look."

"I'm not much of a shopper."

"Well I'm here now," she says. "What size you got?" She moves quickly, yanking samples from the shelves and putting them into his hands. "What's wrong with those?"

Jimmy and he shake their heads together. "They're too low," Shane says. "No ankle support."

"Oh they good enough for Iverson but not for you."

"I'm gonna pass."

"Suit yourself. You got to do something, though,

those are embarrassing." She's as appalled as Lou at his inability to consume.

"I can stand it."

"The rest of us can't," she says, smiling and nodding at Jimmy, her new best friend. "Help your brother, will you?" She glances down at Jimmy's feet, shakes her head. "Damn boy, what size *you* wear? Got you some flippers."

"You know what they say."

She grins. She and Jimmy are getting along famously.

Her last stop is sunglasses and a high-tech fabric handbag that looks like it's made from liquid mercury and atomic waste. "That's bad ass," Jimmy says, taking it out of her hands, running his fingers along the seams.

"Nice, huh," she says.

"Yeah."

Jimmy and Debra keep chatting about her other purchases as they load them onto the moving belt, and this time she doesn't take out her check or anything as Shane pays for the stuff and watches the clerk pack everything into two enormous plastic bags capable of suffocating many babies at once.

They carry everything into the kitchen, piling things carefully on the Formica table in the middle, and then stand back waiting to be told to leave. Kitchenwise, the place isn't much to look at. Dishes crammed dirty into a too-small sink, the lingering smell of instant food. Linoleum gouged and stained and scarred. Fiberboard cabinets. The kitchen sucks. A few appliances sit bulky on the counter: plastic toaster, plastic coffee machine, a boom box perched on top of the refrigerator in the corner. On the front of the fridge, a few magnets hold school drawings signed Sharina and Kaleb, and as Shane steps over to take a polite and closer look he sees it, clinging to the side: a picture of Sam.

To his surprise, it is exactly the Sam he has in his head. The kid's shoulders are back, chest forward, he's puffed up in his basketball strut. Between his strange freckled skin, his bushy hair clipped close to his head, jaw tight, chin up, eyes focused through Shane to the beyond, the kid looks like a draft recruit bound for an unknown war. Despite all that tough, this Sam looks like the thinner, slighter kid of the early days and not the more substantial Sam who later acquired biceps, triceps, deltoids, pecs. This is the Sam he knows: the kid who looks like he's not going to talk to you, no matter what, but then at the last minute his eyes slip to one side, his chin dips, the weight of gravity seems to open his mouth into a childish O, and a low, soft sound escapes. Hey Shane. You on next?

Debra is still putting her groceries away while Shane stares at Sam, building questions in his head. But when she turns back his way she asks the question.

"You smell that gas?"

They sniff in unison. There's a lot of scent in the kitchen and it's hard to tell what's what. She waves Shane over.

"Put your head in there." She points to a gap between the stove and the wall, and when he puts his head in there and breathes in deep there it is: gas.

"You're right."

"Yeah, huh."

"Did you call PG&E?"

"Yeah, right."

"They're usually pretty good about coming right out if you say you smell gas."

"I bet. Up there in Noe Valley."

"Well. I can probably take care of that, you want." He slips out to the van to get the wrenches and tape. When he comes back he sees Jimmy waiting for her to answer him, as if he's started a conversation she doesn't want to have.

"Huh," is all she says, her voice final and flat. A stack of tuna cans comes down on the counter with a loud and solid thwack. Shane edges between them apologetically, pulls the stove out a little bit, tries to get at its important stuff.

"It's all who you know," Jimmy says, "and we know some people, that's all I'm saying."

"That's all you're saying."

"Jimmy," Shane says. "Gimme a hand here."

Jimmy doesn't move, still waiting for something else from her.

"Yeah," she says. "Okay, I heard you. Go on, now, you gonna help your brother?"

They pull her stove out away from the wall. Back behind is a compacted honeycomb of dirt and dust, buoyed by shards of brown glass and a plastic toy and other tiny ruined secrets they don't have time to identify before she's shooed them aside and cleaned everything up. Then she and Jimmy both watch him rub a dab of spit on the connection until he can see it barely bubbling up, watch him close the cutoff and then unscrew the cap and wrap the threads in clean white silicon tape, wrench everything back up tight. He spit-checks the connection again but it seems fine.

"That's it?"

"That's it. Should be good."

"You handy, huh."

"Basic things."

"Yeah he is," Jimmy says.

"Yeah, huh, he know his stuff."

She looks at the clock on the wall but there isn't one. "I got to get my kids." She glances around her in a sudden panic and flaps her arms to herd them towards the door. "Thank you, all right?"

"Any time."

"What about the job?" Jimmy says. Shane's about to ask what they're talking about but decides to let them play it out.

She sucks in a breath and holds it. "You, uh, you got a phone number or something?"

Now they both look at Shane, for some reason. He fishes a business card from his wallet and she accepts it with a confused expression, holding the paper between the tips of her fingers like a dirty wrapper from the sidewalk. "That's my cell," he says, "so we're always pretty much in reach."

"What about your number?" Jimmy says. "In case."

"Yeah," she says, seeming less sure of herself, fishing around for something to write on. "All right."

The door clicks shut behind them as they step out into the late late afternoon, the sky still blue and bright.

"What was that about?" Shane says.

"I told her we'd help her get a job."

"A job." Shane laughs. "What's that, like the deaf leading the blind?"

"Man, she needs out. We got to get them out of here, you know what I mean?"

Shane is about to answer but then they spot someone waiting for them in the parking lot. His Tennessee Titans jersey hangs off him like an older brother hand-me-down as he leans comfortably against the van with the air of someone deputized to guard it. Shit: the van. Shane finds himself walking faster. Tennessee straightens up as they approach, waiting. There doesn't seem to be anyone else around.

"All right," Tennessee says. "What you need?"

"Visiting a friend," Jimmy says.

"Nothing," Shane said.

"Friend, man, I'm your best new friend. Got a one-stop shop here." He's calm, watching one of them and then the other.

"No, man, we're cool, man, thanks. We're not looking."

"Everybody looking," Tennessee says. "Huh."

"Not this time." They've stopped a few feet away from the van. Tennessee doesn't move, slouching comfortably in the way. Shane can feel his blood moving quickly now, the little adrenaline warriors beating their breasts and racing through his veins to battle stations. Ready to run run run.

"Yeah," Tennessee says. "Next time, right." He smiles hugely, bright white teeth shining out at them before he takes two exaggerated side steps away from the van. "Y'all friends a Sauce, huh? You say hey for me, right. Yeah."

They step silent to the van doors. Shane fumbles with the key, unlocks.

"It's all there," Tennessee says. "I made sure nobody touch it. That hardware safe inside."

"Okay," Shane says. "I appreciate that."

Tennessee laughs softly. "Next time."

Shane closes the door. Tennessee stands in the center of the lot, watching them go.

8

A T HOME HE FINDS Lou in the shower, bathroom door ajar. He steps through the steam to find her, his high-tops squeaking against the tile floor.

"Hey lovely."

His wife pokes her head out, green eyes dull and happy in the heat. He pulls at the curtain to get a better look and then reaches with intent. What he wants to do, the idea is to lift his warm and soapy wife against the tile wall, hook her legs around and notch her heels into his lower back. Her wrists around his neck. He'd like to watch her mouth open, flashing teeth, water dribbling in and out of her mouth like a cherub fountain. It's either that or spank her, bite her, call her filthy names. How else to get them out of these new gentle habits: can I? should we? do you want to?

"Hello baby," she says.

He leans in for a wet kiss, copping an excellent feel

but she doesn't take it seriously. Maybe he would slip anyway, crashing both of them to the slick tub bottom, cracking heads and teeth. "I'll be out in a minute," she says, sliding his hands gently off her and pulling the curtain tight. "I'll leave the water running."

A minute can mean anything in Lou's hands, and he heads back to the bedroom to do his push-ups and sit-ups. He can feel this Saturday in his arms and legs—the game, the quick march through the projects, his muscles tensed for danger all day long. Push-ups. Sit-ups. The wall-to-wall crushes down lush beneath him. Maybe I wouldn't go home either if I were you, he thinks. A complicated business being Sam. Push-ups. Sit-ups. It's push-ups again when she finally comes in, gives him the shower nod.

When he gets out she is clothed and scented, hair pinned up, body tucked into an expensive Italian-speaking dress of reds and yellows. Flowery, short, sexy, tight. Short. No hose. A pair of light-colored thin-strapped shoes he's semi-sure he's never seen before. She looks like summer and the evening's in collusion, warm and still. That one hot day, that one warm night a year. No San Francisco girl would ever have bought a dress like that.

"Holy cow," he says.

"It's party time," she says, smiling. There's a little dance to illustrate. "Par-tay."

"An e-party?"

She nods. "Did you forget?"

"It's Saturday, it's early for a party, isn't it? Don't the e-people know that?"

"E is for early." She has laid out a shirt for him on the bed, unbuttoned and ready. Short sleeves, white and blue, with a little festive shine to it.

"E is for." He tries to think of something clever.

"Espa.com," she says. "No shit. I know what you're thinking, but if you don't come, who's gonna laugh at the e-people with me?"

"We'll laugh?"

"Oh yeah. It's gonna be a regular all-star team, laugh-wise. Greed. Lust. Intrigue. Plus I have to go. And I wanna go with you."

"I'll just get drunk and grope you."

"What more could a girl want."

He sits on the edge of the bed and thinks of the rough skin of Sam's ratty couch, crouching there low to the floor across town. "Well, you're sure as hell not going anywhere looking like that without me." That gets a smile. "You'd be snatched up by a dingo. Where is it?"

"The Mission."

"The Mission. They used to look forward to raping and pillaging people like us. The Mission, in that dress."

"What's wrong with this dress."

"Wars have started over women like you in dresses like that."

"Oh goodie." She's happy with him. "I know you don't believe me, but you're smarter than all these people, you know that? You're clever and tan and you're mine." She reaches out to adjust his shirt, evening out the tuck all the way around. She smoothes his collar, and pushes him gently back for an arm's-length inspection.

"Okay," he says, agreeing to something.

"And you're looking really cute right now," she says. "Healthy. Relaxed." He's awkward in the rush of compliments, forgetting to say something back. "Do I look all right?" she prompts him.

"You. You're a story." He doesn't know what that means but she smiles anyway.

"A story," she says. "I'll take that."

On Mission Street, the last scraps of sun cling to the sides of buildings. The neighborhood change of shift is not yet complete. Daytime Mexicans still hurry for final meat and fruit and fish while nighttime whites begin to fill the bars and taquerias. The Mission's good old-fashioned shops are just closing, shutting their gates and doors on unlikely wares: wigs, mirrors, fishing tackle, billiards equipment, miniature wedding dresses. This is not his neighborhood and never has been, this land of the Mexicans and their neighbors, of storefront Jesus Te Ama churches and close quarter hand-to-hand commerce. For years the bloody liberals of the city and the likes of his angry bro have been crying foul, change, gentrification, ruin, but there in the middle of Mission Street it's hard to see what they're talking about. Everything seems as dirty and functional as ever. Still authentic and living and pocked with threat.

"There," Lou says. "That must be it."

A crowd is gathered on the sidewalk, stalled in a wide

circle around a spectacle in progress. Ten feet long, in wild green and red and gold, a chain-linked Chinese dragon serpentines between the storefronts and the curb, as a watching crowd shifts like a wind-tossed flame to make room. The dragon ducks down low, almost scrapes its delicate crepe belly along the sidewalk before floating to face Shane and Lou. The dragon pauses. The huge head peers into their car, baring saber teeth. The painted yellow eyes seem wide with recognition. It shakes its mane roughly and veers away.

"Wow," he says.

"See. Fun already," Lou says, her eyes scanning the sidewalk for a familiar face.

The restaurant's narrow entrance is the newest on the street, renovated into clean lines of ultramodern pseudo-deco that converge on a steel nubbed door of darkened glass and matted steel. What has gone before seems hard to say, but now the place shines out of the ratty block like a flying saucer dealership, gleaming with a grand surety that it is the future, and it will win.

Above the doorway hangs a large fabric banner that reads, *Espa.com—World to World eBusiness Solutions.*

At curbside stands the first valet parking dude Shane's ever seen on Mission Street: a twenty-something in a shiny red zipper jacket waiting for keys. The valet's jaw snaps with punctuation as he chews a real or imagined piece of gum. Shane tries to recognize him, chances are he went to Mission or Wash or Galileo, but the guy's too young. A guy who went to school with Sam, if anything.

They wait behind the line of shiny SUVs until Shane hands over the car and follows Lou inside, where a long hallway drills deep into the city block. Lining the hall on either side, oversized flags hang ceiling to floor: Brazil, Germany, France, the U.S., Japan, China, Turkey. After Turkey some flags he doesn't recognize, including one with a fat green tree perched between orange sky and earth. He doesn't remember ever seeing another flag featuring a plant.

A woman stands amid tall metal vases sprouting three-foot-high sunflowers, beaming at them as they make their approach.

"Lou," the gatekeeper coos as they arrive. She is tall and thin, with long brown hair, high society cheekbones, and small teeth. She uses every one of them as she expands to welcome them, like a friendly, handsome blowfish piranha. Her gums are plenty and healthy and pink.

"Candace," Lou says. "You look lovely." In her tight black skirt and fitted black blouse, Candace looks professionally fantastic, but *lovely*, he thinks, is the wrong word. Lou is lovely. Candace looks bored and beautiful and cold, like she might cause grave premeditated harm during sex.

"Oh, and you, what an amazing dress! It's wonderful."

"Thank you." On cue, they both turn their beaming, congratulatory faces to his. "This is Shane, my husband. Responsible for both my sanity and my dress."

"Really." Candace seems to will her chilly blue eyes larger as she turns her attention to him. "What a brilliant man." It is untrue about the dress but this is an old party trick of Lou's, handing strangers a reason to try to like him, immediately.

"It looks great in here," Shane says, trying to do his part. "I like the flags."

Candace winces slightly, as if he's let fly a medium-loud belch. "Yes," she says, "the flags." They turn to examine the flags together. People are coming in behind them and their hostess calibrates her smile again.

"I'll catch up with you later," Lou says to her in a warm stage whisper. Candace nods in agreement, and he pitches in an awkward little point-blank wave.

As they step through this second doorway a waiter meets them with a tray of lightly foaming fluted glasses, filled halfway. Shane follows his wife's lead as she casually collects her champagne and steps into the crowd, which splits and recombines and bubbles loudly around them. A steady stream of waiters ferries crowded silver trays throughout the busy rooms and he manages a crab cake as one slips into range. He is brutally hungry. His champagne, he notices, is already gone. He looks around for a place to put his empty glass and then imagines spiking it into the ground, the soft explosion, the shards nipping at their ankles like angry fleas.

Lou leans in to him like she has sweet nothings to deliver to his ear, but it's just a movement, an activity to avoid stasis. She is checking out the e-people. They are pale and skinny and young, dressed in new dark clothes. Their voices blend together in a comfortable, optimistic buzz, unhurried, unplagued by doubt, each one confident of being heard. How long has it been since he was at one of these? He used to follow her almost once a week before his injury relieved him of that duty and most others. Some of the same people must be here, though he recognizes no one. He feels incapable of remembering them. He can't stop thinking: Why talk to them? Why get to know them? He already has his wife and friends and family and cannot shake the belief that all these brand-new persons are simply passing through. He needs to make an effort. He needs to grow up. He needs a drink.

Shane leads Lou to the bar, where she immediately cracks up the bartender who pours their drinks. She waves at someone across the way, her bare arm brushing against a young guy who takes one look at her and clears his skinny throat. The kid's a journalist of some kind, maybe twenty-five but from his opening patter he's worked for half the magazines that Lou leaves lying around their living room. They toss some names around while Shane tries not to gulp his beer.

"I had lunch with him yesterday," the kid says.

"I once saw him eat a sandwich with a fork and knife."

"Really."

"Turkey. Cold. Off the record. He's got something brewing, doesn't he?"

"Oh maybe. What did he tell you?" He grins at her as if in no time at all he'll be writing a knowing exposé or sliding his soft young hands up her short dress. Niggas be acting like bitches.

Shane winks at Lou: everything's okay, go ahead and take this call. She winks back, thanks, and lets him go.

Outside, the courtyard is smoking. Twenty-somethings swap cigarettes in solidarity, leaning into the puffs like recent pros. There are far fewer women than men, and most of the women wear skirts but some wear pants, slightly loose and flared, flowing around their legs as they move. Pants that behave in unpants-like ways. Their clothes look highly flammable. They don't shop at the Fit Right. What kind of job, he wonders, what does Debra do? What do these people do. His head feels large and shaggy as he takes in all that hair, freshly cut with shining, expensive scissors, the split ends fused, necks closely buzzed and rubbed with lotion. He is taller than most here, and the head-top view brings to mind a tournament golf course, richly fertilized and lovingly mowed. He pictures a barber moving between chairs in an office, cutting each person's hair as they lash away at their keyboards, gazing deep into computers' eyes, printing money.

The wall at the far end of the courtyard is as big and flat and smooth as a movie screen, and sure enough, high above the crowd, an enormous, silent graphic show is in progress, the blues and reds and yellows filtering the faces of the crowd through a strange, stormy light. He watches as a tower grows up out of the ground like Jack's wacky beanstalk, grows and swells and then stops when words come flapping in from one side of the screen like a mad burst of bats, words in every language and even alphabets, breaking apart, the characters mixing and swarming into the tower. And then they emerge on the other side, calm, tamed, transformed into sentences and graphs and banners, and as the tower morphs slowly into the Eiffel Tower and then the Taj Mahal, the Tower of London, the leaning tower of Pisa, the sand castle church in Barcelona, the sentences organize themselves into colorful Web pages in languages to match the monuments. Finally the shape-shifting tower changes one last time, Coit Tower at last, with the bay behind it, and he watches as Coit Tower merges with the Web page, the bay drains and pools into the big blue letters of *Espa.com*. The Web page fades away until only the imaginary word remains, *Espa,* and there the film holds and dims and slowly fades to black.

No one else seems to be watching.

At the far end of the courtyard he passes a table covered in what seem to be high-end party favors. Hands are snatching at soft black wool berets, miniature electronic dictionaries in eight languages, handsome watches with three interior dials telling time around the world, Belgian chocolates, Chinese silk handkerchiefs, finely printed business-card-size world maps. A guy stroking one of the handkerchiefs catches his eye, raises his eyebrows with significance, but Shane moves away from the table quickly.

Back at the bar he finds Lou's fellow vice president Richard and CEO Sloan. Rich must be just past thirty, but he looks older and heavier than the last time Shane saw him. His hand feels cold as they shake. Sloan looks the same as ever—soft, comfortable, patrician in his beautiful, textured dark blue shirt, loosely tucked.

"Shane."

"Sloan. Rich. How's it going."

They nod and smile in unison.

"Have you been playing?" Shane asks Rich. They both look at Shane blankly. "Basketball," he says.

Rich bows his head in exaggerated shame. "I wish. I haven't, it's been forever. Depressing. At least at Oracle I used to get out at lunch sometimes and run."

"I remember. That was a beautiful court."

"The Oracle complex is amazing," Sloan pitches in. His voice is always too loud, as if permanently tuned for a speaker phone. "You know how much Larry E. sank into that?"

"Shane used to come down to visit Lou, played with me a couple times. You shoulda seen it. He destroyed everyone out there. My boss got so mad at you that day, I thought you were going to get me fired."

"Glanville played basketball?" Sloan laughs.

"Yeah, can you imagine? Anyway, Shane put him in his place."

"What did you do?"

"We won, I guess."

"No, you *beat* him. You beat him like a dog. And let him know about it."

"I blocked his shot, said something, you know, part of the game."

"Not down there it wasn't. I don't know what you said, but he looked like you'd slapped him. Glanville says something back to Shane and the next thing Shane scores like five in a row. It was awesome."

You don't work here, that's not how we do things, you don't belong here, do you. That's what the guy had said. Shane smiles. He can pretend he doesn't remember but he remembers every moment. "The dangers of corporate ball." He used to imagine going back down there with a Firehouse all-star team. Imagine him and his big-mouth brother with Sam and D-One and Alex, just tearing it up on the Oracle court. Jo Jo and Darius, imagine.

"Seems like a long time ago," Rich says.

"Five years."

"Five years. A different world. You're still playing though."

"I've been hurt."

"Oh, that's right. It was your knee?"

"Foot."

Rich nods. How can they not know? How can Lou spend hour after hour and day after day with them and not leak something of their lives? He should know by now that in the halls of Menlo Park, the husband barely exists. Separation of job and home.

"I don't think I've broke a sweat since then. Ridiculous."

"You guys fucking work too much," Shane says. Being close to Sloan makes him want to swear.

"Yeah," Sloan says, smiling. "Work work play work what it's all about, right now." He sounds proud. "But not for long."

A small hand touches Shane's back. "Hey everybody," Lou says, eyeing Rich and Sloan with theatrical suspicion. "Tell me you're not talking about work." She gives Shane the look now. "Or basketball."

They all nod together, one big herd of nodding heads. "So where you been?" Sloan grins in anticipation, knowing that Lou will have something for them.

"Oh, chatting with our celebrity friend over there." The man in question is standing alone near the doorway, waiting to be recognized again. He's short and blond with lots of chin and lash and brow.

"Ah. How does a writer get on the cover of *Wired*?"

"Shameless self-promotion," Lou says. "He *is* a decent writer. He just writes about stupid things." Shane examines the man more carefully. Reading and writing are Lou's domain, and she doesn't give out "decent" easily. Once she even said it: maybe if things work out, that's what I'd like to do. He's pictured her sitting at a desk by the window, scribbling cleverly in a Holstein composition book when he comes home sooty at night.

"Come on, Lou," Sloan says, "you weren't nice to him were you?"

"Maybe. Can he help it that he's so vain and short and has a ridiculous name?"

"Ah, you're so much more fun when you're petty."

"I'm never petty. I'm vindictive and jealous and cruel."

"Do you think he's good-looking?"

"Sure. In that yellow Lab mated with a frat boy kinda way. A friend of mine slept with him. Apparently he's *uninteresting* in bed." They all laugh, Lou leading the way, putting her hand on Shane's arm for support. She likes to touch people when she laughs, and he wonders how many arms she's already touched tonight. When you hear Lou laugh for the first time you want to make her laugh again. Someone across the room is waving to her, pulling her over with a beckoning hand.

"Speaking of vain and cruel," Sloan says, "we should go talk to the Quixo mafia." Lou winces slightly, glancing at Shane.

"Food," he says, "I'll catch up." Lou kisses him quickly and links arms with Sloan and Rich to ford the room. He watches them arrive, joining an attentive crescent of men who lean toward Lou as if trying to catch her scent. Her eyes slide back and forth between her listeners, the fine expressive lines in her forehead forming and disappearing. Her laugh bursts and breaks from her and chases itself around the room, and then the men are laughing too, swept away by her sound. She is their living proof that they're all having a good time. Shane puts his head down and heads in an opposite direction, moving through the difficult crowd.

It is tough going. He keeps leaning to one side, contorting to make himself fit, but when one of the oncomers doesn't pay enough attention or adequately compromise, Shane holds his ground and gives the guy a good solid shoulder that spins the slender youth half around. The guy looks as shocked as if someone shoved a pistol in his mouth. He keeps his glass but the drink spills on sleeve and pants.

"Sorry." Shane shrugs, and looks him in the eye so the guy can say something now if he wants. But whatever the guy sees in Shane's face shuts him up. Shane nods and tries not to smile as he moves past him through new space to food. How long would these people last in the projects? How long on the wood floors of the Potrero Rec Center court? What a weird fucking day. Food, Shane thinks, and then I'm getting genuinely drunk.

What he thought was a full food table turns out to be covered entirely with cheese, more cheese than he's ever seen in one place. Each wedge has been laid out carefully on pale pink plates, but most by now have been long gouged and smeared by silver rounded knives. Little folded cardboard headstones sit smug behind the plates, each toting descriptions written carefully in gourmet-shop calligraphy. He reads a little bit. The cheese is global. He tries a piece of Spanish while a well-dressed man beside him bends down and sniffs deeply at a German. The man tastes it, shakes his head, looks at him. "That cheese," the man says, "that cheese tastes like ass." He looks at Shane as if they know each other. "And I don't mean that in a good way."

"No. I'd guess not."

There *is* something familiar about him: a sort of big guy, broad in the shoulders and snug in his pale green short sleeves with a big beautiful gold and lapis lazuli watch weighing down his wrist. The man nods at Shane as if together they've come to some serious conclusions.

"That one's not bad." Shane points to the Spanish.

"Yeah? I'm not big into cheese. Are you sober?" the man asks.

"Very."

"You really popped that guy."

"I guess so."

The man smiles. A waiter passes nearby with a tray of someone else's drinks and the cheese sniffer steps into his path and plucks a couple off without a word. The waiter stares at him, opens his mouth as if about to say something but then thinks better of it and disappears. The cheese man hands Shane the drink. It's clear, at least, and odorless, a likely vodka tonic.

"Right," the man says. "Do you smoke?" He rubs his hands together slowly.

"Not mostly."

"Well, shit," the man says. "Step out with me for a sec." He slides back from the table and opens a door with a metal sign on it: ALARM WILL SOUND DO NOT OPEN. Nothing happens. The door gives way to a narrow service alley, and over the blinking sounds of the party Shane hears cars, the street. The man steps out and holds the door, looking at him evenly, almost seriously. It's that look of action and reaction they give each other on the court when no one has to say anything. Just: here we are, you know what to do.

The alley is one of the cleanest he's ever been in, the concrete darkened by a recent hosing down. Topped by juiced and empty orange peels, two wheeled and plastic trashbins sit happily overflowing, their square lids propped ajar like the mouth of a hungry baby bird. Down the alley back on Mission Street, he can make out the lively sidewalk with its pedestrians sliced into tiny pieces by a metal lattice gate.

"You were at the gym today," the man says.

Shane stares at him. "I guess I was."

"Our gym with the ridiculous name. Yeah, I saw you up front talking with that Media Matrix engineer. You just join?"

Shane remembers the man, now, in the Paragon entryway, slipping sideways between Shane and Mario, the watch sparkling on his wrist. "No. I." He shakes his head, not knowing what to say. "I play basketball," he says.

Fulton nods approvingly, as if that explains something. "This place is such a town sometimes."

"You've got a good memory, though."

"Well," the man says, smiling slyly, "you went to Cal, right? That's why I noticed, 'cause I thought I recognized you. Must have been a couple years ahead of you, but I dated a friend of yours, Andrea Ross?"

"Andrea." He sees a tall athletic girl with short yellow hair. "Sure."

The man keeps smiling, enjoying Shane's absolute surprise. "I never forget people," he explains. "It's my only talent. There's a lot of Cal guys down at that gym. What ever happened to Andrea, anyway?"

"I don't know. I lost touch with everyone."

"That sounds nice," the man says. He watches Shane

for another moment and then shrugs, removing a loose cigarette from his breast pocket where it has been slightly flattened by the tight fit of the shirt against his chest. "And now we're in this shit, huh. You want to get high?"

"No. Not really." Shane can see it's a joint now, fat and barely wrinkled, twisted snugly at both ends.

"Please."

"I try to commit my energies to abusing alcohol."

"Noble." The man licks his finger and wets the sides of the joint and lights it, the flame glinting off the bright yellow gold of his watch. "Man, you really popped that guy," he says, smiling in fond recollection. "So great. Little dickhead. Bit more of that, and I'd feel proud of this party."

"This your party?"

"Not really. Yeah." He passes the joint to Shane. It is an enormous piece of work. "Please," he says again, more kindly this time. "If you make me smoke that thing alone, it's going to swallow my brain like fuckin' Jonah."

Shane takes the joint and pulls on it politely, hands it back. It's been a while.

"Thank you," the man says.

"Sure."

"I love dope. It's nostalgic. Remember the guys who used to sell it at Cal, that guy, you know him, Randy?" He takes another long hit and then closes his eyes, slowly, like a Lewis Carroll bug. "Randy. I thought *that* was profitable. And now look at all this." He waves his hand to include everything around them, a wave that penetrates walls, sweeps through the building and the alley, to the streets and the city and the nation beyond. He falls quiet for a moment, assessing his self-proclaimed domain.

"You know, dope dealers could be quite good, actually. Distribution deals, bundling, packaging. Traffic. Job market gets any tighter, that'd be one place to look. Night club promoters too. Nonprofit fund raisers. There's a whole alternate talent pool that will have to be tapped. The bright-eyed coeds and sell-out journalists and MBAs are running out. And besides, you look at these kids, you know they're only going to get you so far. Most of them have the imagination of a housefly."

"I guess."

"*Dead* housefly. You know what I'm talking about. You look at all these loaded people, all over the place, and nine out of ten are totally unimaginative cheap wads. They go out and buy their houses or cars or geeky ass tech toys. Design their super sailboats. Expensive bottles of wine, good dinners. But not nearly enough whores." He shakes his head. "Or explosives. This town should be having firework displays every Friday. Tuesday *and* Friday. Parades, motorcades. Sword swallowers and naked dancers in the streets. They're all a bunch of geeks or cheap wads. The most they can think of is some huge new server or an extra wing for their house in Atherton or a tidy little fête like this. People should be flying helicopters to work. Firing guns in the air. Where's the deep-down carnival? Most these people too scared and empty to do shit." He looks at Shane carefully. "You're not in it, are you."

"The Internet thing?" Shane is starting to float a little bit, feeling happy.

He laughs. "Yes."

"No."

He nods. "That's good," he says. "That's damn good. Well I'm with these people all day every day and I just think that if you're going to be fabulously wealthy you either have to do goody good or despicable bad. Both, preferably. But don't fuck around in this middle ground. And whatever you do, you can't be cheap about it. I went out with these guys the other day," he says, leaning comfortably against the brick wall, "none of them with an excuse, every one of them has real worth. We're swapping rounds, and getting some weird drinks, you know, something they really got to make, and the bar we're in, a drink costs eight nine bucks or something. So the rounds are like thirty-something each and these guys are leaving five-dollar tips. I mean, that's ridiculous. They're supposed to be starting bizarre philanthropic cults and buying emeralds for their mistresses. It's like these people don't even fucking know, it's Vegas out here, you got to tip your luck. You got to slaughter goats and virgins." He jabs a finger at the closed alley door, the invisible party beyond. "Got *no* respect for luck, the right place and time. No, they're meeting monthly with their personal finance managers and reading cautionary tales about sudden wealth syndrome, planning on writing novels and figure painting or learning to play the lute. And behaving like that's a normal reasonable thing to be doing at twenty-four, thirty. It's normal, of course, because they, they are special. They're special? What a bunch of shit. I mean, you and me go back in there, look around, are we seeing something special? Are these the Keplers and DaVincis in there? No, they have a few ideas, not terribly good ones, they're willing to work. A college degree, San Francisco area code, who you know, the moment, and luck. They got people in Romania ten times smarter than us driving taxicabs. Engineers, rocket scientists scrubbing toilets, taking out the trash in four languages. It's fucking embarrassing. So finally I tell one of these guys he's a sick, cheap, and stupid bastard."

"Yeah?"

"Nah, I didn't tell him that. I should have. Sometimes I do. Fuck. I'm in it. I'm definitely in the soup. But I'm not a cheap bastard. Therein lies my chance at redemption, I guess. Pretty good pot, huh?"

"Yeah," Shane says. "It's pretty good."

Outside, on the street, a thumping Doppler bass whips by them from a passing car, a tiny thread of reality working its way into their stoned little alley.

"I was a communist for a semester in France. Everyone should be a communist for a year or two. You're here with a wife or something, I guess."

"Right."

"Ah. Because there are three particularly hot French chicks in there right now, we could go get 'em. But you already got one."

"Yeah. Not French."

"Probably hot though."

"I think so. What was it like being a communist."

"Oh you know, I ended up feeling like a tool. You get older and it's kind of ridiculous." His voice turns unexpectedly grave. "You cannot get anything done. So it's like, do you want to actually accomplish something or just get high and fuck hot French girls and complain." The joint has been burning slowly, unnoticed, and now he licks his fingers and pinches it out with a fleshy hiss.

"Doesn't sound so bad."

He squints at Shane slightly, and hesitates. "You know what I mean. Eventually you have to really *do* something. You need a drink."

"I know I do."

"Right."

The man tries the door, pulls it first, then kicks it karate style, with violence. But it doesn't budge and Shane follows him down the alley to the street to circle back in the front way. The Chinese dragon has disappeared. Across the street two scruffy young kids smoke cigarettes in front of a neon-signed bar, watching them. One of them points and the other one laughs, as Shane follows the man inside to walk the walk of flags again.

At the end of the hall, Shane pauses near the orange and white flag with the tree. "Do you know what flag that is with the pine tree?"

"It's a cypress. Lebanon. Next year they say they're going to open an office in Lebanon, can you believe it? All these ridiculous places. It's so great." The man waves his fingers at the unfamiliar-looking flags. "Thailand, Russia.

Totally berserk."

"That's Russia? It's red white and blue."

The man laughs. "I don't remember your name."

"Shane." He puts his hand out but the man ignores it, moving ahead to the door where he pauses in the threshold, poised to enter the crowd and sound.

"It's always a treat to find an outsider," the man says. "In a sense, you're the only one here anyone can really relax and talk to. Because you don't matter, or care." He looks thoughtful for a moment, then extends his hand, you first, ushering Shane towards the bar.

At the bar Shane leans in to get their drinks, but when he turns around the other has disappeared and instead there is Lou. She plants an excellent kiss on his cheek, sniffing quickly at his mouth to collect information.

"Did you miss me?" he asks.

"Yes."

"I stepped outside with a communist."

"I know."

"You've had your people watching me."

"I'm in the loop. He's not much of a communist."

"He goes to your gym."

"Yes he does. How do you know him?"

"I don't exactly. Not even his name. He went to Cal."

She nods. "That's David Fulton," she says, as if the words mean something by themselves. "He owns this company. He owns quite a lot of companies. Your new old friend is some of the biggest VC money there is." He nods but doesn't convince her. "He's like," she tries again, "he's like the *Michael Jordan* of venture capital. What'd you talk about out there?"

"Marijuana, I think. Greed. I'm not sure."

"The man's worth at least $400 million. Personally."

"He smokes really good pot personally, too."

"Sure. How funny. You of all people. What's he like?"

"Talkative."

"Oh come on."

A new band is starting up, something rich and Latin, with horns and an active squad of percussionists. Trumpet, congas, a drum set, cow bell, wooden sticks. The singer has a strong voice, ready to party and mournful at the same time. Dance now because you are all of you going to die.

"They won a Grammy last year," Lou says. "But no one's heard of them. I don't think Fulton likes this company much. Elvis Costello played a launch last week. A month ago he had James Brown."

"I was there!" CEO Sloan has sauntered up beside them, his loud voice competing easily with a trumpet in progress. "People were going nuts. You didn't come."

"No," Lou says. "But Shane's new friend did."

"Now who could that be."

"David Fulton."

Sloan turns and examines Shane closely as if he is a precious stone suddenly for sale. He checks back to Lou to see if she's kidding. "Really." Sloan's eyes quickly scan the room for the suspect. "How do you know him?" His voice sounds higher now, permanently raised in question.

"They were getting high in the alley."

"Just the two of them?"

"It figures, doesn't it," Lou says. They both shake their heads in mild amazement.

"The man is wearing like an $80,000 watch," Sloan says.

"Guess I should have mugged him. While I had the chance."

"You rarely see him out," Sloan whispers loudly. "Reclusive. I mean, he doesn't seem to like very many people." He has a hand on Shane's shoulder, palpating him slightly. "Maybe you could introduce us. We've been trying to get in bed with him for a while." He is saying something else, but the hand is the only thing Shane notices. Lou notices too, takes Shane by the arm and starts to lead him away. "A dance!" she says, tossing the words over her shoulder at Sloan like a wedding bouquet.

They take a few steps towards the theoretical dance floor. No one is dancing. Everyone is talking louder and louder to make themselves heard over the percussive din, moving away from the band. He puts his drink down carefully and wraps a hand around her waist.

"We don't have to," she says.

"Don't we?"

They dance. His feet feel like enormous ski boots but he doesn't care. The music is made for this. He spins her, raising her arm, pushing her waist, turning her body in Olympic rings across the floor. People are staring, sort of, he thinks Lou might whisper halt but instead she throws her head back, shimmies her narrow hips, bares her neck and wrists. They must be terrible but the singer is cheering them on, looping the song again to make it last. He can feel the sweat beading on his forehead as the horns wail and for a moment it all comes together. The band is wailing in a wild crescendo, an enormous octopus banging cymbals, triangles, tambourines, anything noisy within its reach. The trumpet screams, he spins her one last time and she dips low, flashing panty for all the world to see. He lets her fall and fall and then catches her inches from the floor, her body feeling weightless against his fingertips. A few people applaud. The singer nods at them, pleased, launching quickly into the next song.

"Oh my," Lou says.

He lifts her upright and finds his drink. "I could dance with you again," he says. "I could dance or drink or take you home to make babies. I could do any of that."

"You and your babies."

"They're gonna be so damn cute."

"Yes," she says. "I know." He feels like they're in Paris, or Rome, somewhere they've never been. She glances over his shoulder. She smoothes her hair back into place and he follows her eyes to the darkish corner where David Fulton is standing silent with two other men, holding empty drinks.

"But before the babies," Lou says. She's looking at Shane seriously, now, her green eyes flitting almost grim between his eyes and mouth and hair. She catches herself, flashing him her fish face and crossing one eye then the other, a self-trained childhood trick. "I know it's horribly gauche, dahling, but you must introduce me to that man. Really."

He smiles at her show. "I don't even really know him."

"Make me a hero," she whispers. "I promise Sloan will never touch you again. Then we can do whatever you want." She jogs her eyebrows, mock lascivious.

"Okay. What do I say?"

Fulton swivels smoothly toward them as they approach, as if he's been expecting him all along. "Bravo," Fulton says. "Now it's almost a party. You're not leaving, are you? Is this your wife?"

"Here she is. David, right? This is Lou."

"Shane was bragging about you outrageously," Fulton says. "Little did I know he was being modest." Lou smiles, accepting the compliment with her head and nose and neck. Shane is a little bit surprised to hear Fulton say his name. The man's voice sounds different now, more calculated, as his mouth forms each word like soft soap bubbles and lets them float into the room. "Are we allowed to say we've seen each other before all sweaty and panting in skimpy gym clothes?"

"I think so," Lou says. "I won't tell if you won't tell."

"Deal."

"It's a wonderful party," she breathes, "once again."

"You must keep dancing."

"I got you a drink," Shane says, "but I believe I drank it."

"Good man. You've got a keeper there," he tells Lou.

"I really like this guy."

"Me too," she says.

"May I ask a favor?"

"Please," Lou says.

"I have to leave," Fulton says. "Will you loan him to me for another drink?"

If she's surprised she doesn't show it. "I suppose. Can't be selfish, can we?"

"Great. There's something I'd like to talk to you about," he tells Shane, giving him that basketball look again.

"Me?" Shane feels a strange pressure in his head, a sensation that something else might happen. Lou stands there beside him, the hair on their arms just touching, waiting for him to say something. "Sure," he says.

"Fantastic. We'll take good care of him."

"I'm sure," she says, smirking proudly at them both. She goes up on tiptoes and kisses Shane on the cheek. "Have a good time." Together Shane and Fulton watch her go.

"You game?" Fulton says, smiling with mischief in his eyes.

"I guess." He's not exactly sure what's happening, but Lou is happy, he's happy, everyone seems happy. He can keep drinking, dancing, saying yes. He doesn't want to do anything to stop it. "Long as it's worth the interrogation I get tomorrow."

"Right." Fulton raises his hand, points around the room, magically collecting sheep. "Let's blow this Popsicle stand. I got just the place."

"Oh I believe you," Shane says.

9

B Y MIDNIGHT THEY are in the heart of the city, watching
strange women dance and remove their clothes. The
place is famous, but in all the years of bachelor parties
Shane has never been here. In addition to the standard
stage and table routine, this club boasts a pornographic
funhouse, zoo, and circus of naked women in action:
soapy good times in the shower room, interactive flashlight
games at the lesbo slumber party, athletic prowess at the
dildo Olympiad. Fulton pays for everything, laughing,
throwing his arm around one buddy and then another,
throwing his arm around Shane, hooting at the girls like a
corporal set to die tomorrow. Shane doesn't mind, nothing really bothers him right now as he glides across a
calm and drunk plateau where time and place are no
longer problems to be solved.

They finally come to rest in the main room at a table,
with him and Fulton watching the show while two guys

named Dan and Matt argue about something or other. An Ed sleeps comfortably in his chair, dreaming beyond the argument, the music, the flesh. The place is packed. Everyone seems happy, even the girls. You can feel the money seeping through the room like snowmelt.

"Is this what you wanted to talk with me about?" Shane says, as a new woman steps on stage, striking a modern dance pose, hands gripping the pole behind her head.

"Sure," Fulton says. He points at the dancer. "Exactly."

The music starts. Shane watches the muscles in her arms stretch taut. She kneads her enormous perfect breasts as she thrusts against an invisible man in front of her, first circular and then pistonal, as the music moves to a frenetic flutter. The invisible man really has her number, and she comes volcanically, the long hair sweeping wild across her shoulders, her back and neck, as she slips seamlessly into the gentle, longing, post-coital dance for more. Sinking to the ground and slowly spreading her thighs wide. It's her job, but still, he thinks she looks like an A-1 fuck, has won his hard-on fair and square despite the alcohol, the arguments of Dan and Matt, despite the absurdity of strip clubs.

Fulton nods, leaning in and taking a deep breath. He spreads his hands out on the table, steadying his wide shoulders, bracing for conversation. "So does she have it? Or doesn't she?"

"I'd say yes," Shane says.

"I'd say no. The motions are there, but she's not a

real." He makes a fist and frowns, making a mild grunting sound. "You know."

"No."

"Come on. You're observant, you're a watchful guy.
You have your own system, yeah? of seeing through
someone's surface and deciding what they really are."

What do you know about me, Shane thinks. "I guess
I wasn't thinking about that."

"No, you were thinking about her tits, we all were,
thank god. But let's go back to your system for a second.
I'm interested in how you do this."

Shane looks at the woman stepping off the stage,
pausing to talk to a nearby table. "I don't know. You go
first."

Fulton laughs. "Let's see," he says. "She's sort of
caught in a no-man's land. Usually people run mainly on
instinct or psychology or some fantastic mix of both.
She's neither. Not unhappy in any productive way. Judi-
cious in the way she looks around the room, but she's not
really looking for anything. She's bland but she doesn't
quite know it. Now you, how would you get to her."

"Me? I wouldn't."

"I wouldn't either." Fulton waves his hand and Shane
turns to see the woman in question stepping toward
them. She leans over Fulton, who holds her shoulder gently and whispers something in her ear. She laughs, whispers back. He is one of those guys who knows how to talk
with strippers. Soon Fulton points and nods and she is
on Shane's lap, her fingers stroking the back of his neck,

her breasts bobbing slowly in front of his nose. Her pelvis seems to float on some kind of magic steady-cam technology. Her mouth hovers over his, whisks past his eyes and ears, lips and tongue suggesting terrible things. Shane shakes his head and wedges his hands under his thighs, trying to keep them to himself. She grabs his head and presses it against her breasts and then Fulton shoos her away, slipping her cash as she drags a finger along Shane's thigh and moves on.

"No, huh?" Fulton shakes his head.

"You coulda fooled me."

"Come on," he says, "you knew. You can tell a real cunt the moment she steps in the room. I see the way you handle people. I know you know more than you let on."

"We must be drunk," Shane says. "I don't have any idea what you're talking about."

"Then we're not drunk enough," Fulton says. He raises his hand in the air. "We need more drinks here, stat."

Their waitress, however, is nowhere to be seen, and Dan and Matt begin to explain about poor service here, at times. They know, they were here just last week, turns out, the two of them with a big crew.

"It was pathetic, Schultzy was just lobbing money around and no one had an ounce of respect for the guy. There must have been ten of us with him, gonna show us a rock 'n' roll time, what a good guy he was, and we're all just walking up to him, 'Hey, dickhead, give me another couple hundreds, this girl wants to rub her tits in my face.' And he'd just hand it to you."

"Pathetic."

"Loser."

"No kind of money is going change that."

"Better than sitting in the house," Fulton says. They are watching a new redhead with world-class legs in front of them, sink to the ground, mount an imaginary object, give it the business. "Better than the hoarding masses."

"You would have loved it, man," Dan says.

"He'd rented the big Humvee limo." Matt points at his own chest. "We took it. Ditched him."

"Yeah?"

"Yeah, was great, he went back to a private room and we got up and jumped in that bad boy and had them drive us cross town."

"You guys suck."

"The best part is he came and found us. We were over at Z2 and he shows up, all laughing like he's a good sport about it."

"Yeah like, 'Good one, guys.'"

"And Ed, you know Ed when he gets going, he just keeps twisting the knife, he's like, 'Dude, get us a private room upstairs, get us some coke, get us some this.'"

"And he did."

"Of course he did. What a joke. He had no idea, like, how to go about it. Made a fucking fool of himself. Must have dropped ten grand. More."

"They should take equity," Dan says, looking around appraisingly. "Couldn't you see it? Some canny high-class whores in this town who don't need the cash, pick their customers company by company, pussy for shares?"

"Sure it's happening."

"Would make sense. If anyone needs early retirement."

"Least scalable profession in the world."

The waitress who finally comes over to get their drink orders looks familiar, and as she pulls within range Shane realizes he knows her.

"Tanya," he says, before he can think better of it. It's been about ten years since she dated Jimmy but he still recognizes her.

She looks at him blankly, then nods. "I know you."

"Jimmy McCarthy's brother."

"Of course." His companions are looking at him with something new, now—hard to tell if it's respect or amusement or both. "How is Jimmy?" If she's embarrassed she doesn't show it at all.

"He's same old Jimmy. How about you?"

"Oh, you know." She rolls her eyes to the room around her, shrugs her shoulders, smiles. "I'm in transition." She has a pretty wonderful smile.

"I hear you."

She glances around the table at the others before settling on Fulton. "Hey there," she says, giving Fulton one of those smiles too. "How you been?"

"Super," Fulton says.

"Good to see ya. What's everyone drinking?"

"I think we're still tequila, is that right?"

"I can't drink any more tequila," Matt says. "Gimme a Heineken and a water."

"That for everybody," Fulton says. "And four shots of the best tequila, too."

"Are you looking for a job?" Dan reaches out and runs his fingers lightly up her arm, and she pulls it back, glancing at Shane.

"Hey," Shane tells Dan, and the guy removes his hand, still looking intently at her face.

"I have a job."

"I mean, in transition, I thought. Well I thought you might be interested in a highly opportune opportunity." Dan sounds pretty drunk, all of a sudden.

"No, thanks," she says sweetly, although there's just a hint of curiosity in her face. She holds his glance for a second and then ditches him, moving away to get their drinks.

"Don't be a dink Dan," Fulton says.

"Trade shows," he says. "These girls rock the house. Is she smart?" he asks.

"She dated my brother, she can't be too smart." Shane wonders how long it's been since someone punched Dan in the mouth.

"It doesn't really matter. You ask her," he says, leaning heavily in Shane's direction, breathing alcohol in his face, "Seriously, she can make good money doing the trade shows. There is no substitute for putting a hot chick with gazungas at the booth. Trust me. I been to a shit load of shows, and they are all out sausage fests. Free crap and hot chicks, that's what it comes down to. Fortunes have been lost and made on racks like that."

"I bet she pulls down more here in a couple nights than she would doing a week of trade shows."

"Fuck that. There's not company one out there that isn't loosening its belt, so to speak." He laughs at his own little joke. "That bod, she can talk a bit, she names her price. I know a dozen startups trying to bust out that'd take her on. Guaranteed she could work it into a nice trade show consultant racket."

"Unless she's cutting deals here on the side," Matt says.

"Fuck," Dan says. "You want to cut a deal on the side, you cut 'em better at a trade show. You think there's money here? This year in Vegas, I've never seen pockets so deep."

"You know what?" Shane says, rattling the ice in his empty drink, waiting for the next. He finds Dan's small young blue eyes and takes a moment to look inside. "You are really starting to annoy me."

The guy looks at his buddy Matt and then back as if seeing Shane for the first time. "Right, she's your friend," Dan says, smiling. "I didn't mean anything by it. I'm just thinking out loud."

"Come on though," Matt says, "it has to be a better job than this."

"That's all I'm saying," Dan says. "It's no joke. Listen, I'm not sure what you do, but there really are secretaries at Yahoo who're millionaires now. Millionaires. I don't know why anyone wouldn't at least try to get in on it while it lasts. This," Dan says, waving his hand around, "this ain't going nowhere."

"I think his point is," Fulton pitches in suddenly,

"why don't you guys ever shut the fuck up? You see what I'm talking about?" he says, gesturing at Shane with sympathy. "These guys think they're businessmen, and they can't read people for shit, they don't even know until you're about to shove their drinks up their ass." Matt and Dan laugh. Fulton lowers his voice so they can't hear them. "Next time just do it. I'm serious, just fucking do it. No one lets their instincts call the shots anymore."

Tanya returns to the table. When she leans over his shoulder Shane can smell her perfume and a salty patina of youthful sweat.

"Won't you join us?" Fulton asks her. "A quick drink with old friends."

"I'd love to, but." She smiles at Shane. "I'm almost off, maybe I'll get a chance before you go."

"That'd be nice," Shane says.

"It sure would," Dan adds as she retreats.

"Cheers," Fulton says to Shane, clinking tequilas with him.

"I'll drink to that," Matt says, shooting his down the hatch.

Shane shoots his too and then takes a long pull on his beer. What does Lou think he's doing out here? Her clothes are lying in a runway across the bedroom floor, his wife naked and at rest in bed. Deep in dreams, her breath deep and slow. He gets up and walks carefully to the bathroom and then back to finish his drink. It's been too long since he's had five six drinks too many. It has to be done. It's good for the mind, a rare storm that reshapes

the river and shakes dead limbs off trees. Excess is important. Strippers are stripping. Ed is awake now, grumbling
about the lack of drugs.

"There's probably about five dudes within a block of
here selling crack," Fulton says.

"Where are we, anyway?"

"Tenderloin," Shane says.

"I'd come with you to buy crack," Fulton says, "I
really wouldn't want to miss that."

"Yeah," Ed says unhappily. "Tenderloin's right up
your alley."

"Come on. Let's do it."

"Let's do something," Matt says. "This is lame."

Fulton nods, grimly, and they all rise to leave, Fulton
lingering behind to settle up. Outside, Fulton's big black
BMW is waiting for them, the chauffeur stone-faced
patient inside. They sit in silence, waiting for Fulton.
When he finally emerges he has Tanya and another
woman in tow, the three of them enjoying an unheard
joke as they pack into the car. It's cozy in there. Tanya sits
on Shane's lap. He hopes he's drunk enough.

"Where we going?" someone says.

They drive into the middle of nowhere, down near the
abandoned docks off Third Street where suddenly a club
appears, filled with hipster kids. It's too loud in there to
talk but Tanya tries anyway, giving up when Matt whisks
her away to dance. Fulton follows with her friend, leaning down to shout in Shane's ear, "DJ Crackhead's in the

house!" and Shane doesn't know what that's supposed to mean but sits drinking by himself, watching the world have a vigorous good time. Dan and Ed are off looking for more girls and maybe coke. The bar stops serving alcohol and the music turns up another notch. He wanders off to wait for the bathroom and when the door unlocks and opens, out tumbles Fulton with a very young Asian guy, laughing and slapping hands lightly as they part. Fulton winks at Shane, raising his eyebrows in silent question, but Shane brusques by him, pretending not to notice.

When he gets back Fulton and Tanya are tearing it up on the dance floor, both waving at him to come out but he finds his seat and stays absolutely put. Fulton swings into range, otter-slick with sweat. "How you doing?" he yells.

"I'm pretty fucked up."

"Good," Fulton shouts. "We'll load up on girls and drugs and head back to my place. I've got some great scotch. This place is horrible. My friends are assholes, don't you think?"

"Definitely."

"Let's beat the shit out of them later. I'm serious. I'm serious. Tanya's great. You having a good time?"

"I must be."

"I wish you'd stop worrying. Your wife doesn't give a fuck, you know?"

"What do you know about my wife."

"I don't. 'Cept she wants you to be here, I know that, and I know why and I don't care, because you want to be here too. Fuck, don't listen to me, I just talk too much, listen, I'm glad you came, I really am. You," he begins, about to say something else when the music leaps another ten notches and drowns him out. He leans forward very close, and Shane can see the octagons of pores above his lip, smell something recent and minty in his breath. "You're the real thing, you know that, don't you? You and me, we should hang out."

"We're hanging out."

"Yeah. Too bad you won't join my gym. Makes me almost wish I played basketball."

Shane doesn't know what he's about to say but suddenly the scouts return with girls but no coke. They all head outside, a group now, turning Fulton's vehicle into a clown car packed double-decker, boys beneath girls. Fulton sits up front, hanging a mysterious silver chain on the rearview mirror.

"You and your damn trophies."

"No red panties tonight?"

"Not tonight. Now what's this about drugs?"

"Yeah what happened Ed?"

"I don't know." They're cruising down Third Street in the wrong direction, continuing by the old abandoned warehouses and docks.

"Where are we?" a girl says.

"I think my car was towed down here once."

"Dogpatch," Shane says.

"Fucking nowhere," Ed says. "Should have done the Tenderloin."

"I've got some pot," Tanya's friend says.

"Pot." Ed sounds disgusted, searching the streets for a sign.

Shane looks out the window and sees the elevated concrete of 280. On the other side, the Potrero Hill projects wink out from the hill with their hundred points of bright white light. He whispers something to himself but he's too drunk to know exactly what. He feels Fulton watching him.

"Someone knows where," Fulton says. He sounds giddy, meeting Shane's eye and trying not to laugh at the funniest private joke in the world. "Shane knows."

They all look at Shane.

"Where," Ed says.

"Over there," Shane says, not thinking, just talking. He points like a child. They all look out the window, seeing nothing.

"Where?"

"Those lights on the side of the hill?" Fulton says.

"What are those?"

"The projects," Shane says. "That's the projects."

"Yeah right," Tanya says.

"Fuck you, Fulton, don't do this. I'll do the Tenderloin, okay."

"Too late. Call out the turns, Shane." The girls are making noises but he shakes off their protests. "Shane," Fulton says again.

"Take a right," Shane says.

"Right turn!"

"Dude, I don't know."

"Scared?"

"No, just looks like a pretty shitty idea."

"The shittiest," Fulton says. "Shane?"

"Straight."

"Shane." He can't see Tanya through the bodies but he hears the plaintive voice from his past somewhere in the car. They're getting closer now, and the projects look like a prison camp quarry chiseled into the steep hill. The bright white lights blaze from the corners of every building, like warning signals laid out for aviators and drivers and pedestrians alike. Watch out for the mountain. Watch out for black people. Watch out for everything, bub.

"Left." Shane wants them to see it, now.

"Oh fuck," a girl says, almost cheerfully.

They climb the ruined slope and pass the first barracks, doors and windows boarded up with plywood. Below them they can see the highway, cars skimming by on the elevated pavement. Then all views disappear as the projects leap up around them on all sides, a tunnel of rock and concrete. From the shadows up ahead, shapes move from the buildings to the streetlights, three guys sprinting to intercept the big black car, elbow jockeying one another. Shane feels the girl on his lap contract and stiffen, bracing for the impact.

"Stop the car," Fulton says. The car halts gently, clinging to the steep grade. No one says a word.

The guys outside arrive, stooping to peer inside, shouting something. Shane can feel the girl pushing back into him, trying to get out of the way. Behind the first wave, a few more shapes have stood up off the hoods of parked cars, leaning forward to see what happens. A hand floats inches in front of Shane's face on the other side of the glass, one finger rolling through the air as if to will the window down. A face appears, clear eyes leaping through the back seat and then the window hums magic and retracts. Shane can smell dust and metal and burnt rubber. Something else. What does blood smell like, he thinks.

"What you need?" The guy moves back from the car a half-step, getting the angle to try to see them all at once. If he likes what he sees it's impossible to tell. His voice is loud, filling the car with sound. With one hand he is holding off the other two guys behind him and they stay put, trying to peer over his shoulder. He gives Shane another half a second, the look scouring out the inside of Shane's head, seeing everything there in one instant, everything, and not finding one single thing of interest. "What we doing tonight?" the guy says, frowning.

"Ed?" Fulton says. "Would you like to place an order?" Ed seems frozen, looking straight ahead and saying nothing. "Come on Ed. Tell the man what we need. And get a lot."

"Quarter," Ed says.

"Quarter," Shane repeats softly.

The guy stiffens slightly, despite himself. "Quarter," he repeats. He nods, turns his head to the guys behind him and murmurs something. They take off jogging, back towards the buildings. The guy holds out six fingers.

"Red Jetta," he says, shifting his weight from side to side as if dancing to a private beat. Fulton's hand appears, stretching through the car like plastic man, and Shane takes the wad of bills and holds it out and the dancer disappears.

The car is silent as they roll forward, slowing beside the parked red shiny car in question. They stop there, waiting.

"I don't see shit," Ed says.

"Hold on, now," Fulton says. "Just wait a minute."

"They're gonna fuck us, they have to," Ed says, miserable. "Let's just get out of here."

"Shut up Ed. It's business. We're businessmen, remember."

"That guy?"

"Everyone. Fucking us isn't a good business plan."

"Why not? Best case it's light and cut to shit. Worst case we end up dead."

"One day for sure."

"Jesus," a girl says.

From the shadows, a figure appears, tossing a crumpled brown paper bag onto the hood of the red car, right outside Shane's window. Shane watches the kid disappear and then leans out the window into a halo of streetlight, stretching one arm out, trying to reach the bag. He can't get it, they've put it deliberately too far from the edge so you have to get out of the car. No way. Shane's gaze slips up beyond the car where he sees the blue and white jersey catching the light, the eyes above it wide with knowledge. Tennessee nods at him, bobbing his head slowly, smiling with his Cheshire teeth. His mouth moves, a whispered nothing. There's someone standing beside him, and Tennessee turns to face him, pointing at the car. Shane bangs his head in his jerky rush to vanish. The knock jolts faces into motion, as he closes his eyes: Tennessee, Debra, Jimmy, Shane, Lou. Samson. He blinks wide and peers out into the dark, trying to see Tennessee's friend.

The pressure in the car changes as a door opens, front passenger, and now Fulton is striding around the car, through the headlight beams, the sheen in his pants sparkling in the light. He plucks the paper bag off the hood, glances inside, and tosses the bag through the back window, into the car. The bag lands on Tanya's lap and she convulses as if it's a poisonous snake. Ed has the bag now, but Shane is watching Fulton, standing there in the dark facing Tennessee. Tennessee calls out to Fulton, Shane can't quite hear what.

"Okay," Ed says, his voice small and shaky. "Okay, come on, lets go."

Fulton lingers and then puts his hand to his mouth and kisses his fingertips. His lips smack loudly and then he flicks his fingers at the two shapes watching from the shadows. Fulton holds his hand steady, a perfect follow through as he watches the kiss through the air to its final destination. The shapes don't move but Shane can almost see them growing in size, inflating toward a large, loud pop.

"Jesus."

"Get in the fucking car!" someone yells, or everyone, the car thick with sudden sound.

Fulton's hand snaps shut and then he turns and shimmies back across the car headlights, breathing quickly, teeth clamped together, moving fast. He dances the final steps to the car door, quick quick slow. He opens and jumps in.

The car leaps forward even before the door slams shut, Shane hears a voice call out to them, he waits to feel a thump against the car, a body, a brick, a bullet, something is going to stop them, but instead he feels the thank-you-ma'am of hopping over the hill. Music erupts from the speakers in the car, and everyone is talking at once as they plunge down into the city, waiting there below.

"Goddamn, you're a fucking nut, you know that?" Dan is laughing, Tanya is upset, Matt is making out with one of the girls, Ed is snorting their purchase through some sort of nose pipe. Someone passes Shane a flask.

"How about that?" Fulton says to Shane across the din. "How 'bout that, huh?" The girl on Shane's lap is snorting now, reloading. Shane shakes his head but she dips a finger into the powder and puts it in his mouth, rubbing along the gums. The car is filling with pungent smoke as Tanya's friend puffs on a joint and passes it up to Fulton. Shane can still taste the girl's finger. His gums are numb. The car has gotten smaller, everyone expanding in the smoke and coke and drink.

Ed's eyes are bulging out of his head, he's coked up good and shouting at Fulton. "You and your fucking field trips, you're going get us killed, you know that?"

"Shut up and do drugs," Fulton says. "We're alive, aren't we? We're alive as you get."

"Blow them a fucking kiss?"

"Shit, they loved it. All those guys are equal opportu-nity doinkers." Fulton's reaching back and pulling one of the girls into the front seat and she goes easily, laughing. When her thighs have cleared the gap between the seats, Fulton is still looking back, locking his eyes on Shane as the girl settles into Fulton's lap.

"Gotta take me back there sometime," Fulton says. "The real thing. I knew it." Shane shakes his head in dis-agreement. His brain wobbles in his skull, a straightjacket banging angry against walls. Ed passes the nose pipe up front and Fulton takes a fast hit. "We'll leave these jerks at home, just you and me." He leans back to pass Shane the pipe and whispers, "*We* know we can all just get along."

They're passing General Hospital, and as they stop at the light Shane opens his door without warning, slipping from beneath the bodies and tumbling out on the street. He lies there on the pavement, tiny pebbles digging into his hands, expecting to vomit, but instead he pops up on his feet and pulls in an enormous breath. Someone calls after him, they all do maybe, but he's running. He hears his name. He runs.

He cuts through a parking lot, hugs the side of a building, and crosses the wide avenue at full tilt, ignoring the light and barely looking for traffic. He can really move when he wants to. The air sluices by his cheeks, pulling his face back into a smile. He just keeps running, with the short quick steps of a little kid. He passes dark store windows advertising beef, bodegas with their fruit

locked up, an old-fashioned ice cream parlor, Disco-
landia, Mexicatessen, a block of travel shops and money
grams. Shane lets his stride out as he races past stores he's
never seen before, never stepped inside, maybe never
will. His feet hammer against the concrete, smash smash
smash, those hundreds of bones holding steady and
strong. If he follows this street across the valley and up
the hill it will take him straight into his neighborhood, to
a corner four blocks from home. These long veins of San
Francisco are what keep them all alive, connecting neigh-
borhoods that each believe they're the city's heart. He
wants to bring Lou here in daylight, he thinks, it's been a
while since he showed her something. They will walk this
block, the sidewalks crammed with Mexicans and
strollers, walk it as they once walked the hills of North
Beach, the Seacliff trail to Land's End, Baker Beach where
you can see the Golden Gate over gritty sand. Have you
ever seen a Mexicatessen? he'll say, a tamale parlor? a Dis-
colandia? a psychic's shop? a bridal store for little girls?
And she hasn't, just as she'd never seen the other secrets
of this city with which he wooed her, long ago. Fuck the
Fultons and the projects, the live/work lofts and the strippers in the Tenderloin. San Francisco is the pet cemeter-
ies in Colma, the houseboat canals, the reservoirs, the
rooftops of this city, cresting in black tar peaks and faded
waves. It's like he's forgotten until just now: this is my
city. Not the moguls and the gangsters, mine. He'll show
her. Show them all. He runs.

10

LOU IS AMUSED by his hangover, which lasts until Monday. He hears her moving around the house, talking on the phone, vanishing and then returning as he lies in the curtained bedroom drifting in and out of sleep. His urine is an outrageous shade of irradiated orange, he can't seem to get enough fluids into his body to make things right. He still feels slightly foggy when he drops Lou off at the airport Monday morning for a work trip to New York. She kisses him like she means it and says she'll be back soon. Be good. She wants to hear all about it when she gets back. He goes home, cancels his jobs, and drinks coffee for the rest of the day. There's a message on his cell phone from Fulton, a cheerful hey what's up, but Shane doesn't return the call.

He skips basketball on Tuesday and schedules a chimney liner in Pac Heights as a kind of penance. The house is on the same block as one of the first roofs he ever climbed on, almost twenty years ago with Dad. Watching his ten-year-old son crab-walk down that steep roof must have made even his tough guy father nervous. Shane wrestles the 200-pound metal snake up there alone and then crams it in, swearing and sweating. The liner gets stuck and he has to pull it up and try again. The steel scrapes against the brick inside as his arms shake with the effort. There's a problem with the chimney cap, he's brought the wrong kind and has to crimp the oval mouth into a perfect circle to make the fit, jerry-rigging to secure it with drill and wire and ill-fitting screws. Improvise or die. Below him in the guts of the house he can hear a toilet flushing.

When he's done he sits straddling the roof crest, resting in the sun. Pacific Heights is a paradise of rooftop treasures hidden away up high. Antennae and cupolas, skylights and triangular windows in the eaves, small-tiled patios and miniature chairs, benches, tables, plants, gardens, putting greens, sculptures of cats and naked ladies, stiff poles flying unknown flags, bird nests, vanes and wires and metal laundry trees. Steel vents shaped like wild mushrooms or periscopes or tall nuns with flapping caps. Chimneys. Chimneys everywhere. He gets that childhood twinge of looking out and feeling entitlement to every aerie inch he sees. As a boy, he couldn't imagine that he'd want to do anything but leap around on rooftops the rest of his life.

His hand is bleeding slightly, a little cut from the hard edge of something. He wipes it against his pants. He presses the cut and then blows on it until it stops. It seems like he bleeds about every other day. Black vinyl gloves would help but they annoy him. He wears them sometimes to keep his hands from turning black. Dirty hands are damning. People think he's a mechanic. He looks down into the window of the enormous house next door, where a man is pacing a room, gesticulating, talking on the phone. Sometimes the men are naked, the women too, sometimes they're having sex or cooking or staring at themselves for minutes at a time. The man next door is angry. Someone, somewhere, is trying to fuck him and he won't have it. How does he make his money? No one Shane meets anymore understands why he cleans chimneys, although Shane's not sure there's anything to understand. But when he sees the look in people's eyes— if that man glances up and out his window—he wants to tell them: remember seven years ago? Remember that? He was out of college and his dad was dead, his mother's house was slipping from brick to twigs to straw, these were the beautiful cloudless drought years and the economy was a mirthless running joke. He could have gone to work for someone, probably—but his dad had left a $60,000-a-year business already in motion, and there wasn't anything out there close to that. No one had doubted his decision then, and it never occurred to him that his dad's business was also at its limit, that he wasn't ever going to make more than that without changing everything.

By now everyone thinks he should have sold the business, or forced hapless Jimmy to take it over, or expanded it into an army of trucks and soldiers to do the dirty work. Something. He is supposed to have done something. He's done his best to explain to Lou the feeling of the self-determined life, making his own hours, his own decisions, his own regions of responsibility. This is something she can understand—who wants to work for someone else? Not her. Not him. But what's so great about bleeding hands, about rooftops, about wrestling giant metal snakes? Why not trade in the body for the mind, if you've got a good one? Why doesn't he want more? These are the things Lou can't figure out. These he can't convincingly explain. He does want more. He just doesn't want it or expect it from his work. He doesn't want a chimney-sweeping empire, to worry about employees trashing Persian rugs with sooty boots or killing infants in negligent fires or falling off the roof. He doesn't want to trade in his brushes for an office, dust off his Cal diploma and jump into the fray no matter what Yahoo secretaries make. Fuck Yahoo. He knows that Lou's days inside would drive him completely cuckoo. His brothers can do it: Brendan a desk-tied engineer in Marin, Tommy a high-tech salesman in Livermore, even Jimmy who reads all day because he won't get a job and can't be trusted on a roof, they seem to have no problem domesticating themselves to a static indoor life of pneumatic chairs, computers, phones, the unmoving printed word. Why not him? What's so great about climbing on top of steep-pitched roofs to peer down into the rough black throats of houses? Well it's not perfect but it works for him. Okay but for how long? And what about when he gets hurt again?

Alcatraz and Angel Island sit shimmering in the September heat in the rare and glassy calm of the bay. He stands and unzips and pees serenely to the tiles of the roof, staring north into the purple Marin hills as his self-made creek runs to the gutter and disappears into the unknowing world below. Then he checks the fittings one more time and descends to tell his client everything's good to go. You got yourself a brand new chimney system, people. Go ahead and burn.

He's on the roof at Carol's house when his phone begins to ring.

Carol is an older lesbian and pyromaniac who builds enormous fires all year round and has her chimney cleaned twice a year. Once annually for most people is more than enough but in her case twice seems like a good idea. Carol has a basement full of good dry wood and likes to send great hot yelping flames licking up the sides of her chimney night after night, thumbing her nose at the utilities and deforestation and the frequent chill outside. She is the McCarthys' oldest continuous customer, dating from the very first days of his dad. Her house has two chimneys, but one of them was bricked up until five years ago. Shane found a fossilized bird in there, its mouth agape in mid-scream. A newspaper from 1910. His father once discovered a box full of old coins and silverware in a chimney in the Haight. You hear these stories. Beer bottles, tennis balls, tiny skeletons, but he knows a guy who found a loaded gun. Santa better watch his ass.

Carol's chimney has been cleaned regularly of secrets, but it's used so often that even after six short months he can never see the telltale cleaning lines of wire brush there up top. "It's scary Shane," Carol's partner always tells him the minute he arrives. "She's going to burn the house down one day I know it."

"She's made it this far. All these years."

"I know, but that's what I'm worried about. That she wants to go out in her own big funeral pyre."

"God forbid. I've got a new video, give it a shot." The new video in question is one in a series Shane receives from the National Chimney Sweep Association, featuring chimney fire: chimneys blasting a huge, hot, angry spume of fire thirty feet into the air. He's never seen a fire like that with his own eyes, this greedy gleeful kind that would think nothing of gobbling up a city block. The videos are meant to scare clients into regular cleanings and general submission, but Shane mostly gets them for the amusement of Carol and himself.

"You know that video won't help," Carol's partner scolds him. "She loves the pyro porn."

"Well, got to get the girl her fix."

They're watching the video right now, he can hear the sound of the television filtering up the chimney and out the top. He answers his phone.

"This Shane?"

"Yes." A woman.

"Yeah, you said to call?" They have the volume cranked up down there, he can almost hear the whoosh of the recorded fire. Is someone singing? "This Debra."

"Debra." He feels a jolt of panic. He's in Fulton's big black car, a young buttock rubbing against his matrimonial thigh.

"Debra Marks. You, uh, what you doing, you with your brother?"

He sees the apartment, Sam's picture on the fridge tilting in the breeze. "No, yeah, how are you?"

"I wanted to talk to y'all, about that thing?"

"Okay, sure, yeah." He waits for her to talk about it but she waits right back. "Hello?" he says.

"I'll be home in twenty minutes," she says. "You could pick me up."

Never. "Okay," he says. "Give me an hour."

"An hour." She sounds pleased. "I'll see you." The line goes dead. Downstairs Carol is laughing, thrilled by the cataclysm of fire, and he steps away from the chimney, suddenly not wanting to hear the private world below. He should be used to it by now, stepping into other people's lives.

He collects Jimmy first for backup and drives them to the projects while his brother narrates the highlights of Tuesday's game and then speculates on Sam. Jimmy's been thinking about the kid and can't wait to talk to Debra. He's got theories, ideas, plans. Shane sits there nodding but not exactly listening. They halt at a stop sign on top of Potrero Hill.

"It's left," Jimmy says, pointing one sure finger into the orange roofs and ruined pavement waiting for them again.

Shane knows exactly where it is, but his foot won't move and his hands are pulling right. He heard a story once about anarchists in England who would buy lion shit when the circus was in town. They'd put it outside their little anarchist houses, and when the police came with their dogs, the dogs would smell that shit and refuse to cross the line. Those dogs had never seen a lion before but they knew whatever made that shit was big and wanted to eat them.

"Left," Jimmy says again, more forcefully, and Shane clears his mind and feels his feet and hands obey, sending the van on its way. That's what Jimmy's for.

The streets are empty. Shane knows the way but for some reason doesn't recognize a thing. Is that where the red Jetta parked? Is this Tennessee's nighttime stoop? If they'd been shot that night, if he'd crawled out of a car of corpses, fairy-dusted with bad coke, what would he be able to reconstruct for the cops and jury and wife? He can't quite look closely at the streets around him, now that he has an inkling of how dangerous they must be.

He pulls into the lot and Jimmy hops out of the van without a second thought. I need to tell him something, Shane thinks. I'm going to get my brother killed. Jimmy takes two steps toward Debra's door when it opens and she slips out, like someone trying to keep cats inside.

"Where we going?" she asks when they're all safe in the van, barreling out of the projects as fast as Shane can manage. Jimmy and Debra both look at him as if this expedition were Shane's idea.

"I missed lunch," Shane says, and despite the fact that it's four o'clock, Jimmy and Debra nod and quickly begin discussing their impending meal.

"I don't care for Mexican food," Debra says.

"How can you not like Mexican food? That's like you just don't like food." Jimmy is appalled.

"Get on." She glares back at him, enjoying their disagreement. "Taste like sweat."

"Without Mexicans, this town wouldn't even eat. It doesn't matter what kind of restaurant, nine out of ten there's Mexicans cooking in the kitchen."

"Aw, now you playing."

"Without Mexicans, this city'd starve to death. Shane, back me up here. Wait, I know a place," Jimmy says.

Shane follows Jimmy's directions toward the bay, under the highway and over the railroad track that runs from downtown south near Third Street, past Potrero Hill. From the van Shane can make out the tunnels below where the city swallows up the double-decker trains coming in from San Jose. A couple of kids are leaning against the railing above the tracks, eating chips and flicking crumbs onto the rails below. Shane drives them past trucks and camper vans where people are obviously living. Homeless encampments marked by tents and shopping carts. This is a part of the city where you can still disappear.

"Any news from Samson?" Shane hears himself say.

Debra doesn't look at him but shakes her head. "Now you got me hungry," Debra tells Jimmy. "Where we going?"

The place is Cajun and good. They sit at one of the small tables crammed near the front, even though Jimmy lobbies for the counter. Debra nixes that. She doesn't want to watch them cook. She asks if she can still get breakfast and orders poached eggs, bacon, biscuit, grits. Jimmy gets a catfish po'boy. Big bowl of gumbo for Shane.

"Well?" Jimmy says.

"It's adequate," she fires back, smiling. "'Cept for the biscuit. Can't do too wrong with breakfast."

"Where do you go to eat?"

She shakes her head. "If I'm out I'm eating pizza, chicken or something, you know, something quick. Mostly I cook. And if I want soul food I make it myself."

"This is soul food?"

"No, like real soul food. Chitlins, hot-water cornbread, black-eyed peas. You got to clean the chitlins right and lot of people don't clean 'em right."

"Come on," Jimmy says. "People don't really eat chitlins." They stare at one another, and then Debra smiles.

"You messing with me, now."

"Nah." He leans back and looks around. "Well I like this place," Jimmy says. "Even if they don't have chitlins. Least it hasn't been colonized by yuppies yet."

"Oh, you not a yuppie."

"Me?" Jimmy can't believe it. "I don't even have a job.

And I'm living at home." He sounds almost proud about it. "That's not too yuppie, is it?"

"Oh boy," she says, shaking her head, "you one a those. Let you momma take care of you 'til she drops, I know that one." She looks at Shane with solidarity, smiles knowingly and he smiles with her. He likes the way she handles Jimmy. Jimmy seems poised to explain something, then thinks better of it and shrugs.

"Yeah," she says, still looking at Shane but talking to Jimmy, "bet you got all the opportunity in the world, too."

"Oh, sure," Jimmy says. "I'm thinking of running for president."

"You fool enough to fit right in."

"Yeah. Well enough about me," Jimmy says. "Tell us about Samson."

"What about him."

"What's he, you know, who are his friends? What's he like to do besides basketball? How long's he been going to this gym?"

"You think you the po-lice or something?"

"I thought maybe we could help you find him."

"How y'all gonna find my Samson? I don't think so. I wanna talk to you about that other thing."

"What other thing."

"You want to help me out? Help me out. Maybe you still living with your momma but I *am* the momma. I need to find me a job or something. I got to get up out of there, you know what I'm saying?"

"I been thinking about that," Jimmy says. "I didn't forget. She should talk to Lou."

Shane pictures Debra sitting across a conference table from his wife, chatting about page views and butterfly models, unique selling points and calls to action. He stares at the black lines of dirt embedded in his knuckles, keeping a straight face. Debra is watching him carefully.

"My wife," he says. "She knows a lot about the current market, business."

"She owns her own damn business," Jimmy says. "And it's growing."

"It's this Internet thing," Shane says. "They." He shrugs. "Yeah, I mean, maybe. We can talk to her, it can't hurt."

"I think it could be perfect," Jimmy says. "They're hiring all these people, and no one knows what they're doing. And don't those dot-commers talk about diversity initiatives or whatever? But there's just a whole bunch of whiteys, man, they don't have no diversity. It's a fucking joke. Lou could totally make this happen."

"Jimmy."

"If not Lou herself, she knows somebody. You ever use a computer?"

Shane is horrified. He expects to see her reach out and smack his brother across the face but Debra just glances back and forth between them, trying to gauge what's going on.

"Yeah," she says. "Not really."

"It's pretty easy. They want you to think it's rocket

brain surgery or something but mostly that shit's just glorified typing."

"Why don't you have no job, then?"

"Hey, I could definitely do that crap except..." Jimmy waves his hands as if swatting invisible flies. "I've got my own things I'm working on. What I'm saying is that you sit down with someone and poke around a little bit, you could do half these jobs these little fuzz-faced twenty-year-olds coming in and getting fifty grand to do *nothing*. Nothing."

"Fifty thousand dollars?" Debra says. She checks Shane for confirmation. "Is that right?"

"Listen." Shane debates about what to say or whether to grab a fork and stab his brother in the thigh. "Let's just put this topic on hold until I talk to Lou, okay. You have to forgive my brother. He means well but he never has the slightest idea what he's talking about."

"Yeah, huh."

"Yeah. I will talk to her, though."

"So what does Samson do?" Jimmy asks, unfazed by slander. Shane can hear the cook and the waitress talking about a movie or something, the thick sizzle of something wet hitting the grill. "Does he have a job?"

"He had a job," Debra says finally. "For a while. He was working in a mailroom? Right now I don't know. I really don't know all what he's doing."

"Why not?"

The two at the counter laugh. Fun continues in their world. The woman at the table behind them swirls the ice around in her empty plastic glass. Debra and Jimmy are having a mild staring contest, which Jimmy seems to win as Debra looks over to see what Shane thinks about all this. A mailroom. Sam working in a mailroom. Did he wear a button-down shirt? Shane tries to picture him walking out of Debra's door in khaki pants and a light blue oxford, hiking the scrappy project path, waiting for the bus to take him downtown for six bucks an hour. No, that couldn't be right. How'd he work a mailroom and hit the Firehouse at noon? And hit the gym, too? Did he ever try to get a job at the gym? Shane shrugs to tell Debra: no help here, only questions. She quickly returns to Jimmy.

"So you just get in people's business, huh. That what you do?"

"When I care about them, yeah."

"Oh you care about him. I never heard your name. I never seen you before."

"Five years. He been balling with us for five years, and you never knew about it. Makes you wonder, huh."

"Don't make me wonder. You don't know me. You don't know Samson."

"That's why I'm asking. I want to know."

"Oh you miss your little friend, huh."

"Don't you."

She stares out the window, tapping a fingernail against her teeth. "I don't know where he got to this time." Her voice has dropped down low and soft in the sudden quiet of the restaurant. "He don't stay with me too much anymore. You know, he a man now and all that.

Big twenty-year-old baby. He don't like it up there. I mean, nobody like it up there. But they mess with him, you know, and they ain't no children anymore."

"Why they mess with him?" Jimmy asks.

"Why you think."

Jimmy ignores the mad in her voice and considers. "I don't know. He's a good ball player, that's got to count for something. He can kick half their asses on the court if he wanted to."

She searches his face, like she's trying to figure out if he's making fun of her. "Yeah he good, huh," she says finally, keeping something in. "I don't know that make it better or worse."

"Better."

"Come on now. He can ball, but he's not street, not even. I'm his momma and even I know he don't look right. Where they're concerned—if you ain't hard or run your mouth, you're not in the game? You're nothing. I kept him away from all that. My boy a high school graduate, know what I'm saying, my boy's never been inside, nothing like that. He got another place to stay? I don't blame him."

"But a month. And you don't even know?"

She shrugs, looks around the restaurant for sympathy, somebody who can tell her what to do with these two morons.

"What about the police?"

"What about 'em?" Now she's fishing, Shane thinks, like we know something. What could we possibly know?

"They find him, I guess someone tell me about it, huh."

"Maybe not. We got a cousin on the force, we could ask around."

"Look," she says. "Reason I called, you know, it's difficult, see." She's tapping her nails against her teeth again, then clenches her fist tight to stop herself. "I got to get us out of there. But you talking about a job and you don't even have a job. I don't know why I'm wasting my time."

"We can help you, there's no reason we can't."

She nods in disagreement, weary. They're all wasting their time, the three of them, but what else do they have? "What about you, you all quiet over there, what do you think."

Shane watches her mistaking silence for knowledge and shakes his head, his tongue thick with nothing but questions. Where's your family? Where's Samson? How do I get out of this? He pictures Debra in a cubicle typing away, her right hand darting out to flick the mouse. Click click. Sam climbs up a long ladder to a rooftop where Shane's waiting to show him how to snap the brushes together. Sure—and they all live happily fucking after. Debra's still waiting for him, her eyes skipping around his face, his hair, his mouth. As if what comes out might actually mean something. She waits.

"It's a good time for jobs," he finally manages. "I'll talk to my wife. Maybe she can help."

They drive her home in silence. As they turn into her parking lot, Shane spots the telltale light blue jersey floating past, Tennessee and friend on an early evening stroll. Then Jimmy sees him too.

"That's the guy," Jimmy says.

"What guy." Shane pulls the van forward a little faster, trying to stay unseeing and unseen. Tennessee is not someone he wants to see right now. But Jimmy is adamant. He reaches forward, touches Debra's shoulder, points.

"That guy. Dude was here last time. Waiting for us. He knows Samson."

"Everybody know everybody," Debra says. They park in front of her apartment.

"They're friends?"

"Naw, he." She changes her mind. "Listen, y'all don't want to talk to him, he a drug dealer, okay. He one a those, you know, police come for him in the morning and he back by lunch."

"Huh. They got special police for up here?"

But Debra doesn't seem to hear him. "He coulda got out," she says softly. "Not one of those got a new car every week or something. Sent his parents back home, they from Memphis? He built them a *house*. He go build his parents a house and then stay up here to sell drugs? Naw, he gonna end up dead though."

"Did Samson," Jimmy says. "Was he messed up in that?"

Debra shakes her head. "Naw." She reaches for the door but doesn't open it, clicking the handle lightly back and forth.

"I guess not, huh." Jimmy's looking out the window, searching for Tennessee, for Samson, for someone. "First time we saw that dude, he just walked up and tried to sell us something, right off the bat."

"Oh he try. What you think? He try with me, I seen him from a little boy he still come up and all 'Auntie auntie, what you need.'" She almost smiles, shakes her head. "And he know I don't do that."

"But we coulda been anybody, right?"

"Who could y'all be?" She opens the door to leave but stays seated and then shuts it again, slowly. "Listen, these people up here." She shakes her head. "Y'all can't be coming around, okay. Yeah, people think I'm talking to the—they don't know who. People be talking. Talk up here like you don't even know."

"We can call you," Shane says, too quickly. Jimmy shoots him a look, hearing it, like the date gone wrong: yeah, baby, I'll call.

"My phone's not working."

"Do you want me to look at it?"

"You can look at it, but that's not the problem."

Shane blinks. He's getting better at not answering, at refusing to fix the problem. "Okay." Would you mind, then, if I walked out that door and disappeared off the face of your planet? But she's not letting him off the hook. He slips another business card off the dash and hands it to her. "Call me in a couple days, then."

"Couple days," she repeats. He can't tell if that's a long time or surprisingly soon. She scans the business card in her hand: the jolly chimney leprechaun in rooftop boogie with his broom. She points at this ridiculous character, almost smiling. "You do this, for real?"

"For real."

"Huh. Okay. All right now." She slips out the door and flips it shut behind her.

They watch her amble away from them, hips swinging, singing or talking to herself.

"What the hell," Shane says. His brother moves up to the front seat, settling smug beside him. "Lock the door," Shane tells him. "You're not gonna talk to me first about your little scenarios?"

"When? Besides, you'd probably say no. But you wouldn't say no to her."

"Jesus, Jimmy. I mean. I wanna help but shit."

"Shit what. Shit because she's black?"

"Oh sure, that's it. That's the only issue we're dealing with."

"Come on, I know it's not all computer geeks. They need marketing, salespeople, receptionist, customer service, office manager, you know, everything."

"That's not even what I'm talking about."

"What are you talking about."

"And what do you know about office managers?"

"I read. I listen to the radio. They're always bitching about they can't find warm bodies. Any idiot can get a job."

"Except for you."

"I'm not an idiot."

"Says who."

"Listen. Who knows what she can do, but whatever it is, I bet she could do it for Lou." He snaps his fingers three times, summoning a genie. "She's quick, she got a spark, you know. Come on, you have to admit, for a guy with nothing, I'm a brilliant super genius. You gotta talk to Lou about it, at least."

"I will. You know I will. But you got to let me do it my way. All right?"

"You got it."

"And what are you gonna do?" Her phone. Computer. Résumé.

"Me? I'm gonna find Sam." Jimmy jerks his head, spotting something. "Hold up, hold up," he says and Shane obeys before he sees why. By the time Jimmy's downed his window and calling out, it's too late.

"Yo, what's up. I ask you a question?"

Tennessee stares a little murder and then smiles at them as he steps their way, his body rocking in a limping strut. He reaches out and Jimmy meets his hand, the two of them doing some variation of slap grasp bump like they're old friends.

"S'up chimney man," he says, eyeing Shane with deep recognition. "Your lucky day, it's happy hour."

"We're looking for Sauce," Jimmy says.

"Yeah," Tennessee says. "What you need Sauce, you got the king now. He with me. You made it to the well, don't gotta worry now. Well don't run dry."

"No," Jimmy says. "It's not our thing."

"Aw I seen you do your thing," Tennessee says, staring at Shane. "Chimney and the rock stars. Y'all forget about Sauce, I gotcha. What I say, he with me, you know, his land is my land."

"It's not like that. We're friends of the family. We're trying to help his momma out."

Disbelief tightens the muscles in Tennessee's jaw, where a knot pulses briefly like an angry tumor. "Yeah?"

"Yeah, she don't know where he got to, and we're trying to help her out."

"Help her out? She your friend."

Jimmy nods.

"That's good," Tennessee says, frowning, waiting for someone to change their mind. But no one does. "She needs a friend. 'Cause that bitch owe me money. Sauce owe me money. Everybody owe me money, the whole motherfucking cosmos owe me money. And I'm getting paid. Maybe you owe me money too."

"Naw. Not us. We just looking for our man."

Tennessee and Jimmy stare each other down, and to Shane's surprise Jimmy doesn't look away. It's the look of having nothing to lose. Tennessee glances over at Shane, calculating something, sucking in the difference between the two. "You," he says to Shane, "you see Sauce, you tell him he better take care of his momma and my money."

Shane nods. He doesn't know what else to do.

"How we going to tell him," Jimmy says, "unless you help us find him. You got any ideas at all where he might be?"

"I got all kinds ideas." Tennessee steps back and examines the side of the van. "A man ain't nothing without ideas." Then he begins slowly chanting numbers: "Two, seven, nine." He keeps chanting and Shane thinks it's impossible, how could anyone owe anyone that much money, until he realizes it's not a mathematical figure but Shane's own phone number which Tennessee is reading off the van's painted flank.

"Forget it," Shane says. "Fuck this." He slams the van into gear but keeps his foot on the brake as Tennessee grabs the doorjamb and leans his head inside.

"You want business? Sauce can't handle no business. I seen you, boy, you think we playing checkers up here? This for keeps, motherfucker, you ever wonder why you ain't got a hole in your head? Shit, I'm keeping you alive, bitch. You wanna keep fucking that ho' somebody better keep her breathing too. We got debts to pay, mother-fucker. You know who I am? I'm the nigga who gets paid, that's who I am." His hands grip the rim of the window as if he's trying to plunge his fingers through the metal, or restrain himself from diving through the window and ripping them apart. "Ask your rock stars where Sauce at, where my paper." He pushes off gently, now, and backs away from them, smiles, his teeth straight out of a tooth-paste commercial. "And have a nice day," Tennessee says.

Shane slips his foot off the brake and the van starts rolling forward. His left knee is shaking and he reaches down to steady it with one hand.

"Tough guy," Jimmy says, watching the world fade behind them in the side view mirror. He's grinning.

"That's what I'm talking about. Fulla shit. Whoooey." He hunches his shoulders, rolls his neck like he's getting loose for something. "That'll wake you up, huh. You see Samson up here with these assholes? No wonder he cut and run." Jimmy waits for Shane to join in, but Shane is just driving. "You okay?"

Shane's not sure he could speak right now, and doesn't know what he'd say if he could. Instead he nods and drives, doing his quickest best to get them off the hill.

11

L OU RETURNS FROM New York unhappy. Her meetings have not gone well. Despite the market and the optimism, the bankers want to delay their IPO. Bankers are morons, Lou says, thriving on acronyms and incomplete sentences. She swears to Shane she's sick of this shit even if she knows it's all she does or talks about. She mentions a novel by Balzac.

"I missed you," he says.

"You did?"

"Yep. Nothing good seems to happen when you're not around." He kisses the soft skin at the hinge of her jaw. He slides his hand across her stomach and slips it slowly down her pants.

"Well."

They take the afternoon off and have sex on the floor of the living room, rolling around inside the red oval on their imitation Persian rug. They work hard to get her there. She does not come easily, but this time he feels her with him at the end. Afterwards they lounge on their bellies in a patch of sun, their pale butts seeming innocent in the blinding light. Lou looks happy, her eyes closed, lying there in silence while he rubs her legs.

"I needed that," she says, finally. "Scary how much I needed that." He closes his eyes, not wanting to speak, enjoying the physical calm. She drapes her body over his. "Can I just stay here for a while," she says.

"Yes."

She lingers for a few minutes. For a moment he thinks she's fallen asleep. Then her body stiffens and she sits up. "I can't. I gotta go."

"Where? No," he says, "I'm getting the handcuffs. I'm putting you under house arrest." She makes her move and he grabs her with his legs, pins her firmly between scissored thighs. She struggles briefly.

"Okay." She relaxes. "I'll stay, but we have to *do something.*"

"Handcuffs isn't something? How about ice skating?" A brand new rink has just opened downtown.

"Really?" She's amused. They went skating together before, years ago at the Embarcadero, where Lou glided while Shane stumbled behind, providing comic relief.

"Not really. Or let's go tonight."

"What about now?"

"How 'bout a walk?"

"A walk?"

"A walk."

They eat grape Popsicles and hike up the long serial-killer stairs near their house, climbing through a stand of eucalyptus to the very top of Diamond Heights. The warm weather is holding on miraculously into its second week. Shane asks Lou about the things she ate in Manhattan. She tells him about seeing some guys playing basketball in a chain-link cage. She checks her watch a few times, but she's not wearing one. She shows him her purple tongue. On the bay in front of them, two enormous freighters arrive like floating cities, riding low in the water under the weight of treasures from Korea, Hong Kong, Japan.

"Where's the first place you want to go?" she asks.

"I don't know. Mexico?"

"Farther."

"Brazil?"

"Not Brazil. I think rule number one is never let your husband see Brazil. How about Spain?"

"I haven't thought much about Spain."

"I've always wondered about it. Christians and Moors. Picasso, Gaudi, Goya, Cervantes—just seems like something wonderful and strange goes on there, you know? Maybe we could buy a place on the coast and live there. For a year or two or ten."

He sees blinding white buildings under a cloudless sky, a winking blue sea. "I would try that," he says. Two-hour lunches, he thinks. Siestas. That salty ham.

"Supposed to be cheap in the south."

"Our kids would speak Spanish."

"With that snooty accent. How great would that be?"

"Do they have." He's about to say *basketball* but decides against it. He's pretty sure they do. "Chimneys?"

"You'd never have to look at another chimney in your life."

"Oh. Right."

"Hot nights."

"Sangria."

"Stupid shitty bankers."

When they get home Shane makes them cocktails with lots of rum and mint. He finds Lou smiling and alert at the sliding doors, listening to the portable phone.

"I want to ask you something," he says.

"Guess who that was," she says, hitting a button on the phone and holding it to her chest. "Your buddy ol' pal. Something about dinner?" She examines him happily for secrets. He shakes his head. "At a certain David Fulton's house?"

"Really."

She smiles. "I'll still pretend it's a surprise." She holds out the phone for him to listen, but he hands her the drink instead. She takes a sip and aahs with satisfaction. "Do you like his friends?"

"They're banker-like."

"Oh but you had a good time that night. You two totally hit it off."

He wants to tell her she's wrong but doesn't know where to start. "Well, you know, he's a partier. But I'm not exactly their kind of people."

"No, you're exactly not. That's why he likes you."

"What time."

"Soon."

He nods. "That's not what I needed to ask you though," he says. She is on the way to the bedroom as he follows close behind. "Do you remember the kid I play ball with? That kid I'm always talking about?"

"The Dragon?"

"No, the kid, the young one."

"What kid?"

"Samson," he says.

David Fulton's house is tall and narrow and elegant, wedged between two nondescript buildings in the foothills of Pacific Heights. The style is unusual for the city, almost Franco-Prussian gothic, stern and gray, with a beautiful copper-green roof pitched extra-steep as if for snow. Poking out up top are two serious chimneys seemingly built for Nordic storms, not California fog and drizzle. It seems strange to Shane that he's never seen this house before, which looks like it's been extracted from a quiet city in Austria and potted here full grown.

"Shane!" Fulton shouts, as if they are unjustly separated friends from the old country. He wears very blue jeans and a tight white ribbed long-sleeved shirt. Shane notices his body now, the wide practiced chest, thick shoulders, solid arms. The gym. I'll have to ask him about Samson, he thinks. "And the lovely Lou. What luck! Come in, come in. Let's recreate!"

The entire front of the house seems devoted to hall-way, long and wide, built with a four-abreast processional in mind. An excellent hallway for a swordfight. The ceil-ings sit up high enough that they disappear, and light beams out from obscure fixtures along the smooth white museum walls. Shane trails behind Lou and Fulton, observing their soft banter about the house. He reaches out to touch the surface, his hand brushing against cool, hard stone. Marble, perhaps. He pulls his hand back quickly, checking to see if he's left a smudge.

Their host leads them to a mammoth living room suitable for Christmas caroling or impromptu wedding receptions. Piano. Two large Northern European couches, perversely elongated past any usual size, face one another. Neither one of them would even fit in Sam's house. The wide windows frame a perfectly coiffed backyard of big squared shrubs, baseball-diamond grass, and flowers, with a flagstone patio to one side sized for small helicop-ter landings.

"Everybody, meet everybody," Fulton says. "This is Lou. Shane. You know Ed and some of these bums."

They smile, laugh, offer pleasantries. "The bums need a drink," Ed tells Fulton. "Before I tell you the won-derful tale of Texticom."

"Yeah?" Fulton looks interested. "I thought Phil said no."

Ed nods, smiling tight-lipped. "Yeah. Well I broke his rice bowl." Dribble the ball once hard, hit the shot, stare into those eyes. That's right: you weak, bitch. That's why you sitting, nigga.

"Unbelievable," Fulton is saying, shaking his head and smiling. "I want the bloody blow by blow." They wouldn't last two seconds on the court.

Lou touches Shane's elbow and gives him a cautious look: where are you, come on back. He's not a hundred percent sure how okay they are after the Debra conversation but he winks at her and she winks back. That poor kid, she said. That poor woman. But. It's not that simple. Once he would have agreed but now he isn't sure. Maybe it is that simple. Maybe you give a woman a job, you find a disappearing Sam, you do these simple things and make things right. He follows her now, as Lou pulls him away from Fulton and Ed and slips them into another conversation with two tall women by the window. Hawaii is a topic. Fulton's house is a topic. He watches his wife listening to everyone at once, her senses spidering out to recognize the footsteps of new arrivals in the distant hallway, smell the cologne cocktail of the three men behind her, hear Fulton whispering into Ed's ear. If he puts his hands against her wrist and neck he knows he'll feel the quick blood beat of her sharpest self. She is excited, something is happening here even if it looks like nothing. The two tall women are behaving dull and she keeps herself in check, rounding her edges, making pleasant, saving herself for someone who'll appreciate a stabbing. Despite Lou's best behavior, the women don't like her. Most women don't. But she doesn't give up, filling in their hollow smiles with a funny self-effacing monologue on her three most embarrassing pairs of shoes, and Shane leaves her there to win their hearts alone. He takes a few steps and inserts himself into another group nearby.

"Shane."

"Rick."

"Celeste."

"Lynn."

"Loren."

They wait for him to say his piece and when he doesn't they slip back to their show in progress. "I wish you'd come in on that."

"I know."

"Step up and pet the pony."

"Who took 'em?"

"Sachs."

Someone mentions kissing frogs as he nods to the conversational beat, riding the sound, letting the words fall apart. He is on a collision course with drunk.

"So how does David know you?" a woman asks him suddenly. She has long brown hair without an errant strand or split end in sight. Everyone turns to hear the answer.

"We don't really." If they're expecting more, they're in for their first of many disappointments of the night. "And how do you know him?"

"Everyone knows David. The question is more how does David know us."

The couple next to her laughs.

"Biblically?" the woman says, smiling.

"Fiscally," someone pitches in.

"But I haven't seen you before? Who are you with?"

He glances over at Lou, still deep in conversation. Why not, he thinks. "I work on chimneys."

He enjoys the small ensuing silence. "Chimneys? Like." She points a tentative finger at the rooftop above them. He nods. She nods. "Ah," she says, "you're a real person." She trades a meaningful look with one of her pals.

"David's latest favorite?" the pal says.

"Chimneys," another man says, musing, not quite getting it. "What's the Web component?"

"Black widows, mostly." He's made the joke before, it works, it's serviceable, but this time no one seems to hear him.

"You *could* do something, though, couldn't you," one of the women says. "The house-services portal. Everything from chimneys to painting to foundation to whatever, everything. Like an online contractor."

"I-contract. Rightman.com."

"Housecare.com. Homecare. Upkeep."

"It's got to be out there."

"Classic middleman play."

"Maybe Home Depot's on it."

"No, that's it, you build the thing and sell it to Home Depot. Or bid it out between them and isn't there another one?" She points at Shane to give him his cue.

"Lowes?"

"*Lowes,*" she repeats, making it sound somewhat nasty.

The conversation continues. The drinks continue. Cell phones detonate with peppy tunes and are duly answered. Shane slips away to find Lou again but Fulton finds him first.

"The escape artist," Fulton says. "Now I suppose I see why." Together they watch Lou holding court in the corner, her laugh rippling through the room. "Where'd she come from? Are there more?"

"I found her at Cal."

"Sweethearts! My god. She's going to be king someday. I need to have you over again before she takes her throne."

"She'd like that. She thinks you're important."

"But you don't." Fulton grins.

"I don't know anything about it." He finds himself staring at a line of incredibly expensive-looking lighting fixtures around the mantle, above the fireplace. "Did you do a lot of work on the house?"

"You like?"

"What's not to like?"

Fulton laughs. "This couple spent five years fixing it up. I didn't have to do a thing."

"You bought it like this."

"Sure. Everything in it, too."

"Everything?"

"They took their clothes, I guess. Some people have the gift. Some people like nothing better than to march around the world, looking for this stuff. You imagine?" He points to a simple yet elegant chair in the corner, a silver antique clock sitting on the mantle.

"And they agreed?"

"Some people are good at things. Some are good at money. I said a number and they moved to Paris in two weeks." He scrutinizes Shane's face, looking for a reaction. "Totally obscene, isn't it," he says, smiling.

They arrive at the front room, far from the guests, where Fulton produces a bottle of scotch and pours for them both. "So when we going to party again?" he says as they clink glasses. "The projects, man, I'm telling you, those projects are a trip."

Shane shakes his head. I've got to get out of here, he thinks. Fulton's eyes dart across his face, reading him, and he kneels down quickly in front of the fireplace to change the subject. "So what can you tell me about my chimneys?"

Shane squats gratefully beside him. "Not much. They're big."

"What do you do when you clean them? Are there chemicals?"

"Brushes."

"Old school. So you stick a brush up in there."

"Down. From the top."

"Of course. From the roof. It all makes sense now. You're the guy who spends days on the roof. While the rest of us. Yeah, I gotta see that." He leans forward with a big smile on his face, a best friend suggesting an evening caper. "I always wanted to go up there." He points upwards and nods.

"I should have brought my ladder."

"The painters left one." Fulton squints with mischief. "Let's go."

"Now?"

"Why not."

The sun has set but the sky's still incandescent as they sit atop the crest between two chimneys where an attic window pokes out like a ship's cannon. Fulton sits carefully at the roof crest, his bare feet propped against the cannon barrel. He stares at the waves of roofs stretching in every direction as Shane gazes down into the dark hole in Fulton's house. Below he can hear the conversations in progress, the buzzing words floating up the chimney like sparks. From the sound of things, he and Fulton are not missed.

"Fuck it's nice up here," Fulton says. "Do you think I could build a deck?"

"I don't know."

"With a hot tub? It would look like shit I guess but who cares. Sit up here in the tub. Naked, with a bottle of good wine and cheap dates and a sniper's rifle. There's got to be a way." He glares at the roof, calculating its demise. "I think I'll call my architect. The very idea of it is going to cause him physical pain."

"You can find someone to do it, I'm sure."

"Oh, always. No matter what *it* is." He half rises and crabs his way along the top of the roof to meet Shane. "So where you been hiding? You didn't join my gym."

"No."

"I swear it's not all pussies. They got tough guys, too, there some ghetto boys, plus a buncha good dudes from

Cal. You should join. I'm always there. I guess your work keeps you in pretty good shape. Me, three days I'd turn into the blob."

"Do you know a kid named Sam?"

"Probably. The gym has no names. One of the best things about it."

Shane describes him, quickly. "My brother and I been looking for him."

"Intrigue. Come back down with me sometime, I know everyone, we'll figure it out. Goddamn." He points out to the west at two small streaks of clouds turning orange and red. "You must be a better person. Anyone who spends most of their time up here has to be a better person."

"It's all right."

"Gotta be better than all right. You could be doing a lot of other things, you wanted to."

"I don't know about that. I like being outside, I like houses. I like being my own boss."

"Sure. But it can't be the best money in the world."

"It's okay."

"How much do you make?"

"About sixty." He doesn't remember anyone ever just asking him like that. "Before taxes. But I deduct everything."

"And your wife?"

"She does all right, I guess."

"She can't be paying herself much. They're stalled out on the IPO, what I heard."

"Everybody knows everybody," Shane says.

"You're betting on her."

"It means a lot to Lou."

"And you?"

"I want her to be happy."

"But not rich?"

"I don't really think about it."

"Maybe you should. Would she be happy if the company's successful but she doesn't make a lot of money?"

"I don't know. Is that possible?"

"Of course it's possible. Everything could change tomorrow." Fulton laughs. "But tomorrow isn't coming, not for a while, I'll tell you that right now. There's a lot more to this than people realize. People don't even know. By the time tomorrow rolls around? She'll probably be starting her fifth company by then. You guys'll be living across the street, up in those beauties somewhere." He nods off into the heart of Pacific Heights. "I don't see you as a South Bay kinda guy."

"This might sound stupid," Shane says, "but I don't really know anyone to ask."

"Shoot."

"Does that mean you really think they're going to make it?"

"Of course," Fulton says. "Why wouldn't they? Come on, look at all this. And look at her." Fulton rubs his shoulders in the slight breeze. "You can tell the difference between the parasites and the ones who have the magic. You can smell it. Not everyone can create things. Some people just want the path of least resistance. Some people just want to get rich. But she's a creator. She'll build this one and do another and do another. She's got the bug."

"I don't think so. I don't think that's what she wants."

"You never know. You never know until they've got their fingers wrapped around the golden ring."

The light is fading hard, as the window sparks of downtown blink brighter in the growing dark. The rooftops' waves are shadowy now, a quiet winter sea.

"It's a great time to be breathing," Fulton says. "A lot of kids hated history, but I was one of those geeks who liked it. I always wondered what it felt like when everything changed. Those moments that got their own chapter." He holds his head above the chimney, listening to the strange distorted sounds below. "Now we know. It feels…gooood." He shakes his head with pleasure, surveying his domain.

The lights of downtown stare back at them, well-lit offices telling tales of late hard-working nights. "Can you help her?" Shane says. Were the downtown people getting rich too? He feels Fulton watching him, but he doesn't look over. "I don't know if she needs it. She seems to think she does. But if you can, I'd be really grateful."

Fulton lifts his head, following Shane's gaze, looking for something he's never seen before. He nods, slowly. "One wrong move up here and that's it, huh."

"That's it."

"What about my chimneys."

"What about them."

"Can you fix them?"

"Sure. Is there something wrong with them?"

"I don't know. But they can't be perfect, can they?"

"I guess not."

"So make them perfect."

Shane laughs. "I'll come back sometime and check them out."

"Deal. As long as you bring me up here with you."

The roof is steep, and Shane offers Fulton a hand as he creeps down toward the ladder. Fulton grabs it, hangs on tight. He moves well up there, a strange absence of fear in his eyes.

"Makes me feel like an idiot I've never been on my own roof," Fulton says when they're on the ground again. "Makes me think of all the other things I've never done."

They sit at a long maple table in the dining room, fourteen of them eating lobster, corn, and small roasted potatoes. Somewhere, an invisible cook has been cooking. Bottles of pinot noir move freely at all ends of the table. Shane is drinking beer. Everyone wears cheap plastic bibs with cartoon lobsters strutting large across their chests, waving their happy claws like cruise boat tourists.

"Forget New Hampshire," someone is saying. "The whole primary thing is ridiculous. New Hampshire is over. The East Coast is over. Might as well make California first and call a spade a spade. Who gives a shit about New Hampshire? Iowa?"

"Yeah. Except that most of this country has more in common with Iowa than California."

"Who needs 'em. The fifth largest GNP in the world, right?"

"End State."

"Technology. Hollywood. *And* farming. Who's gonna mess with that?"

"Farming?"

"There's New York."

"New York. They have no idea what's going on in New York."

"No idea."

"We've even got our own chimney sweeps," Fulton says. "What do we need with New York?"

"A chimney sweep," one of the other women says, looking at Shane. "There's something romantic about that."

"I found him first," Lou says.

"The key to San Francisco," Fulton says, looking sly, "is mixing the power of tradition with the absolutely new. You know, like, human society is changed forever but people still think it's good luck to shake the hand of a chimney sweep."

"Is that true?"

"Supposed to be," Shane says.

"How on earth do you know that, David?"

"The man has heard of everything."

"A master of idle conversation."

"There's more, isn't there?" Fulton says, winking at Shane.

"Yeah," Shane says. He feels like he's been set up.

"Which one, the king and the horse?"

"What I heard was they used to invite the chimney sweeps to weddings and have them lie in the bridal bed. For marital good fortune."

"Oh, that's tasty."

"Lie in the bed?"

"Unclear if that's with or without the bride," Lou says. "The chimney folks had great PR guys." She winks at Shane. "Naughty."

"What else?"

"Well," Shane says. "They're all luck-related. Like kissing a chimney sweep is supposedly good too."

"Kissing?" Lou says. "You told me humping."

"Can't hurt." The table is smiling. Lou leans over and kisses him theatrically on the cheek.

"What about," Fulton says. "What about this. In architecture, they say the chimney was the technological leap that allowed for class division."

"We have got to get you a day job, David."

"Something. Selling Slurpees at the 7-Eleven."

"I never heard that," Shane says, searching Fulton's face for motive. Definitely a setup. But why?

"Think about it. In the castles, apparently everyone used to eat together in one big heated room, with a fire in the middle, and an open hole in the roof for the smoke. The duke, the duchess, the piss boy, everyone in one big room. Then chimneys come along, and suddenly you can heat rooms separately. With chimneys," he says, removing the slender piece of meat from the bottom jaw of a lobster claw, "people could finally get the hell away from one another."

"Says who?" someone says.

"I read it online."

"Well it must be true."

"Where do the top hats come in?"

"So the Internet's even worse," Shane says, "right? Because now people never have to see each other if they don't want. Like everyone's got their own personal chimney."

"Not at all," Fulton says. "What was the important stuff that used to live in the privileged rooms? Was it the people or was it what they knew? It was really language, books, maps, knowledge, ideas, memes, the conversations of power. And now that lives everywhere, right? Now anyone can find it. And use it."

"For free."

"Free can't last. Someone will invent new chimneys," Fulton says. "*We* probably will." He's trying to catch Shane's eye but Shane won't have it. He drinks his drink. Did Fulton make this fable up?

"Data encryption."

"Embedded copyright protection."

"Paid content."

"Place your bets."

"Funny to think about someone looking back on this as medieval."

"Ah those heady times of possibility."

"Days of kings and feasts and parties."

Drinks continue to disappear at a rapid clip. Fulton throws a corn cob at someone. A lobster claw puppet show ensues. The table is abandoned for the deck out back. Lou is telling a dirty joke about a parrot screwing chickens. Shane has heard it before and starts laughing before she gets anywhere near the punch line. They're all laughing, Lou too, holding onto someone's arm for support. A cell phone rings, then rings twice more before Shane realizes it's his.

"Excuse me," he says, embarrassed, although no one pays him any mind. He steps back into the house. "Hello?"

"This Shane?"

He sees the phone tucked into the curve of her neck. "Yes."

"I need you to come over here."

"Now?" he says. He means to ask *why?* or *what?* but somehow *now?* gets there first.

"Yes," she says. "I need your help. This Debra. Debra Marks?"

"I know." She waits for him to say something else, but he doesn't.

"Shane?"

"Yes." Lou is still holding court outside, telling another story. Her audience leans as one, as if her hands are tugging gently at the end of their marionette strings.

"Can you do that for me?"

"Okay," he says.

"Are you coming?"

"Yes."

"Okay," she says, "I'm here waiting." She hangs up.

12

Lou's car climbs up the slope into the projects, purring healthy and quiet against the steep incline. As he slows to turn into the parking lot, his mind flips through a quick slide show of monstrosities: stabbings, shootings, dissections, strangulations, bludgeonings, forced drownings, anal rape. He wishes Jimmy were here, although maybe it's for the best.

He parks the car, sits in it running for a moment before he kills the engine. Slipping off his jacket, he tosses it in the back seat, then opens the glove department and removes the miniature can of mace that Lou keeps inside. He holds the can briefly and then puts it back. The seaweed smell of lobster lingers in his shirt. He checks around for signs of life and death and then gets out of the car as slowly as he can make himself, closes the door behind him, speed walks to Debra's doorway. The familiar graffiti sits waiting for him: God help us all, Niggas be acting like bitches. There's one glowing in the dark that he hasn't seen before: a date, Ray-Z, R.I.P. His fists are balled up tight. Glass sand crunches beneath his feet, the sound of fight or flee.

Behind him, out in the parking lot, a voice calls out, impossible to know what it says or who it's for, but it sends an electric jolt up his spine. There's someone there. He doesn't look back, just pounds on Debra's door. Quick. Music's coming from her apartment or maybe the one next door, pretty loud, the bass rattling the brass doorknob slightly, the hard low voice rapping promised threat. It's a good soundtrack for a killing.

On knock number five her door opens and her face appears, level with his, hair slicked back carefully, lips wet with lipstick just applied. Her perfume staggers him back a half step, and she slips through the door, closing it behind her.

"You look nice," she says, as if this is the most normal occasion in the world, his dropping by on a Thursday night.

"I was at dinner." He fights not to look behind him. If she notices the wobble in his voice or hands, she doesn't let on.

"Huh." She sighs softly and nods her head in the vague direction of the world beyond. "I'm sorry," she says, not sounding sorry, "I just need to get out of here."

"Are you okay?"

She shakes her head. "I need to talk to you," she says.

***

They end up in an upscale diner down near the Embar-cadero, almost on the edge of North Beach. He doesn't know why there, where he has never actually been, he simply gets out on the road and starts driving. They barely speak. He's expecting some kind of explanation but it seems like she's decided to wait until they arrive. They drive by the new ballpark in full construction, rebar bursting up like a field of magic beanstalks, they drive under the massive girder legs of the Bay Bridge, they drive by the ferry building made small by downtown around it and the empty piers in renovation and then he sees the diner and the perfect parking space out front. He stops.

They sit in a big red booth. In the mirrored wall, he catches a glimpse of them: his pink-white skin looks red and blotchy next to hers, his light cotton pants and black sports coat wrinkled compared to her fitted white blouse over tight blue jeans. She takes her time, in no kind of hurry, reading the large menu carefully before choosing crab cakes, a small Caesar salad, Diet Coke. He orders a beer.

"Last time I was out for dinner," she says, "like out, at night? I don't even know. I do *not* even know," she says again, slowly, as if the words themselves might drag back the memory by force. She examines Shane, then checks out the rest of the diner. "I like this place. Reminds me of a soda shop. You ever go up there to Trays?"

"No." Is this why she's summoned him? Is this how she works her way up to the truth about Sam?

"It's known," she says. "Kinda like this, if it's even still around. Used to be. I haven't been there for years."

"I'll have to look for it."

"It ain't much, nothing to look for. It's like more down home, know what I'm saying? This here's better," she says, nodding her approval, making clear that she has no problem with change, advancement, progress.

The drinks come, and he gives his beer a good gulp while she stabs her ice with the straw. Her nails are long and perfect, red to match her lipstick, although her hands themselves seem huge and ancient, too big and too old for her body. Deeply wrinkled at the joints. Those hands must have done some work in their time. Why does the rest of her look so young? She has young skin, that's it, what is Lou always telling him: it's all about the skin. Up on a hill somewhere, his wife is being clever or listening with furious concentration or sparring with whoever's game: an Ed, Celeste, a Fulton. What was the look she gave as he left, lying his way to the door? A question—do you need me?

"You a quiet one, huh?"

"Not always."

"You are though, you happy just to sit there and chew your tongue up."

"Sorry. I'll try to do better."

Through the window they can both see the bridge, which is something else from here, large and lit, its clean steel lines slicing up the dark sky behind it. Beneath it, the revamped Embarcadero with its rows of healthy uplit palm trees in the median, edged by new curb and stone.

She shakes her head.

"Straight out Disneyland down here."

"I know what you mean."

"Yeah, huh, you feel me? It's going on, they got the made-for-TV city. You ever see them doing that show they do?"

"Which one's that?"

"Right here, you know, it's like in San Francisco. Come on, now, you seen it. With that puffy head Miami dude wearing little pink yellow jackets. Every time I see that show, I'm like, for real, unh-uh, it's too cold be wearing that golfing get-up. Not in my city." She looks back out the window again, as if the film crew might be there, right now. "They must got a headquarters down here somewhere. Always got that shot, you know, in the show, of the bridge through those big-ass windows."

"I think I saw that."

"Yeah," she says. "Me, I don't care for it, but I seen them making the show one time on the hill? They had the big ol' trucks out there and lights, daytime right? but they had it all out there. Seal off the block and the whole nine. I didn't see that dude though or nobody famous, but that's what they all said it was. I'm like, put me in the show I give you something more to look at than ol' puffy head and that little Mexican. Nah, I don't care for that at all."

"I don't really watch it very much, to tell the truth."

"What shows you look at?"

"Nothing consistent. I guess I do watch some TV, but it's like I don't even notice."

"You just zone out, huh."

"That's it."

"That's what Samson do," she says. "You could dynamite the door he don't hear it."

"Where your kids?" he says, not meaning to but the thought of Samson brings the other faces out of the ether around him.

"They with my momma for the night. Over in Oakland."

"But everything's okay?"

"Nah, everything's not okay." She shifts in her seat and leans in to tell him a little secret. "Shit. Look at me." He does. She's frowning hard, summoning wrinkles into her forehead and shaking her head softly. She looks angry and scared and maybe even a little like she wants to slap him or something. He doesn't know what to think. "Look at me," she says again. "What am I doing here."

"I don't know. Tell me. What's going on?"

"My shit's fucked up," she says, "why I got to talk to you. I can't sleep. I can't think straight. I can't do nothing. And now that punk come hassling me? I got to ask you something."

"Okay."

"I gotta know something."

"I'll try."

"You and your boys play with Samson, y'all homosexuals?"

He shakes his head, squints, not so much denying, but trying to make sure he's heard her right.

"Yeah you," she says, "the other guy, y'all you play with, y'all homosexuals?"

"No. Not that I know of. I'm married."

"Married don't mean nothing."

"Maybe not. But no. I'm not a homosexual."

"The other guys."

"I doubt it. Not that you'd notice. It doesn't really come up."

"Samson's a homosexual," she says, staring at him hard. "You know that?"

"No, I didn't." He can feel the vinyl of the booth irritating the skin of his thighs, seeming to tighten against his flesh like shrink-wrap plastic. "Like I said, it doesn't really come up."

"Oh, it comes up," she says. "It comes up and up and up. Are you religious?"

"Sometimes," he says.

"Well I'm not religious. My momma was, though, she pray more than she eat. She the one named him Samson. You know why?" He shakes his head. "Cause I was 14 years old, and I was drinking and drugging already and gonna have a baby, and she told me God was giving me a gift, like He gave Samson to the Israelites. And she took me to that Bible and that Bible said I must drink no wine or do nothing else unclean—and everything but everything I was doing be unclean, know what I'm saying?—so I had to stop cold if I wanted to have me a little king, a little somebody. And you know what? I just stopped. I believed her. 'Cause it did feel like a gift, and I wanted to have the baby, and I did. Didn't I?"

He doesn't move, focused, listening.

"Yes I did. And I cleaned up. And my momma, they got me in the hospital and pushed out Samson and she said now you got to go with God and take care of this child. Like that for years, my child and God all she cared about." She takes a deep breath, lets it go through her nose. "My momma here right now, she'd tell you all about it. She tell you all about God and Samson. Oh yeah, how my little boy's gonna burn in Hell." Her voice is hard and shocking, not just words. Hell a place as real as Burlingame or Daly City. "Well, if he do end up in Hell, least his daddy and friends be there soon enough, keep him company. But uhn-uh," she says, shaking her head, wicking those thoughts away hard, "that's not for me. Maybe he's all right, out there somewhere." She looks off out the window, watching a car drive by, then stares at the food at the table next to theirs where two huge plates of fries are being consumed by a couple of frat boys. "Those fries look good. I could eat a world of fries right now, you feel me?"

"I don't know. I don't think I understand really, no."

"Least you honest," she says, half laughing to herself. "Samson gone, y'all show up at my door like I dunno what, then that punk roll up on me and what am I supposed to do?"

He is fidgeting with his water glass, tilting it back and forth, watching the level change, and she reaches across the table, puts her hand flat on top on his hand and stops him. "I don't know now if he hiding out or what, I don't know if it's true he owes money, I don't know if it's true y'all know where he's at."

"I wish I knew where Sam was at. Who told you that?"

"This little gangster, Ty. He say Samson staying with your friend."

"He's just making things up. He's just trying to scare you."

"Well it's working. Bottom line is I got three other little ones take care of and I got to get out. And you got to help me, that's what."

"I will," he says instantly. "I want to." He does. He wants to more than he's wanted anything for a long time. Get her out of there. Get her a job. Find Samson. These are tangibles, pins to aim at and knock down. She's breathing heavy through her nose, holding her head in her hands. She's going to cry. Is she going to cry? If she cries he doesn't know what his own body will do.

"I'm going to help you," he says. "I'm going to do whatever I can." She nods. She looks angry is what she looks.

"That boy," she says. "What's more fearful than being a momma? You think of anything, let me know." Her hand is still on top of his and they stay just like that, her holding him in place as they watch each other, until the waitress returns with the food and she lets him go.

"This looks good," she says, not missing a beat. She digs in, eating slowly and steadily, absolutely confident in her appetite. She knows how to eat. He orders another beer. She eats and doesn't say another word until she's finished. He can still feel the warmth of her hand on top of his, like she's burned a mark there that will blister up tomorrow.

"Why you not eating?"

"I'm not hungry."

"That beer, boy. Beer will fill you up. You a drinker, huh?"

"Sure." He's tilting his empty glass again but this time he stops himself. "Want to go?"

She looks around to see what's wrong with being here. "All right. Where we going?"

"I don't know."

"You don't know, you don't know. Man, what are you, scared or something? I scare you, all this shit scare you?"

He tries to smile. "You're scary."

"Yeah, you should be, you should be huh. No," she says, "you gonna come through for me, you gonna be scared but you'll do it." She smiles, her mouth and face expanding in anticipation and when she's done it turns out to be quite a smile, a dime-sized dimple on either side. She looks like a teenager when she smiles. "I could go for a walk. A little stroll around Disneyland, see what's going on."

Outside they stand side by side while he looks around and figures out which way to go. She reaches out and takes his hand. Her skin is cool and rough, her long fingers wrapped around his. A light and comfortable grip but he can feel the strength in there ready to squeeze water from stone. He feels their skin touching as if from a great distance, a sensation beamed up to satellite and then back down to earth again. He tries to let go, at least he thinks so, but their hands stay peacefully joined.

"All right, Mr. Man," she says, pulling him gently. "Let's walk."

North Beach is buzzing. The crowded sidewalks slow to a syrup crawl as they hit the neon center. They make their way mutely past the gaudy strip clubs, past the packed bars and restaurants. She keeps his hand like a flashlight as they walk the narrow sidewalk. The oncoming pedestrian traffic thins single file to the outside to let them pass. His favorite North Beach café is crowded with its usual mix of regulars and tourists, but there's a table opening up right in the window, prime for people-watching. He suggests a coffee. Her hand is still cool in his.

"I don't drink coffee."

"No coffee. A glass of wine or something?"

"I don't do no substances, nothing. Don't drink, don't smoke, don't drug, nothing. I did, was in the whole game back in the day but uhn-uh, like the song say. Ts'all over now."

"What song is that?"

"Now you playing, huh? What, you too lazy to walk? Gots to have your coffee, wine, and beer."

"Sure you not some born again?"

"Once was enough for me." He gives her the smile she was waiting for. "Yeah," she says, "you getting there, huh. Some things better than coffee and tea."

They walk. They get off the crowded restaurant drag and she finally drops his hand, casually, and slows her pace to pause in front of the shops, examining the show windows packed with shoes and used guitars, comic books and space-age wedding dresses, the empty racks of sleeping bakeries, second-hand clothes shops packed with faded suits and cashmere sweaters. He trails a step behind her, his hands jammed in his pockets for protection.

At Washington Square he leads them around the perimeter, stopping in front of the big lit-up church of Sts. Peter and Paul that lords over the square, stretched out tall in all its fancy glory. The wide doors are open, an unusual Thursday night something under way inside. When he turns around she's sitting on a bench, watching both him and the church.

"They even got Disneyland for church," she says.

He sits down beside her. "They must be doing some sort of special mass tonight."

"You go to church."

"Sometimes. I grew up with it."

"What are you?"

He points at the church. "Catholic."

"Oh you Catholic." She laughs. Catholic is funny. "So the big pope and all that. But you ain't got no kids."

"No."

"Huh. That's Catholic, huh. You go to church lately?"

"No."

"You go on in there now, you want to."

Inside there is no mass, just a heavy gold and marble church at rest. A handful of people sit or kneel in the pews under the high gilded ceiling. There's plenty to look at in there. Debra stops almost in the doorway, uneasily eyeing the full-sized marble angel at the entrance, while Shane crosses himself and slips into the aisle seat of the back right pew. The only times he goes to church now are holidays or an occasional Sunday trip with faithful Ma. Lou doesn't go. Maybe she'd like it at night, when it's empty and quiet and personal. If his dad had been alive they would have been married in the Church. He's been sitting there a little while before Debra appears on the side aisle and sits down in the farthest seat of his same pew and they watch each other across the expanse. He nods at her and they meet outside without a word.

They walk a block out on the street before she says, "So, what, you pray in there?"

"Yeah."

"You pray for Samson?"

She is making fun of him. "Maybe."

"You pray for me? You oughta pray for me, boy." A thin trickle of anger creeps into her voice from all sides. Something about the church has pissed her off.

"I'm not too good at it. But I'll do my best."

She gnaws her lip as she watches a car parallel parking in front of them. "Where you think he is."

"I don't know." A boyfriend, Shane thinks.

"This afternoon," she says. "I couldn't find Demetrius? And then he out there with that drug dealer, sitting on a car? With brand-new Nikes, you know."

Shane isn't sure he understands but he nods anyway. "What drug dealer?"

"This kid Ty, y'all know him."

"With the Tennessee jersey."

"Yeah, he the one say Samson owe him money. I owe him money. You."

"I don't believe him."

"Don't matter, do it, what you believe."

"No. I guess not. Were they friends?"

She stops and he turns around and looks at her with the twin spires of the church behind her reaching for the black sky above. "What do I know about Samson's friends. Shit."

He wants to step to her and hug her tight. It's not her fault. None of this is her fault. "I'm sorry," he says. "He never talked about us, either, I guess. All those years. The game up at the Firehouse."

She shakes her head. "He don't talk to me much about anything, though."

"You ever watch him play?"

"When he was little, yeah. Not for a while."

"You should watch him some time. The moment he steps out there." He sees the gold chain dangling in front of Sam's chest, swaying side to side before he bursts into the middle, rising above the crowd.

"What." She wants more.

"Something happens to him. It's like…everything's easy on the court. Everything makes sense out there. He doesn't hesitate, he always knows what to do. I wish I could describe it. I wish you could see it."

She wraps her arms around herself as if her body's coming apart. She opens her mouth but instead of speaking pulls in one long breath and turns and walks off, back into the meat of the city.

He follows her through the crowded streets, walking behind her, trying not to watch the bare skin of her neck or the stitched seams of her jeans, walking behind just any ol' stranger on just another North Beach night. Too easy to follow, he thinks. Where are all the black folks here. Where my niggas at. Even when they hit the crowds she doesn't look back as she picks her way through the bodily traffic with the exacting step of a woman at night, alone. Beyond her swiftly moving shape, the city's big best and brightest buildings crouch behind the illuminated triangle of the Transamerica, waiting for her or for him or for anyone who chooses to sign on to downtown ways and disappear in there. It can be done. Even at night, the tessellated blocks of light suggest enterprise and fortune, a never-ending load of things to do that tomorrow or tomorrow or maybe even tonight will send people scrambling into action. To be one of them you only have to find the right window, Shane thinks, the right tiny block of light that's waiting for you. There must be a window down there waiting for everyone, even those of them who've never made it into the office after all these years. Debra, Jimmy, Samson, Shane.

Maybe that's the answer, straight ahead. Or maybe he

should stop walking altogether, take a sharp left alley turn and let her disappear and go home and try to live happily ever after. He's afraid to be alone with her again. Talk to her about the job. Ask her about Sam's boyfriend.

She waits for him at a light, standing with her hip cocked, sure that he's there behind her.

"I'm sorry," he says.

"Where to?"

"I got to go."

"All right." She doesn't sound like she believes him.

"Should I drop you off at home?"

"Where else you wanna drop me. Might as well return me to my cage."

The city is quiet as they retreat, winding back through the empty streets the way they've come. "You've got an interview," he says when he can't bear the silence anymore. It's not remotely true but it disrupts the air inside, changing the molecules around them.

"Oh yeah?" She leans against her door, cranes her head back, gives him a far-sighted look still half-smiling. "Where at?"

"With my wife. She's got that company."

"Okay."

"I don't know when. I'll let you know."

"What it pay?"

"I don't know. Do you have a résumé?"

"A little bit. Not really."

"I'll help you. I can help you with all that."

"When."

"This week, I guess. Can I ask you a favor, though? Will you let me talk to the police?"

"You want to talk to the police?" She's angry again, but this time he's ready and tries not to flinch under her stare. "About what?"

"About Sam. Samson."

"Listen," she says. The car is paused at a stop sign with the steep eastern cliff of the projects in front of them. It looks like a strip mine at night, bright lights and gouged rock. "The police, you know, what they gonna tell you? What's it gonna be, you know? He in jail? Or they need a perp for something and here's a black man missing. Or here's a body. That's what you wanna talk to the police about?"

He stares at the stark white prison lights waiting for them up ahead. "But don't you want to know?"

"Talk to whoever you want."

"You tell me what to do," he says. "You tell me what you need."

"I *been* telling you," she says.

A car is coming up behind them, honking and flashing its brights as it swerves alongside in a loud rumble of angry engine. He catches the face of a kid Sam's age yelling obscenities at him as the car passes, tires screaming down the road. Shane watches it fly down the dip and then up the steep street into the projects, whipping familiar around the curves. He feels like he's sitting on a platform ten feet above the car, watching his life happen. See Shane sit. See Shane run.

"You all right," she says, and he can't tell if it's a question or a statement of fact. He thinks: what would it feel like to smash one car into another with malice and intent? The airbags popping out to save him while the sneering kids bled to death, their guns embedded in their laps. What would it be like to get used to this?

"I could hire him myself," Shane says. "It's not a bad way to live."

"Hire who?"

"Sam. Samson."

"Samson," she repeats.

"I never knew," Shane says, pulling his foot off the brake and following the roller coaster ride into the projects. I never knew about any of this, he thinks.

They pull up beside her door and he waits for her to go back to her life, but she's waiting for something too. "Call me," he says, finally. "Call me tomorrow."

"I will." She doesn't move, though. "You any good?" she says.

"I don't know." He's not sure what's she's talking about but that seems like a safe answer.

"Playing ball."

He smiles. "Not bad for a thirty-something white guy."

"For real?"

"Me and your boy battle out there, that's for sure."

"I gotta see that," she says, smiling. "I hope I do. Bet you surprise some people, huh."

"I guess."

"You surprise me. You surprise me all the time."

"You surprise me too." He can't see her eyes in the night shadows, and he's glad. "Did he ever get hurt?"

"Samson?" She sounds disappointed in the question.

"Yeah. Injured."

"Naw. Not really."

"I was just wondering. I got hurt once. Made *me* want to." He swallows the word: *disappear.* The parking lot seems nothing less than peaceful in the moonlight, empty and still. "Just to realize you're that close to nothing, all the time. One minute you're happy and jumping in the air, and the next minute you're a useless piece of shit. You're that close to letting everyone down."

"Damn," she says, "everybody get hurt sometime." She laughs. "You ain't never let anyone down in your life. I know you ain't gonna let me down. You're a good man, you know that. You one of the good ones."

He finds himself nodding slowly. "Well." He checks the parking lot but it's still calm as a summer lake. "You going to be all right?"

"Yeah. I guess you got to go, don't you?"

"Yeah. Call me," he says.

"Tomorrow."

She leans in to say goodbye but instead of saying anything she cups the back of his head with her hand and presses her cheek on him for enough time to count, the bones of her face digging in hard against his. Then she releases him and swings out of the car and walks away to her door.

13

PARKING IN PACIFIC HEIGHTS is ridiculous. Thursday night after eleven and everyone is tucked in tight, their shiny cars dug into every nook and cranny he can think of. He cruises by Fulton's house twice, but someone's sleek blue Mercedes in the driveway stays put, a sign of continuing festivities inside. Nothing to do but widen the loop, head for the steep hard-to-park hills, murmuring teenage blasphemy under his breath: hail Mary, full of grace, help me find a parking space....

This is Disneyland, he thinks, here in Pacific Heights, these are Debra's fantastical houses of Mickey and Donald and Goofy. Tall and painted perfect, they stand up straight, peering proudly over the bay or looking back at the city with mild disdain. There are mansions here, designed for awe, gated transparently for all the world to see. Some blocks Shane can actually trace the competition of long-dead silver barons who whipped their architects into frenzy, hurrying to outdo one another on prime visible city real estate. Who lives there now? Movie stars, doctors, lawyers, businessmen he's never heard of, financial mavens, foreign consuls. The occasional newly titled duke or duchess of the Internet, perhaps.

His slow tour brings him by one of the more minor mansions, a house he's been inside once, a high school party, a thousand years ago. Some rich girl from University with plenty to lose, you had to respect her a bit for daring the real rager. Her parents' home was begging to be looted and defiled. Even back then, he thinks, there was a little science fiction to the city, you'd be going along living your own small Sunset flatland life and then find yourself high atop Pacific Heights snorting speed off antique refinished dinner tables and feeling up trust-fund girls in imported tiled bathrooms. Not his regular scene exactly, but the Catholic kids could kind of have it both ways. They could go high or low. Usually low. Parking up here was a bitch then too.

He's almost forgotten why he's driving around when he spots a tight space on one of the hills. The car behind it has just arrived, the guy climbing out and watching as Shane moves into position. He cuts too hard the first time and has to reset, but before he does the guy walks up beside him and shakes his head. Shane eases down his window.

"You can't fit in there," the guy says. Same age, maybe younger, dressed like he's just come from the gym. His shorts look like the skin of some rare synthetic lizard, new and expensive. Shane wonders if he married that

University girl, moved into that house, stored his loafers in closets they did their best to cover in vomit and piss.

"Of course I can."

"You'll block me in."

"We'll see, won't we."

"Hey," the guy says sharply, but Shane throws the car into reverse and whips the car back into the space, getting the angle right this time, knocking the car behind with gusto and then front back bumping into place, whirling the power steering like a great ship's wheel. The guy watches him angrily from beside his own car and when Shane gets out is bending there at his bumper, running one finger along the rubber and steel to check for subterranean damage. The guy stands up and stares at him.

"I guess I fit," Shane said. "This city's still got room for me, after all."

"You're an asshole," the guy says.

"Really," Shane says. "That's not the problem. You don't even belong here."

"*I* don't belong here? Who the fuck are—"

Shane steps quickly to him before he can finish, grabs the guy by the throat and pushes him back against the car. The guy reacts too late, smacking at Shane's arm as he tightens his grip. He's about to pulverize the guy, he's about to punch him in the face as hard as he possibly can, he's about to break all the bones in his hand on this guy's face.

"Listen," Shane says. "Shut up, and go home. And I mean home, wherever you came from." He lets go and leaps back as the guy takes a weak swipe at him, sputtering something. "I'm serious. Shut the fuck up." Here's a problem he'd be happy to solve.

The guy is rubbing his neck, thinking about what to do. While he's thinking, Shane turns and walks away, the blood still rushing through his head, preparing for the sudden attack from behind. For the first time in a while, he doesn't give a fuck what happens. But nothing happens, although his heart's still going good as he stomps off through the empty well-lit streets toward Fulton's house.

A woman whose name he doesn't remember is leaving as he arrives again at the tall grave door. She watches him approach, waiting patiently and holding the door open for him.

"Shane," she says with slightly intoxicated concern as he steps into range, "everything all right, I hope?" Her earrings sparkle in the light from the hall behind her. He slips beside her and takes over the door's substantial weight.

"I think so." That's all he wants to say but he can see on her contracted face that something more is required. "I'm sorry to have run out on all of you, missed everything." The words come with difficulty.

"We were sorry too. Your wife is really lovely," she adds. "In every sense of the word." She purses her lips at him, blinks at him a little drunkenly.

"Thank you." She needs a spanking. This whole neighborhood needs a spanking.

"I hope to see you again?"

"Sure," he says, and slips inside.

He doesn't hear a sound until he's halfway down the long hallway. Two voices, no more no less, mingle comfortably in the big living room. He can hear them leaning back on the soft bright white couches, crossing their opposing legs, sipping blood-red wine. They sound like old friends. They sound like they shared a goddamn crib together.

"If we hadn't wasted all that time with those clowns," Lou is saying.

"Who knows where you'd be," Fulton finishes for her. "The woulda coulda shoulda is brutal."

"My only worry is that somehow he could sue us."

"Sue *you*? You should sue *his* ass. You should have him drawn and quartered. Killed."

Without even noticing, Shane has taken the weight off his heels the last few steps and then stopped entirely in the hallway, leaning against the wall out of sight. A hunk of Kryptonite, nearby, seeping into his bones. On the far side of the hall is an enormous painting for Shane to stare at while he sticks his hands behind his back and digs in against the wall and listens. As far as he can make out, the painter has captured a bunch of parallelograms at an orgy. They're not much to look at but they're boning each other silly, having a rocking good time.

"He'll bad-mouth us."

"No he won't. He'll see you going public without him, Wall Street ready to come all over you, and he'll be begging to get back in. That's about the only thing they're scared of, you know—not even losing money but getting left out, looking bad."

"So you're saying we shouldn't wait."

"Absolutely not."

"And what, we pretend Quixo never happened?"

"No. But *you* define the space. And it's bigger than Quixo. Quixo is for small people with small minds. That's what the mezzanine round needs to say. It needs to be fuck-you money. We will eat your children."

"That's nice," she says, laughing. "Have you used that one before?"

"No. That was just for you."

"Really."

"Not really. I just cut and paste."

"I'll drink to that." It's only half a second before the glasses clink. How close together are they sitting? "Then who should we talk to, you think?"

"You're talking to him, that's who."

"I swear, David, don't play with me."

Fulton laughs. "Let's talk dirty. What was the first round?"

"Sixteen for thirty-five, fifty seats, two-year burn."

Oh just blow each other and get it over with, Shane thinks. He creeps quietly away from them, down the hall. They're laughing now, a bright prosperous sound walking him to the door. He slips outside and takes a long pull of fresh air. He sits on the stoop, watching the cars go by. Who are they kidding. Who is anyone kidding, here. He stretches out his legs, rolling his right foot in circles clockwise. There's a soft pop in his ankle each time his toes pass ten o'clock. Pop. Pop. He rolls it back the other way and eventually the popping stops.

How did Sam ever find us anyway, Shane thinks. How does anyone find each other? You take an econ class with your future wife in college. You hit the gym or step outside to smoke pot with a zillionaire. There were lots of games in town. Did someone tell Sam about it? But who would tell him? Shane listens for footsteps inside Fulton's house, but the house is quiet. The house wants nothing to do with him. An accident, then, a single moment when the kid walked out of Mission High one day after third period, algebra or something gruesome, slumped down the hallways to the huge front doors and stepped quickly down the wide, shallow steps. Walked down the steps, shrugging off the period bell behind him. Right across the street, in Mission Dolores Park, the bad kids, boys and girls, were smoking dope and fingering one another up behind the trees. He ignored their gropes and clouds of smoke as he turned right up Eighteenth Street, through the Castro. Bored, disgusted, alone, no particular place to go. Not like he was going to hurry home, now, was he. The houses got nicer and nicer as he walked, freshly painted Victorians with moldings, detail, plenty of care. Some guy like Shane sitting on a stoop like this, watching him walk by. But not like Shane at all. He hit the garish corner of Eighteenth and Castro and hung a right past the tourist gay-bar strip, the leather shops, the souvenir joints, ice cream parlors, past the big marquee of the Castro Theater showing something classic or slightly strange. And all those men and boys—he'd come through here before, hadn't he? Just to look or be looked at or something more? Fifteen. Probably something more.

But today he kept walking and crossed Market, winding up and up the hill through steep, clean residential streets. Leaned into the hill, the tendons stretching out, the ligaments unlimbering, and he climbed and climbed. He climbed to the very top of the good-sized hill that loomed above the Firehouse court. He sat staring out across the valley at Potrero Hill where his mom didn't know anything about him, where he was just another endangered species, and then the wind changed and suddenly he could hear the familiar percussion of the ball. The sound drew him quickly to the ledge to see the game. On the sideline two guys sat waiting on the green-red painted pavement where they stretched, pointed at the game, gesticulated, rolled their necks and flexed their backs. One of them was Bruce. One of them was Shane.

Sam sauntered down. He could hear it now so back went his shoulders, out prodded his chest and hips. The disembodied sirens of noon sounded throughout the city as he rolled up to the chain-link fence, leaned, slipped two fingers through, hanging there, watching them play. Shane remembers: the unfamiliar kid with skin half-baked between white and black, freckles, brown hair on the verge of shrubby, full lips, pointy nose, small dark eyes too close together. He wore shiny red sweatpants

with a white stripe down the side, a black matte sweat-
shirt with a hood. That thin gold chain, the old brown
watch. Red and white Jordans, almost new. Sam stood
young and lanky against the fence, trying to project disdain, with all the muscles in his face pulled tight. His nostrils flared, he was breathing just a little bit too hard, and
his eyes kept jumping ahead of the ball to where he knew
it was going to go. Ho, ho, he wanted to run. He wanted
in. Shane saw Sam and saw himself, a kid trying to act all
supercool but lusting for the game. Sam looked young
and skinny and lazy but he had that curious body that
made you wonder what he could do.

Shane waited for a minute and then asked him. The
kid gave him his best deaf-mute, blinked.

"You wanna run?" Shane said again.

"Pah," Sam said, as if he'd suggested something outrageous and boring all at once. "Nah."

But Shane could see. He passed the kid his ball on the
bounce and Sam let it ride up into his hands where it
continued spinning softly against his palm like a class-
room globe. Sam put his other hand on top and then
dribbled it hard, twice.

"They're almost done," Shane said, pointing at the
game in progress, and the kid nodded at him, a barely per-
ceptible motion. Shrugged. He saw what was being
offered: a decent game, far from home, total anonymity,
minimal bullshit. He could play in this game and never get
better, never have to face the crazy Rashons and courtside
Tennessees, never have to worry about anyone waiting for

him with guns and malice after the game, never know what it was like to compete against the ghetto best. He shrugged and he took it. Rolled up his sweats, tied down his shoes, stepped onto the court, and played with them for five straight years. Became one of the guys and the youngest loyal subject of the Firehouse court until the day he stopped showing up.

The cell phone on Shane's hip rings angrily.

"Hi."

"Everything all right?"

"Yeah. I'm very close."

"Okay."

"Parking's a bitch. I'll call you when I'm outside."

He stands and listens at Fulton's door one more time for secrets, but the house knows better than that. Then he marches off to get the car.

Lou's electric. He means to tell her where he's been but can't get a word in as they cross town. She is reliving the night before his eyes, and the longer she talks the less sense his story seems to make. By the time she asks him, he has decided something else even if he doesn't know why.

"Jimmy broke down," he says. "I had to go jump him."

"He ever heard of Triple A?"

"I don't know. I don't feel like going home," he says. There are too many things wrong right now to go home. "It's like I missed out on my night with you."

"We'll have other nights. And if things work out, we'll remember this one for a long time, too."

"Let's go out."

"Out?" She's surprised. "Where?"

"The ice rink's closed, but I have another idea."

"Out," she murmurs. "You realize that I'm going to be working for the next seventy-two hours straight to get ready for Monday. You realize that."

"All the more reason to get my night in when I can."

She smiles, and then starts to laugh, the low lusty sound filling the car. "I'm too wired to sleep anyway."

"Goodie. Follow me."

He drives them to a place he barely remembers, down in the hinterlands of Daly City, an all-night bowling alley they used to hit in high school. Lou calls her people en route, Sloan and Rich, to shout the news. "I know!" she tells them, "I can't believe it either! He said Monday. What a weekend. Okay. Okay. See you tomorrow." She clicks off and grabs Shane's arm, her small fingers digging almost painfully into his arm. "David fucking Fulton," she says. "Did you know about this?"

"No."

"I can't believe it," she repeats. She bangs her knuckles together, thinking, letting out breath as if practicing for childbirth.

The DC Bowl is still there, thank god, and halfway crowded on this Thursday night. They've added a karaoke setup in the side bar and he can hear bad singing blending with the sounds of clattering pins. Lou has removed her watch and put on the funny shoes, absolutely game. A memory in the making, Shane thinks. Remember the time? Remember that night? They bowl. He feels better already. The way she launches the ball toward the pins, crossing her body and holding the position for just a tiny extra comic moment. She's not bad, actually. They bowl.

"He's serious, isn't he?" she says. "He wouldn't do that to me. He wouldn't do that to you."

"No."

"No. I'm just being a spaz. I'm gonna throw this bowling ball into the wrong lane." She massages the marbled green and white bowling ball in her small hands.

"Matches your outfit," he says.

"What am I going to wear?" she says. She shakes her head and takes two steps and rolls the ball slowly down the lane. It seems to take several minutes to arrive at its destination, where it calmly knocks down every pin in the vicinity. She hops lightly into the air, claps her hands.

"Who knew?" Shane says.

"I could probably do anything tonight. I could probably cure cancer."

"Yeah?"

"Sure. But I think I'll just bowl instead. I should confess. We do go sometimes, Thursday lunches, bowling with the office."

"Do you have your own ball?"

"Sure. Shoes. Shirt."

"Monogrammed."

"'Lou' in little blue cursive on my tit." She struts over to him and kisses him on the mouth, hard.

"That tit?"

"That's the one."

"I'm up."

"Yes you are." She fixes his collar, runs a rearranging finger through his hair, as if he's going to meet someone important. She pinches his ear, hard. He sits there, content to be treated like a doll. "So you think he's for real?"

"You're really asking me?"

"You're a good judge of people. I just wonder what he's like in cold morning light. A businessman. A great white shark with something bloody in his mouth."

"Why should he be any different?"

"Please. You don't get to be a David Fulton doling out points or feeding the homeless."

"I guess not." He can't see any way to talk about something else.

"If this happens?" she says. "This isn't just money. This is success. That's what Fulton means."

"Fulton means I'll get you back?"

"So back you won't know what to do. I'll be following you around like a duckling."

"Good."

She steps over to the line of waiting bowling balls, picks one up and plops it onto his lap. "Hurry up, now. Some have greatness thrust upon them, but it's still the biggest school night of my life. You think you've seen me work hard? Three days. You ain't seen nothing yet."

He tries to think of a way to say the simple words: Debra Marks. But he can't do it. "We're pretty lucky, aren't we?"

"Yes we are. But." She shakes her head in self-disbelief. "Luck is luck. It's the one thing you can't worry about. You just do everything else and stay ready to take advantage when it swings your way."

"What if it doesn't."

She points at their lane, the waiting pins. "Then there's nothing you can do to stop me from beating your ass."

"Yeah?"

"I'm gonna beat your ass and then we're going home."

He stands up, holding a bright pink ceramic ball in his hands. She winks at him. They've never been bowling before but something about being here with her drags him back through time, a wave of nostalgia for a moment just like this that never happened before. The night you took me bowling and Fulton made us rich. It will join the time she slipped her hands under his leather jacket to hold him on a motorcycle, her fingers warm against the soft skin above his waist. The sand rubbing between their thighs on beaches, grass beneath their bare backs on top of seaside cliffs. Their first awkward garlic-flavored kiss.

What am I waiting for, he thinks. He kisses her again and steps forward and takes his best shot.

She beats his ass. They go home.

***

Does he sleep that night? He must sleep, if you have to ask you probably do. But it feels the same to him when the morning light creeps down the hall and nibbles at his eyes, that feeling when something bodily happens that prevents you from switching off, shutting down. He feels not only like he hasn't slept but that he'll never sleep again. Maybe it's the sex that wakes him up, the yelling breakage kind of sex that ends at the dressing mirror, watching: the hand knotted up in her long hair, the veins set to pop out of his neck, her cheek pressed against the dresser and her tongue visible, the muscles in his chest and shoulders pulled tight. An expression of unpleasantness or pain on both their faces. Who are these people? What is that? When does that happen? It happens. It happens but not often and not without embarrassment. And afterwards when her features have gone slack with sleep and she is once again the beautiful girl he married and loves and mother of his unborn children then he goes back to the mirror to recognize himself. That's him. That's his living body again. He pinches it. He punches it. He flexes his whole weight up on the foot, up and down, he bangs that foot against the frame of the bed and then he's awake. Maybe he should go to a gym right now and work out all night, run in place, ab crunch till he cramps, jump rope and pump until he can do no more and collapses into some happy exhausted sleep. Maybe he should play ten games of basketball or have sex like that with anyone five or eight more times. Instead he lies in bed thinking about thinking and waiting for morning to come.

14

THE CAFETERIA at General Hospital doesn't even look open. At the register sits a still-drab figure that could be a manikin, and the food service area beyond lies dark, the fluorescents dim or off. The main room is empty except for two guys staring at their coffee cups as if expecting them to speak. Outside on the patio, three homeless soldiers in headbands and fatigues chain smoke and yell conversation at one another. He sits inside at a long table toward the back, a little delirious, waiting for Debra.

The room holds no organized distractions: no television, no music, no newspapers, no colleagues cracking good ones over Diet Coke or pale iced tea. He tries to look over some material that he's brought from Lou's company, a press kit, brochures, trade show flyers. The brightly colored covers give way to interior diagrams where incredible things are apparently occurring, and Lou's power verbs in bullet points explain all. Her words.

He stares out the window. The homeless guys out there are having a better time than the rest of the world, chopping it up, smoking professionally. It's hard to imagine the last job any of them might have had. Perhaps just killing people, far from home.

After a while a nurse comes in and sits at the table next to his, and he watches her read the paper. He can make out the headlines. The brouhaha for mayor continues. City budget surplus debates. More folks up in Humboldt are building bunkers for the impending Y2K apocalypse. Too much traffic, not enough housing in Silicon Valley. Little companies are springing up from the ether faster than the big companies can gobble them up. He remembers Sister Carrigan talking about maggots and spontaneous generation. The nurse glances over at him, her tight frown scolding his reading manners. He wonders if she's seen anyone die today.

Hospitals have a way of making him regret everything, absolutely everything. He checks his watch. He thinks about asking the nurse for part of her paper. He tries to think of something to think about. He waits.

His last visit. His last time in his doctor's waiting room decorated with framed pictures of obscure local heroes. Baseball players, mostly. THANKS DR. CHO FOR GETTING ME BACK ON BASE! There were never any baseball players around when he came in for his appointments. Would he have noticed if there were? Month after month, he sat in those plastic chairs so absorbed in his own broken foot that he hardly remembered seeing other patients. They must have had their problems too. They must have had their wives and husbands and et ceteras who didn't think a dirty cast or neck brace or sling was very sexy or cool. They must have lost some swagger about the future. A few of them must have lost faith in themselves. He didn't know because he didn't talk to anyone. He'd just sit there and stare at his foot, trying to weld the thin crack closed with superhero eyes. He imagined what it would be like to have no legs, no arms. Or to be close to death, to reach out and touch it with your hand. He and Lou didn't know how to be unhappy together. They'd never done it before. An overweight man with his arm in a sling walked into the office. Across from him, a leg-casted girl fidgeted next to her mother. Shane sat there for the last time in the waiting room while they avoided his healthy eyes except for the girl, who killed some time staring at him with her red mouth open.

By the time the nurses called his name he was fidgeting himself, gazing out the window at the bright afternoon like a dog longing for the grassy yard. His doctor led him to the small examination room, arranging his X-rays on the light board. They talked about the Giants and looked at the pictures together. His eyes skipped back and forth between the images, comparing that day's set to the one from a month ago. The changes were subtle, almost imaginary, the triangle of new bone filled in one more subtle shade of fibrous white.

"How does it feel?" Dr. Cho asked.

"Good."

Cho ran his thumb along the side of Shane's foot, starting at his little toe and working back toward the heel. Two-thirds of the way back he found the spot and pressed along the fault line. "Any soreness?"

"A little."

"There's still healing going on. It'll keep healing for another year. Actually longer." The doctor released his foot, let his leg slide back to dangling.

"Well. What do you think?" Shane asked.

"My permission certainly isn't a guarantee of anything."

"I know that. But your judgment's a whole lot better than mine."

"We could wait another month. We could wait another year. But the additional growth at this point is very slow. The next year or so is about the last five percent." He leaned back in his chair.

"So what does that mean? Does that mean there's a one in twenty chance I'll break it again?"

"No."

"What would you put it at."

"I don't make odds."

"Damn. I was hoping to bring some odds home for the wife. She likes statistics. Pie charts."

"Well." Cho closed Shane's file and stuck out his hand. "I'm sorry to disappoint her."

Me too, Shane thought, shaking the doctor's hand and leaving the office for the last time.

***

He's been waiting at SF General forty minutes when Debra finally appears, busting through the doors with the tavern drama of the cinematic Wild West. Even the two guys look up from their engrossing cups, expecting smashed whiskey bottles, gunplay. She doesn't see him right away. She doesn't seem to see anything. She runs her hands over her face and hair like someone who'd been caught in a rainstorm. She approaches the counter manikin. All of them watch her show, leaning in to hear what she might say, but none of them can pick out the words. Then Debra's head twitches slightly in his direction, as if she's caught his scent. She turns definitively and strides his way.

"Did you call the police?" she says, first thing.

"The police?" Something has happened, some combination of the police and Samson. "No," he says, trying to sound calm. "I didn't call them."

She slumps down into a chair, staring at the pile of brochures from Lou's office.

"You're late," Shane says, when it seems like she might not speak again.

"I don't have time for that," she says, jabbing a finger at the pile.

"I don't have much time either," he lies. "I've been just sitting here. This place depresses the hell out of me."

"All right, all right." She seems surprised by him today. "It's near my bus stop," she says.

"It doesn't matter," he says. "I'm going to take us

somewhere, we'll get some work done and you can tell me what's going on. You in?"

She frowns. "In?" she says. "I guess so."

The closest Internet café he can think of is up on Valencia, so he drives up that way and hunts along South Van Ness where parking is theoretically possible. He finds a space and they walk the four blocks through the early evening Mission, past the shabby rent-a-cops and BART-dispensed commuters and Mexican men murmuring love or drugs or forged documents in other Mexicans' ears. They cross the thin green line to the fresh paint and clean windows of the new economy. There's a new bike lane there. Slipping between the Viet-Cal fusion on one side and tapas bistro on the other, they enter the café for business. He gets himself a double latte and her an iced tea.

"This one of your places?" she says. "This a place you go?"

"No," he says. "I don't know where I go." If someone were to search for him, where would they look beyond the court, Ma's place, and home? Maybe Shane could disappear as completely as Samson. "Tell me what happened," he says.

Debra sighs, sniffs her iced tea. "They say they found him."

"Who?"

"The po-lice. But it ain't him."

"Where? When?"

She shakes her head. "It ain't him."

"Tell me," Shane says.

***

The police said the last Cal Train south for San Jose left the First Street station that day at 10:42, plodding through the crisscross track yards South of Market and crawling with its single yellow eye into the no-man's land beneath the 280 spur downtown. The tracks there were lined with trash, with abandoned cars, with tents and tarps and old RVs, the makeshift homes of the homeless. At Twentieth Street the train disappeared from view and rumbled through a tunnel for several blocks, emerging very slowly at the platform-only station of Twenty-second Street where it stopped to pick up the occasional passenger. This was the closest station to the projects, a five- to eight-block walk away, depending on which side of the hill you were on. Sometimes you'd see kids hanging out there near the station and the barbed-wire bus lot, and sometimes they went climbing around that train tunnel because that's what kids do.

The train couldn't have been going very fast, but when it hit Samson he was right in the middle of the tunnel, so it was going faster than it would have been had it met him closer to the platform. The driver reported seeing the shape of a person on the tracks appear one instant before that shape vanished beneath the wheels, which meant that either Samson had jumped on the track at the last minute or been pushed or maybe that train driver wasn't paying much attention. The body was smashed and ripped and crushed almost beyond recognition. By the time they tracked down Debra, it was a few weeks old, too.

A suicide, the police said. Or maybe an accident. They'd found some dope on him, too, three tiny little ziplocks of marijuana. Not a robbery, then; someone would have taken it. Not an overdose, no needle in the arm. And not a drug killing, either—those you always found with a bullet or eight in the head. Trains were too complicated for murder. Doped-up suicide on the tracks.

"Bullshit," she says. "That's all they say." The café music rumbles low around them, a repeating chord hungry for attention.

Shane wants to ask her to tell him again. He wants to go to the train tunnel and see the blood on the tracks. He wants something more than this flimsy little story, because he doesn't believe it either. Sam isn't dead. "How bullshit."

"First of all, ain't no suicide. No one kill themselves, up there. You fighting for your life every day, you gonna kill yourself? Shit."

Is that true? Shane thinks. It sounds true. "And it wasn't him," Shane says.

"No."

"Why do *they* think it's him."

She shrugs. "They caught this graffiti kid down there, tagging in the tunnels. Said he saw Samson go in there."

"He knew him?"

"I guess. Everybody know everybody."

"But you know better."

"Listen," she says. "I don't know what he saw. I just know when they call you up late one night, when they say they got the body of your son—that's a call you been waiting for since he was old enough to walk out the door. You feel me?"

"Okay." He's trying, but she shakes her head, his voice not convincing either of them. She tries again.

"Well you been waiting for it. And you show up, and they tell you some reasons, and they ask you some questions and you just thinking: shut up and show me. Time they show you, they already know what they want you to say. They got their case closed." She ripples her fingers in front of her mouth like she's playing a flute, trying not to bite them. She sees him watching and closes her hand into a fist. The music drones on. She's lying, he thinks. She's not making any sense.

"Okay." He's going to figure this out. "You saw this body."

She winces at the word. "Yeah. And I was ready for it to be him, too. They told me it was. And I believed them. But when I saw it, hell no, that ain't him! You know, a mama recognize her son."

He looks away. He sees it: Jimmy crushed dead on a metal tray downtown. He feels something jerk through his muscles, a silent electric sob.

"What did you say?"

"I said yeah."

"Yeah what."

"Yeah that's him."

"Why?"

"Because the po-lice never helped nobody. You sure you didn't call them?"

"Sure."

"You gonna call 'em now?"

"I'm not."

"Sometime maybe you better off if everybody thinks you're dead." She says it slowly, as if she knows this is something he won't easily understand. "So they want to tell the whole world Samson's passed, I say, go ahead."

Shane pictures Tennessee's young face smiling menace out over the light blue jersey. "You think that will protect him? Maybe. But maybe not, maybe he needs help."

"Who gonna help him. The po-lice?" She snorts. It's one of the best jokes she's heard in a long time.

"Debra." Her head whips at him as if she's surprised he knows her name. "How do you really know? I mean are you sure? Tell them the truth, you know, and they can run some." Some what? "I don't know, tests."

"Don't need tests."

"You're sure?"

A woman at a nearby table laughs, a fat obnoxious sound. Debra doesn't seem to notice. "Yeah. They didn't find any of his things, either."

"What things?"

"His watch. His daddy's gold chain."

"Maybe someone took them."

"You didn't see that…body. Nobody gonna take a cheap-ass chain and ten-dollar watch offa that, I'll tell you right now. Take a cheap-ass chain off that neck and leave three bags a weed? Nah, that don't make no sense."

They sit in silence. From across the café, the sound of chattering keyboards explodes in conversational bursts.

"He never took them off when he played ball, either," Shane says. She stares at him. He can see it—for the first time she's looking at him like he actually might have known her son. "Never. We used to argue with him about it, when he first showed up. But he wouldn't take them off."

She shakes her head. "Uhn-uh. My momma gave him that watch. And the chain belonged to my baby-daddy. Samson never take them off."

"We used to give him hell. You know, you can't wear a watch, you gonna hurt someone. You can't wear a chain. And Sam just look at you like you were speaking Eskimo or something." Year after year after year. When we gonna plant that tree. Sam, when you going to take off that damn watch and chain.

She finishes her tea with a big gulp, examines the lemon and ice left behind as if for fortune-telling signs. "You remember that first day you came to my door?" She's smiling, now, like this is a choice piece of nostalgia from their long shared past.

"Sure."

"You know what I was most scared of?"

"My brother's feet."

"Nah," she says, almost laughing. "Nah, I was scared I'd open up that duffel bag and find that watch and chain. And then I'd know he's gone. You know, and I mean gone."

He knows. He understands that. But where is Sam, Shane thinks. She can see the questions building in his face and she shakes her head.

"I don't know where he is."

"Staying with a friend."

"Yeah. I don't know." She glances up at the counter, eying the clock on the wall. "It's getting late."

"I thought we were going to work on the résumé."

"Don't have time for that."

"I already set up the interview," he says.

She squints at him. "Yeah?"

"Yeah. You can't back out now. You back out now and that's it."

"That's it, huh? You do me like that?" He shrugs. "Oh you a tough guy today, huh. Yeah," she says, grinning. "Okay. Tough guy."

The café's computers are set up on little painted kiddy desks, and the two of them have to crowd together to share. The place is packed now, and Shane feels elderly and unpierced. Debra eats a scone suspiciously, the dry debris crumbling to the wide hardwood floors. She watches the glowing busy screen while he shows her Lou's company's Web site. Pastel blue and Mexican yellow, an animated page of moving chalkboard squares and circles laboring to illuminate all. He explains as best he can, but she's not paying much attention and he isn't either. Both Debra and Shane keep sneaking peeks outside, where Friday cars are honking and the sidewalks are crowded with twenty-somethings renting videos and buying six-packs, crossing the street at a jogging run.

He goes to get another coffee and leaves her alone with the computer, letting her browse there on her own. The counter guy is not friendly but when pressed has some things to say about the CD in play. Counter guy answers questions. He's from Texas and doesn't think much of the San Francisco music scene, for instance. The city is too expensive. He's thinking of moving up to Portland or Seattle. Café work doesn't pay for crap. One month he had to put his rent on a credit card.

You see that woman over there, Shane wants to say, you see her? Don't give me this Texas shit. I've had my foot woes and you've got your little rent dilemma but it's a bunch of crap, isn't it? Isn't it? How selfish can a mammal be? Selfish. Life seems too hard for us to really give a rat's ass about one another. He wonders if Texas knows that people in the projects don't kill themselves.

When the kid is called away for lattes, Shane sticks his back against the counter and watches Debra for a while. Debra online: a ridiculous thought, although she seems as comfortable with it as anyone else. But then he notices the way she moves the computer mouse, touching it delicately with her painted fingers as if waiting for Ouija forces to guide her hand to truth. She doesn't click on anything. Her mouth moves silently as she squints into the unchanging screen. One hand slips toward her mouth and she starts to bite her nails before she jerks away, clenching into fists. She stares at the girl typing and laughing vigorously at the adjacent computer, and then swings around and waves him over angrily.

"All right. Can we go."

"No we can't go. You've got to have a résumé."

"What we gonna put on it?" She shrugs. "You think I'm really working there?" The way she points into the computer screen makes it seem unlikely. Really, in there, there's a job for her?

"Maybe. Worth a shot, isn't it."

"Well let's shoot then." That neighboring girl, her fingers flying over the keyboard, her hand reaching out to point and click and drag and cut and copy and paste— that girl pisses Debra off.

Afterwards he takes her down the street to eat Thai. The restaurant is crowded for early evening, and they sit in silence, worn down by an hour of trying to fill an empty page with Debra's past. Maybe everybody's right: this is never going to work.

"You play basketball today?" Debra says, suddenly.

"No." He smiles. Imagine a woman you could talk basketball with.

"Next time you come up the hill, you tell me. I'm coming over to watch you play. See what you got." She laughs, the best one he's heard all day. Him playing basketball is very funny.

"You ever play?" he asks.

"Naw, but I used to go see games all the time. I met Samson's daddy at a basketball game."

"Yeah?"

"Yeah. A white boy, too. He could play, though, shit. And good-looking, hmm."

"This was in Oakland?"

"Oakland, right. By the time I had the baby, though, he was gone. I heard he maybe joined the army but he might just a moved away, you know?"

"You never saw him again?"

"Uhn-uh. He not important though, you know. Some is, some isn't and he's not. Not like he could come around anyway. My momma woulda killed him."

"She's still in Oakland, right?"

"Still in that same house. One person, that's just fine, but you shoulda seen us then. My momma, Samson, sister and brother, in a one bedroom, know what I'm saying? You eat this stuff a lot?" An appetizer has showed up and they are digging in.

"Sure. It's a favorite."

"Some serious garlic."

"You don't like garlic."

"Oh I like it, it don't like me. Garlic don't like nobody. Don't know who you're fooling." She winks at him without quite doing it. "Your wife ain't getting near you tonight. Y'all don't eat dinner together?"

"Your mom a big cook?"

"Oh yeah, sure, when she around. She work over at the Kaiser? She used to be daytime but when Samson come along she switch over to night on the Emergency. So she take care of him in the day while I was in school.

No teenage drop-out here, not in her house."

"He was a good kid, I bet."

"He was good, he was cool you know, didn't cry too much. My momma crazy, you know, the religious thing but she good with children. She just happy to have another soul in that house worth saving. Gave up on the rest of us sinners, long long ago. I was there you know but she raised him practically."

She tells the story. Her second son, her third. A boyfriend in the Tenderloin. Drinking and recovery and the warehouse job they put on the résumé. Her daughter. Losing the job. The projects.

"Let the good times roll. I mean things were bad before that but least 'til then we weren't in no projects. You must be thinking my family tree like poison ivy, huh?"

"No." Lou, he thinks, luck—how could you hear Debra out and not feel something? Maybe it will work after all. "How old was Samson then? When you moved to Potrero?"

"Fifteen, I think. Yeah."

So he found us right away, Shane thinks. The kid, standing with his fingers hooked through the fence, pretending he didn't want to play. "Can you tell me?" he says. "The last time you saw him."

"Okay," she says. She looks around for last bites but everything is gone. She taps her fork against the empty plate, trying to get her own attention. "The last time I seen him was a Wednesday. Just like every other day 'cept he left in the morning and didn't come back."

Wednesday, he thinks. The day after Sam left his bag up there, his last day on the court. "What did you think happened at the time?"

"I don't know, like I said, he stay away before."

"Didn't you wonder where he was. Don't you think he was staying with a." He looks around the restaurant like there might be someone listening. "A boyfriend?"

"Probably," she says.

"But you don't know who."

"I don't know what I know. Yeah, he probably has a friend, you know. Now I don't know, that little gangster Ty be bothering me, I don't know what to believe."

"Was he selling drugs."

"How he sell drugs if he never had no money? When he work at that mailroom, he give me money every two weeks and I never even asked him."

"This guy Ty says Sam was working for him."

"I don't give a fuck what he say." She snaps the word at him. "You trust him? You like his information?"

"No. I don't like anything about him."

"All right then."

"What about the gym?"

"What about it."

"Maybe he met someone there," Shane says, suddenly, speaking the words even as the thought comes to him. "Someone totally unconnected. And when things went wrong, that's where he went. Maybe that's where he is now."

"Whole lot a maybe."

She's right—Lou maybe, gym maybe, Samson maybe. She's right about all those maybes, but for the first time in a while he's starting to feel sure about something.

15

THEY HIT PARAGON in the evening crush, Jimmy
waiting impatiently as Shane slips into the locker
room to change into workout clothes. Men in many
stages of undress traffic between the showers and the
sinks, filing off to a steam room and a sauna down the
hall. Could be any one of them, Shane thinks: the monster with the neck tattoo, the skinny fat guy diving into
his branded knit, the pair of frat boys tugging on their
baseball caps. A sugar daddy, Jimmy chanted in the car,
but Shane is not convinced. The gay kid from the projects
who works out with the yuppies and the body goons,
plays ball with aging amateurs a long way from home. Is
that someone who finds a sugar daddy or simply runs
away from home?

Shane meets Jimmy in the hallway and they find the
manager in his office, not far away. The guy surprises
them—a home-grown Dave, went to Wash, worked here

when it was Mike's, held over from the good old days. He knows Mario. He knows Sam.

"That's his name?" Dave says. "I though it was like Sonny."

"Samson, actually."

"Yeah? You know, I feel bad about him. He seemed like a good guy to me. He been coming in here forever, too."

"Since Mike's."

"Yeah, since Mike's. There a few kids that started coming, you know, back in the day, neighborhood kids like Sonny. That bus stop always been out there, where they transfer up for Mission High."

"And they'd join the gym?"

"Not many. Usually someone bring 'em in, you know, and Mike used to do a special for them, couple bucks a month."

"Mario and those guys," Shane says, "they brought Sam in."

"Yeah? That's cool. Not too many left, now, but when Mike's switched over I got them grandfathered in, you know, lifetime pass. Seems like the least I could do."

"Right on," Jimmy says.

"Yeah, that's what I thought. And Sonny seemed cool, the coolest, why it tore me up to kick him out. Hate that shit."

"What shit."

"Good guy like that, you know, these guys got tough backgrounds I guess, but this is where I work, shit. I mean I'm not blind, I know there's drugs in here but if I catch you, man, you're fucking gone."

"Drugs."

"Yeah. Not just weed, you know, hard stuff."

"You caught him selling?"

"Twice," Dave says. "I don't think there's another dude I'd a given a second chance to, but Sonny, you know, he's such a kid. He was just messed up with the wrong people, you know. I thought maybe he could work it out." Dave sighs. "I didn't press charges or nothing, he's just out."

"When?"

"'Bout a month ago. Let's see." Dave taps at his computer, mouses around a bit. "Yeah, I got him in here under Sonny, just Sonny, like one of those stars who only has one name?" Shane waits for more, resisting the urge to lean over and stare at the screen for himself. "August," Dave says. "First time was in July, but that time I just eighty-sixed his friend. He was bad news all the way."

"What friend?" Jimmy says.

"I don't know. He was in here on a pass. Fucking drug dealer all the way."

"Black guy wearing a light blue jersey," Shane says.

Dave nods. "Something like that. Yeah."

"Sam have a boyfriend?"

"Boyfriend? You mean like." Dave frowns. "I don't know. If he was that way, there's always hook-ups going on I guess. Though we're doing better on the monkey business. Boyfriend, huh. I never saw that. But I don't really pay attention. No one comes to mind." His phone rings and Dave glances at it angrily. "I should get this. You find Sonny, see him, tell him hey. Maybe he gets things straightened out, we can do something for him."

"We'll tell him," Shane says.

They find Mario in the big room, sitting glumly on a shoulder machine, cracking his neck. He brightens at the sight of them until they tell him their news and watch him shake his head. Poor kid. What a fucking shame.

"I had no idea."

"Sounds like no one did."

"Well, someone did. If he was selling, someone was buying. It must have just been recent. His locker was right near mine and I never saw anything funny."

"Shane!" another voice calls out. The three of them turn to see a sweaty David Fulton striding past in short shorts. He points at Shane, laughing. "I'm disgusting!" he says. "Are you here?"

"Kind of."

"I'll find you," Fulton says, power-walking around the corner, out of sight.

"You know him?" Mario says.

"Kind of. You?"

Mario whistles low. "Yeah, I mean, I've never talked to him. He owns my company."

Shane shakes off the image of Lou and Fulton, sitting close together on those long white couches, cooing numbers at one another. He doesn't want to talk about companies.

"Think he knows Sam?" A good candidate, Shane thinks, with drugs involved.

Mario laughs. "I don't know. There's an interesting conversation. You should ask him. I bet Fulton could have the kid reinstated here tomorrow. He pays for all our memberships. For all his companies, I heard."

"Keep those worker bees healthy," Jimmy says. "Productive."

"I'll ask around," Mario says, ignoring him.

Shane hands Mario a business card. "That'd be great. See what people know."

They find Fulton crunching on the ab machine, doubling his body again and again and again but snapping out of it the moment Shane pulls into range.

"I'm shocked," Fulton says. "I thought you'd never join this gym."

"I didn't."

Jimmy watches them carefully, seeing something in this transaction he doesn't like.

"You know, in the end I'm glad. That would completely spoil my image of you." Fulton smiles slyly. "The natural man."

"I wish I liked working out."

"Oh you have basketball. We all have our holy trinity of pleasures."

Jimmy snorts. "What holy trinity would that be?" he says.

"This is my brother Jimmy. David Fulton."

The two of them examine one another.

"You know," Fulton says, answering Jimmy's question. "Sex, drugs, rock 'n' roll. Except rock 'n' roll is just a metaphor, right? Rock 'n' roll is just that other something physical where you lose yourself in your body. Basketball, for instance. Me, working out's my rock 'n' roll."

"Oh Jesus," Jimmy says. "You work with Lou?" He snaps the words like an insult, but Fulton doesn't seem to notice or care.

"Not quite yet," Fulton says, smiling with his teeth and giving Shane a conspiratorial wink. "I do *work* with several different companies like hers. What about you, Jimmy, you work around here?"

"Oh no," Jimmy says. "Not at all. I'm a loser by trade."

"I see."

"Very good at my work."

Fulton squints in a show of amusement, but he hasn't quite figured them out.

"Where are you from?" Jimmy says.

"I grew up back East. Shane and I went to Cal together," Fulton says, answering the question he thinks Jimmy must be asking. "And then met up again at a party. Quite a party it turned out to be. You missed one there, Jimmy."

"Where back East," Jimmy says, zeroing in on the differences. "*Connecticut?*"

"Sure," Fulton says. "Why not? We all have to come from somewhere."

"But we don't have to stay."

"I bought a house here. It's pretty nice. Shane's been there. Besides, there aren't many other places that can compete with San Francisco, are there?"

"I wouldn't know," Jimmy says. "Do you mean compete in terms of pretty hills or the business opportunities of the moment."

"Oh, am I being set up or what?" Fulton says to Shane in a good-natured voice. "Is he a hit man?"

"Aspiring," Shane says.

"Everyone was new to this city once." Fulton watches Jimmy, wanting to see how each word strikes him. "The Indians. The Spanish. The Irish. The hippies. The faggots. The losers. The dot-com kids."

"Parasites come in bunches. The difference is this last bunch just came for the money. First sign of trouble, they're gone."

"You two should get a room," Shane says.

"A padded one, no doubt," Fulton says, rising. "One way or another, this gym never disappoints for entertainment. What should we do now? They do have boxing in the other room. Or maybe you're more of a wrestler?"

"Whatever you want," Jimmy says.

"Tempting." Fulton holds Jimmy's stare, purses his lips, deciding something. "You're totally brothers," he says, finally, in a completely different key. "So really, are you guys on legs or arms or what today?"

"We're looking for that friend of ours, actually, this guy named Samson. Sam. Sauce. Lots of different names. I heard they called him Sonny here."

"Sounds interesting."

"You remember I mentioned him? Young kid, half black, bushy hair. Freckles. We play ball with him."

"Ahhhh," Fulton says, nodding slowly as if everything suddenly makes sense. "A bosom ball buddy. How old is he?"

"About twenty."

"Black and freckles, huh." Fulton nods. "Why you looking for him?"

Shane hesitates. "It's complicated."

"I bet." Fulton smiles again. "Who knew that you were so interested in little boys."

"What?" Jimmy says.

Fulton ignores him. "I think I know who you're talking about. Sonny, you said? Guess I don't know the names too well. It is the *gym,* you know, people leave their names at home."

"But you haven't seen him lately?"

"No. It's funny how little you can know about someone who's just right there." He reaches out a hand to pantomime Sam standing next to them. "That's one of the nice things about the gym. Or basketball, I guess."

"You don't play basketball," Jimmy says.

Fulton flips his small white towel over his shoulder and takes a step back. "No," he says, looking at Shane instead of Jimmy. "Good to see you," he tells Shane. "Give me a call sometime." Then Fulton turns and leaves them, striding with purpose through the aisles of machines and settling on a bench press without looking back.

"What the fuck," Jimmy says. "Why do you put up with those guys? Why have you been to his house? Why do you party with him?" Jimmy's voice drips acid, burning holes in Shane's head. "What the fuck?"

"The thing is," Shane says, "the thing is that guy remembers everyone." He watches Fulton across the room chatting briefly with a guy beside him. "I wonder. The whole drug thing, it's possible." He tries to remember. Fulton outside the car in the projects, Tennessee calling out from the shadows.

"They'd never kick that guy out, huh."

"No."

"Although why would Sam stay here. This place makes me want to maim."

Shane looks around again, trying to see it through Sam's eyes. Escape, he thinks. Who wouldn't choose a world of Fultons over a world of Tennessees. But even here, Sam couldn't keep them separate. He couldn't keep the projects out of Paragon, so Paragon had sent him back. Why does Shane think he can do any better? He is already thinking about Lou, Debra, the conversation that's overdue.

"Can we go?" Jimmy says, staring off in the direction of the bench press.

"Yeah," Shane says. "Let's go."

16

FOR THE FIRST TIME in weeks, it feels like the weather's about to change. The temperature plummets as the sun sinks, revealing the familiar San Francisco: a jagged stone that won't hold heat, carved by wood and winds. With their apartment shut up tight and every window closed, the place feels small. The outside roars around the hundred-year-old clapboards, huffing and puffing to blow something down.

Lou is home for the first time in three days. That's not quite true—she has been home, returning late and rising early, a phantom moving through Shane's first and last hours of sleep. But they haven't said sixteen words to one another since their far-off Thursday night, since Lou began her Fulton preparations, since Shane reverted to fending for himself. Now she lies draped across the couch like a limp chenille throw.

He decides to build them a fire. It took him years

after they moved in to get around to reclaiming the fireplace, something about the separation of work and home. In the small cache of stacked wood on their deck, he finds a largish spider, something menacing, a widow or recluse. He waits for it to walk away, strutting on its six legs, taking its dangerous sweet time.

Shane feels her watching him as he builds the kindling log cabin and stuffs the classifieds inside. Soon the flames are dancing their crazy gassy dance. He stares into their black-blue middles, listening to his wife sip wine. He'd like to hear her low maniac's laugh. He'd like to hear her tell the joke about the mouse screwing the elephant in the butt.

"You feel like a movie?" he says. Shane rolls around to face her. He dimly remembers her leaving this morning in a skirt, but now she's dressed for nuclear winter: a thick East Coast autumn sweater, fleece sweatpants, thick wool socks. Even so, she clasps her arms around herself in a pantomime of cold. Cold equals unhappiness, in Lou's world. He's not sure she's heard him but she shakes her head: no.

He goes to their music collection and reaches for the first thing he sees. It's the second Replacements album, songs he hasn't heard forever. Lou's head tilts at the sound and now she smiles at him, silent. They've been together a long time, haven't they.

"Remember this?" he says, lamely.

"Yeah."

"I didn't even know you yet."

"Dinosaurs roamed the earth."

"I owned condoms."

"So did I."

The fire cracks and pops, the dry wood burning with gusto. Her eyes float back to the magazine folded on her lap and he sees her prepare to dive inside.

"That kid is in trouble," he says suddenly.

"What?" Her voice is soft and almost dreamy.

"That kid I play basketball with. He's missing. He might be dead."

"My god," she says, automatically, her eyes snapping back to him, suddenly alert.

"Yeah. No one knows."

"I'm really sorry, Shane. Christ." She puts her head in her hands, briefly, as if trying to stop a headache, and then pulls her hands away. "I'm really sorry."

"Yeah. I've been meaning to talk to you."

"To me?" she says, shaking her head in disbelief: what on earth does this have to do with me? "About what?"

"About his mother. Do you remember? I mentioned her."

"No," she says. It's a reflex and she doesn't try to think if she remembers or not. No is her answer and she's sticking to it.

"I told you," he says. He sounds like a little kid. "I thought maybe you could talk to her."

"To the mother." Her face expands: the eyes wide, the nostrils flared. She looks away. This on top of everything. "About what?" she says again.

"About a job."

"A job?" She stares at Shane. He is speaking Hungarian, some very difficult language. "What are you talking about?" She's holding her head again. She seems to think it might fall off.

"I know," he says carefully, trying not to yell. "I know you have a lot going on, but we're trying to help her. You said maybe."

"Maybe what?"

"Maybe a job."

"Oh," she says. He can't tell if she remembers or not. "Doing *what*?" She sounds like she's trying not to be annoyed. She sounds annoyed.

"Receptionist?"

"I just hired one."

"I don't know, Lou, something. It's like the hiring rush of the century, right? It's like they say, send warm bodies."

"They who?"

"There must be something she can do."

"What? What could she do. She lives in the projects, right?"

So she does remember. "I don't know. Whatever the rest of those idiots down there do. Whatever all you people do."

"Why don't you hire her? Why don't you wrap her up in bristle brush and shove her down a chimney." Lou inhales deeply, ready to breathe fire.

"All right," Shane says. "Fuck it." He is ready to make

his grand exit when he sees tears rolling down her cheeks, running quick as raindrops across a newly shingled roof. She doesn't blink, doesn't even squint or make a sound, but she is surely crying. He feels something crack inside him, a balloon of helplessness bursting in his chest. He sees the tears and moves towards her without thinking, the only thing left in his brain is you must do something to stop that now.

"I'm sorry," she says, softly, her voice slipping up high. He can barely hear her. He's trying to hold her in his arms and she lets him, briefly, before pushing him gently away. "I don't even know why I'm crying," she sobs.

"It's okay," he says. "I'm sorry."

"No," she says, and continues to cry. He doesn't know what to do. She never cries and now she has her face in her hands and is sobbing on the sofa where he sits next to her, thinking, how do you fix this? What do I do?

"Lou," he says, "Lou. Aw Lou, come on, it's okay. Lou."

She shakes her head, waves him off. "Wait," she says. She gets up and goes to the bathroom, shuts the door. He hears her running the water in there. When she comes out her eyes are red and her hair is wet across her brow but she has stopped crying.

"I'm sorry," he says. "I just wanted to."

"I know," she says. "I freaked out. I can't even fight right. I don't know what, I think I'm just so…stressed… out." She tries to laugh at herself but no sound comes. "You know?"

"You've been working so much."

"It's insane. God. I don't think I even know some-times how insane this is, this life. I'm sorry."

"I'm sorry."

"Okay," she says. "Everyone's sorry." She takes a deep breath and smiles a tight-lipped smile. "Of course I'll talk to her," she says. "She's not on drugs, is she?" It's meant to be a joke but she doesn't make it sound like one.

"She doesn't do drugs," he says. I hope, he thinks, I hope at least that's true. "She doesn't drink."

"That's a start," she says. She's through with crying but she still seems like she's fighting to keep herself calm. "But I seriously doubt," she says, "I just thought that after all this time you." She tries one more time. "That you know this business, it's not like anyone can just come in and do it. Jokes are one thing but it's not like that at all."

"You mean it's not chimney sweeping."

"I didn't say that. You're the one calling people idiots."

"I didn't mean that," he says. She shrugs, not sure if she believes him. He's not sure she should. He feels the anger rising again, a tide pulling back into the dry land left by her recent tears. When do I ever ask you for any-thing, he thinks. "I just want you to talk to her."

"Yes, okay." Lou lets out a sudden hoot, a release of tension that echoes through the room. They both startle like wild animals. "Damn," she says. "There, that's easy. Yes. Of course I'll talk to her."

"Thank you," he says.

"Just one thing. I just want to make sure."

"What."

"That you don't promise things."

"I didn't."

"Because I don't know what I can do. It's like...I don't even have time for you, how do I have time for her?"

"She can have my time for once."

Lou doesn't seem to hear him. "We will though. We will finally have time up the wazinga, if I can just do this right. If we can make this happen with Fulton this week. Then you won't have to deal with the dot-com bitch ever again."

"I'm okay," he says. "You don't need to worry about me."

"Sure," she says. "They'll put that on your tombstone. *Don't worry about me, people.* Come on, Shane. I know it's been hard."

"What."

"Me. You. I mean look at us, we're talking about some stranger and you'd think we were insulting our own mothers. Why do I feel like that?"

"I don't know."

"Stakes is high," she quotes to him, a movie or song he can't remember. She leans awkwardly, nuzzling into his chest. "Stakes is so damn high."

He puts an arm around her. Where will this conversation go? "Mmm, steaks," he says. He kisses her on the temple: a loud smack of a kiss, to end it. "Let's see what I can find for dinner." She glances at him and sighs. Okay. They're okay. They smile at each other, but he wonders if her smile also dissolves the moment they turn away.

Later that night his cell phone rings. Lou has gone to bed, but Shane is drinking a Bud longneck and watching classic sports: Celtics–Bulls '86, game two, one of civilization's great achievements. Jordan goes off for sixty-three, including the drive where he jab-steps Bird on the wing, fakes once and then again, and when Bird won't go for it Jordan freezes him with a through-the-leg dribble, back forth twice and then fades away as McHale jumps out to help. Swish that shit. He backpedals down the Garden's parquet floor and the hostile home crowd gasps. It's the most simply spectacular move that they or Shane have ever seen. He burns two of the best guys who ever played, makes them look like fools. But McHale and Bird still win. That's the beauty of it. He punks them but they're still too much. Jordan will have to wait.

Shane leaps from the couch to swipe the phone off the kitchen counter with one hand. Jimmy, he thinks, although there's a moment before he answers it when he hopes it's someone else.

"Hello?"

"Chimney man." It's a cell to cell connection, bad, filled with crackle and pop. "You got my money?"

"Who's this."

"Yeah, you know who this is. You heard about your boy Sauce."

"Heard what."

The low voice laughs. "Come on now. You know how we do this. He still got family, and they still owe me money. You the fairy godfather, right, now y'all wanna take care of business or bury that bitch? It's up to you."

Shane hangs up, switches off the phone. He looks around the room for witnesses, but there aren't any. There's no reason to believe that just happened, he thinks. On the TV, in the first overtime, Bird is backing down his defender in an isolation on the right side. It's a crucial time, and important play, but Shane can't remember what Bird is going to do. Either fade away or up and under, one of the two. Get rid of the phone. Don't go back. There's a way out, he thinks, I know there is.

17

HE PICKS UP DEBRA on Thursday morning. He feels nervous, as if he's the one headed for an interview. Imagine: putting on his best high-tops and strutting through the parking lot to offer himself as drug dealer, pimp, armed robber, con man. A non-stop job fair up here.

They talk about nothing in particular on the ride down. Weather, traffic. Crappy, crappy, they both agree. He doesn't bring up the gym, the drugs, the phone call. He mentions she looks nice. It's true. She wears a synthetic fabric business suit in a light cream color white people can't do, and in that color her skin looks particularly smooth and rich and shiny, as if she's been buffed and waxed and soft towel washed. It's not a particularly nice suit but somehow it makes her look long and elegant. Her short hair is sculpted into tiny waves along the top of her head, a slightly extra-spiked look that makes her seem extra young. Her eyes clear and alert and blinding black and white. Small gold earrings. He has explained to her as best he can about the casual office deal but he sees she doesn't trust him when it comes to clothes. Can't blame her. She looks too good for the job, although he doesn't tell her that.

The 101 slips by with its monster billboards, touting companies of the day: Sybase, Cysive, Sapient, Cisco. Names like James Bond–villain business fronts or the sinister hissing of Disney snakes. They listen to the radio, the station still set where Jimmy left it last. *This is K-P-O-O,* a young boy is saying, *San Fran-cis-co,* maybe seven or eight years old, charming as hell. *Bay-ba bay-bay!* He glances at Debra but she is elsewhere, staring at the office parks blurring by.

The interview is set for 11:00 A.M., and they pull into the lot early, with plenty of time to spare.

Lou and company are dug into a corner of their own office park, one enormous room in a steel-glass building they scored before the Bay Area went all-out office mad. The Lever.com leadership has no idea what they're going to do when success requires a bigger space, although the assumption is that vast sums of money will settle everything. He doesn't remember what they pay per square foot but he knows the newest tenants in the building are forking out a good bit more than the going rate in the Empire State Building. That's a cocktail stat he's heard more than a few times. He knows that every company in the building is a technology company, that despite appearances this is a prestigious address. Every outfit listed on the building directory is worth millions, although none of them has ever made a dime.

The Lever.com office space is open and newly neutral carpeted, with a bathroom and tiny so-called conference room that must have been an oversized broom closet in the architect's original plans. Sixteen tables made from unfinished doors dominate the space, clustered in fours that each form a loose cross configuration. At the end of each table, a black metal file cabinet sits at a right angle, squaring off the work area to give the illusion of personal space. With the tables in a cross, the file cabinets arranged like flags flying the same direction, the clusters actually look more like swastikas than anything else, Shane thinks. There's not a lick of privacy here, and the sixteen people who work long days together each stare at their neighbor's ear, catching every word that passes through the boxed air around them.

He has warned Debra about the silence. Sixteen people work here but the place is crazy quiet. You swing open that tinted glass door, step inside, and hear nothing except an insect clicking of plastic keyboards, the tiny squeak of a swiveling pneumatic chair, the high metallic tympani of someone's rock 'n' roll music seeping from firing-range headphones. Few phones ring, few conversations break out. He has heard his wife insist that the office isn't always weird and quiet, but it's been like that the few times he's made it down here.

A wave of tilted heads and curious eyes hits the opened door. Up front, at the nearest table, a very young guy wearing the headset of an operator-standing-by holds Shane's glance from a seat that faces the door. The receptionist. The guy with Debra's job, Shane thinks.

"Can I help you?"

"I'm Shane McCarthy. Lou's husband?"

"Oh, yeah, I'm Mark." He points a gotcha finger at him. "I've talked to you on the phone. How are ya?"

"I'm fine." Shane introduces Debra, who is looking around the room suspiciously, waiting for somebody to jump them. No one's going to jump them, but everyone's staring at the new arrivals: the devil's husband, in a rare appearance, with a black chick sidekick, overdressed. Everyone else here is white or maybe pink at most, dressed in fine fabric Valley casual or baggy Techno slob. And there she is, wearing the wrong skin and looking ready for a sit-down at a Midwestern bank. She must feel inappropriate already, and Shane tries to think how to make things right.

"Right, right," Mark is saying, his fingers flying across the keyboard, his hand darting out to swivel click and then back again. Debra watches his darting hand as if it were a rat. "Eleven o'clock, right?" He taps his thumb against the lower right part of his screen where in thick red numbers the time's displayed. They are thirty-two minutes early. The traffic wasn't so bad after all.

"Do you want me to see..." Mark says, trailing off, looking back and forth between Shane and Debra and their enemy the clock.

"Oh, no," Debra says, in a voice that's smaller than

any noise Shane has heard from her yet. Debra the Small. "I'll wait."

"Yeah," Mark says. "You know, she's on the phone."

"She's always on the phone," Shane says. "She has dents in her head."

"That's fine," Debra tells Mark, ignoring Shane's best try.

"Cool." Mark guns his finger at two chairs pressed against the wall. Debra looks at them as if trying to decide something. She picks a chair, puts her purse on the other one and her manila folder on her lap. No seat for him. She's on her own, now.

"I'm gonna wave hi," he tells either Debra or Mark, he's not sure whom. "And then I gotta go." According to their arrangement, Lou will organize her ride back. It's Thursday. He's going to try to make it back to the city in time for basketball.

He makes his way to Lou's marketing cluster, waving a silent hello to engineering Rich who gives him a quick victory salute before diving deep into his keyboard to resume his two-fingered typing prayer. Rich's cluster consists entirely of guys, the coders, and designers perched behind enormous monitors, ridiculously young, dressed in brightly colored T-shirts and loose multi-pocket pants and maybe a baseball cap, rocking back and forth to headphone beats or slumping demi-0lifeless toward the floor. As he passes, he sneaks a quick glance at their screens. One of them seems to be working, flinging words and mathematics together, his fingers flying as if defusing a bomb. The others are slacking: downloading music, watching a Stickman cartoon Kung fu animation. None of them notice him as he moves by.

Lou's group sits against a wall of windows that look out on careful grass strips and the fresh-paved parking lot outside. Lou herself isn't there, but he recognizes the two women and the guy. The women face each other, typing in short conversational bursts, giggling at one another across the table. Shane has heard about their incessant computer conversations, typing electronic notes to one another like high-tech schoolgirls. The clicking stops as he gets closer and they turn to greet him.

"Hi!"

"Hey hey. How's it going?"

"Good. How are you guys doing."

"Aw, you know."

"Lou around?"

"She's in the conference room." The woman's name comes slowly to him: Trish. Pretty and blond and elfin and very, very clean. Athletic. He had a conversation with her once about lacrosse.

"I'll peek in," he says. He excuses himself and moves towards the door, hearing the chit-chat typing crescendo in his wake.

Inside the ad hoc conference room, his wife is on the phone, talking cheerfully about money. Fulton. Today might even be the day. She waves him into the seat beside her, but he stays standing, not wanting to linger though he must say something before he leaves her and Debra alone.

"Sure," Lou is saying, "no problem." She nods at him and tells him to hang on with one raised finger. "Okay." She leans back in her seat, pulls the phone away from her ear, puts a hand over the receiver. "Hey baby. I'm on hold."

"Who's holding you. Fulton?"

"One of his minions."

"Oh you little tramp."

"Sure. They don't call it the new economy for nothing." She smiles, bites her lip. "We're this close to an offer sheet," she whispers, finger and thumb held pincer close.

"That's great."

"I know it." She listens to the phone for a moment. "We're talking fourteen right now for twenty-two, which would value us at sixty-four, post-money." He sees now the well-scribbled pad in front of her.

"That sounds good," he says, trying to remember what that means.

"Yeah. We're trying to get them to twenty-one." She's barely talking to him. She's barely there.

He kisses her on the head. "Good luck. I'm gonna run. I just wanted to pop in. We got here a little early." She nods at him, but she doesn't know what the hell he's talking about. "Debra Marks. We're a little early," he repeats.

"Debra Marks." She's listening to the earpiece, to see if Fulton has come back on the line. "Oh, shit. That's today."

"You thought I'd just come down for a visit."

"I don't know what I thought. Shit. Oh baby."

"We're early, though, you got time."

"I don't, though, I don't. Shit. I'm sorry, I totally forgot.

This is going to be all day, this thing. Lawyers have been activated. We're supposed to head up there this afternoon."

"Great. It'll be easy to drop her off then."

"She, uh." His wife's forehead is folding in on itself, wrinkling into the problem. "We have to do it next week," she says.

"Next week?"

"Next month?" She smiles ruefully. "Year?"

"Lou."

"Baby, I can't. You know what this is. Without this there isn't any that, you know?" She stabs at the paper in front of her with the pen. "Please," she says. "First things first."

He looks at the paper with all those numbers, and the calculator that still reads 66.666666.

"Thirty minutes," he says. "That's all. Twenty."

She shakes her head. "Please."

"No," he says.

"No?" She shakes her head again. She's heard him wrong. "Please," she says again, as if it were already settled. "Tell her I'm so sorry, we'll reschedule for next week. It'll be better. I'll know more then. Explain the situation. She'll understand. She doesn't want to meet with me on a day like this. Really."

"No. You explain it. You tell her you can meet again next week."

"Yes," Lou says, but not to him. "I'm here. No, please, I know exactly how that goes. Don't they always?" She smiles into the phone. Wait, she mouths at him, but he shakes his head and opens the door and shuts it not so delicately behind him.

He sits down next to Debra and together they wait. For thirty-five minutes they sit there, silent, watching the office operate around them. An early lunchtime is in progress, the office filling with the hollow hum of the microwave and humid air of reheated dinners. People must start here early, to beat the traffic rush. There is something with bacon in it; leftover pungent yellow curry thick with onions. A delivery man arrives with a pepperoni-sausage pizza for the programmers' table. Receptionist Mark eyes Shane nervously from time to time, careful not to catch his eye.

"She's still on the phone," Mark says, at the forty-minute mark. "It looks like maybe noon?"

"Noon?" Shane says, disgusted, but Debra touches him on the wrist and nods, meets his eyes.

"I'm fine," she tells Mark.

"Okay," he says, relieved.

"I'm sorry," Shane says to Debra. He hears her stomach growl, sees her swallow nervously.

"You should go," she says quickly, "Really, I'm fine."

"Are you sure?"

"Yes. Go."

"Okay."

He stands, glancing at his watch. If the traffic's cool, he'll still catch some game. His morning cup of coffee and the lunchtime office smells poke him in the guts.

"Bathroom?" he says to Mark, even though he knows where it is.

When he steps into the bathroom he can hear Lou's voice loud and clear. Even this private part of the office has one of those lowered ceilings where sound seems to travel freely between the rooms. How embarrassing, he thinks. But to his relief her voice disappears, he hears the door open and close, and he can get down to business. He's still in there, finishing up as he hears the door open again and the voices begin.

"Nothing?" Lou is saying. "Coffee, water, Coke?"

"A Coke," Debra says.

"Diet or regular?"

"Diet." He can picture them here, facing each other, doing their best to smile. So far so good, Shane thinks. One question, one correct answer. Lou comes through.

He hears them settle down at the table in the cramped conference room. He flushes the toilet, turns on the water to wash his hands and leave. He closes his eyes. In the next room, Lou is smoothing back her hair behind her ears too many times as she always does when she's distracted. He turns off the water. They are sitting there in silence while his wife looks over Debra's résumé. She's never seen anything like it. This woman hasn't worked for three years. He holds himself steady against the sink, picturing, listening.

Debra waits quietly, busying herself with nerves. He

knows that the only interviews she's been on in the last three years were with social workers, housing authority administrators, school teachers—very different sorts of interviews indeed. In these encounters she's learned to be needy, pushy, deserving of help and ready to fight for her rights. He remembers telling her: no need to push but be yourself, confidence without presumption. He listens for Debra, listens for her to do anything at all.

Say something, he thinks, leaning his head against the wall. Is she afraid to open her mouth? Does she think her voice will sound too loud? Is she imagining all the wrong things she's about to say? It occurs to him that her nervousness is not that fear of how will I impress, what will I do to dazzle. Her fear is that her grammar's wrong, her suit is wrong, her skin is wrong, and Shane is wrong. Her fear is that she is about to royally fuck everything up.

"So." Lou breaks the silence finally, rustling papers. Setting the résumé gingerly to one side like a court summons. "Shane speaks quite highly of you. You impressed him. Which takes some doing, let me tell you." Where does she get that voice, Shane thinks, why does she talk like that? He's sure that she is smiling her biggest smile, showing her well-kempt teeth.

"Thank you," Debra says. He hears the sip of soda, thinks back on the growling stomach. She's trying to calm it down.

"He must have told you a little bit about what we do, here."

"Yes he did."

"Probably confused the heck outta you," Lou says. She's trying to joke but then jumps in quickly, doesn't want Debra to take that as an insult. "I mean," Lou says, "I love him to death but it comes to the Internet? he doesn't really know what he's talking about."

"I see," Debra says, unsure if she's joking or not. Yeah, Shane thinks, come on, give her a laugh. No laugh. Lou waits for Debra to volley something back her way, but Debra must be busy with fear. If *he* doesn't know anything, then what does Debra know?

"So," Lou continues, quickly. "Let's see. Why don't I back up and try to give you the big picture." And she begins. Shane sits on top of the toilet's water chamber, his feet resting on the toilet seat.

Lou is good. He has heard her customize the Lever.com story for the e-people and the bankers and the cocktail crowd and the old-economy standbys. She can reduce her work to a glib one-liner or expand it to fill the farthest corners of an evening. But she has no version that makes one lick of sense to Debra. Debra does not know what business-to-business means. She doesn't know a click from a clack, a server from a sump pump, a page view from a donkey show, she simply does not know the lingo that fills Lou's hours and mouth and mind day after day after day. He's tried to prepare Debra, hasn't he? He thought he did. But he has forgotten what it's really like, that what his wife says to him at night is as simple as she goes. Lou has learned to talk to him but he has learned to listen too, and they've both forgotten that there are people who do not know what "content" means, who've never heard of an IPO. The difference between a Web page and a Web site? Then visitor, browser, HTML, XML, JavaScript—forget it. Debra has never opened an email attachment, never logged in or out of anything, never you name it. Hell, he thinks, I sent that woman in there and she's probably never switched on a computer by herself. How can she have followed even five words of what his wife has been saying? By the time Lou finishes her pitch, Debra must be lost, frozen in her chair. And Lou is ready to wheel and deal, has got herself worked up now, forced herself to the task. Lou is on a roll.

Shane glances at his watch. Of the thirty minutes she's allotted for the interview, his wife has just killed fifteen. In two hours she will be somewhere in SOMA with Sloan and Rich and Fulton, debating how many millions of dollars her company should be worth. Maybe if she just keeps talking and fills the whole interview with her voice, maybe everything will be all right.

"So Shane told me you'd like to do something in administration or customer service. Maybe you can talk a little bit more about what you're looking for."

Silence. Here we go. Does that seem like a trap to Debra? Maybe it is. If she says the wrong thing, Lou says well we don't have anything like that right now. Come on Debra, what do you have to lose? Say something.

"Yes," Debra says, finally, and Shane can breathe again. This is ridiculous. Leave them alone. Go. But he can't go. "I'm a people person, so either way, administration or customer service."

"If you could choose, though."

"Anything is fine," Debra says. Focus coming into her voice. He guesses: all this time she hasn't been able to decide whether to meet Lou's eyes or not but now she's locking in on his wife's eyeballs, attentive as can be. Here we go.

"Okay…" Lou says. Doubt—does she think this woman is staring her down? "In thinking about those two kinds of positions, maybe you could talk a little bit about the relevant experience you might have."

"It's good," Debra says. "I always had good experience in the jobs I had."

"But what kind of training, or, I guess I mean, what kind of work have you done that you're hoping to build on now?" The rustle of résumé returns.

"Everything I got there," Debra says. What if she can't remember what they've written together?

"I guess I was wondering if there are things you'd like to expand on."

"Oh, yes. Definitely I would." Hesitant again, faced by an enemy: this man's wife trying to trip her up. She is going to trip up, no doubt about it. Catch her in a lie. There are dates Debra can't remember, approximations she can't prove, names she can't recall.

And Lou. Lou waiting for something to make sense, and while she waits staring not at Debra's eyes, but at the painted lips and then the smooth skin of this woman's chin and neck, the deep rich color even in the florescent light. Lou, feeling small and pale, suffering one of her moments of pale dwarf there on the other side of the table from this strange taciturn black woman who has appeared in her husband's life from nowhere. The woman who keeps staring. Is she trying to intimidate her? What has he promised her?

"I see that you've done some receptionist work."

"Oh yes."

"You answered phones?"

"Yes."

"Tell me a little bit about that."

"It was fine."

"What kind of office was it you worked in."

"Normal. It was a normal office."

"Big?"

"I wouldn't say big. Normal size."

"What did they do?"

"Construction."

"What else did you do there?"

"At the construction? Phones, I just answered phones. Wrote down the messages, you know."

"And computers?"

"They had computers."

"Did you use computers?"

"There? Yes, I did, a little bit."

"And that job, it was something you enjoyed doing?"

"Mm-hmm."

Silence. Lou waiting her out, Debra trying to shut up and stay quiet, not say anything wrong.

"You liked the, what did you like about it?"

"You know, the people you talk to. I like that. Talking to people, helping them out."

Leave now, Shane thinks. Leave on a good note. He glances at the door. Her best answer so far. Leave now and leave them be.

"And you used computers."

"Yes. Mm-hm."

"What kind of computers did they have there?"

"Like these."

"PCs, Windows." Silence. "Which programs did you use?"

"I've used different ones. I just use the ones on the computer." Her voice is very quiet, Shane has to close his eyes tight to hear her.

"Word?"

"Yes, I believe that's right."

"Anything else? Excel, Outlook?"

"It could be, I don't really know the names so much."

"Explorer? Netscape?"

"I'm not sure. I believe I have but not for a long time."

"If you don't, that's fine too," Lou says. She hates him, Shane thinks, she hates his guts but she refuses to hate this woman at least, this woman who doesn't know anything about anything, but it's not her fault. "Most of us only use one or two programs day to day, and they're easy to learn."

"Yes, that's right. I agree with that."

"There is a lot of multitasking around here. You feel comfortable with that?"

"Well, how do you mean exactly?"

A gimme, Shane thinks, and Debra lets it drop dead to the ground. He hears Lou's sigh, disguised into a cough. "Doing lot of different things at once. You're sending a fax over here, answering the phone there, sending an instant message to me, you know, all at once."

"I got kids," Debra says, "that all comes natural to me."

Lou is trying to imagine it, right now: Debra sitting up at the front desk when David Fulton walks in with the CEO of whatever and Japanese investors and British journalists, Debra saying hello to them. Debra asking: what you want? Or Debra not speaking. Don't do it Lou, he thinks, don't do it, don't go after her, don't do it just to prove me wrong.

He steps toward the door. He is going to open and shut it loudly, destroy the moment and go back to his life. Ask his wife innocently that night: so how'd it go? But before he can he hears the mild hiss of a soda screw top coming loose. He sees Debra tilt back her head and finish it, swallowing as she places the bottle back on the table and finds Lou staring at her. Weakened by nerves and hunger and agitated by sixteen ounces of Diet Coke, her body jerks once, quickly, wracked by a grand hiccup, and then in its wake comes the enormous burp she's been carefully holding at bay. It bursts from her mouth in a froggy baritone, filling the air with its gaseous ring that seems to hang in the silence before Debra can speak.

"Excuse me, oh, I'm so sorry. I have a uh, digestion. Problem."

Lou is laughing as Shane flees, opening the door and letting it shut behind him, but not before he hears Debra laughing too, quietly and sadly, perhaps still tasting the acid unquiet of her stomach, perhaps thinking the ice is finally broken, that the interview is just beginning now again.

18

I T'S TOO LATE but he goes to the court anyway. The last
game is under way, tired guys dragging themselves up
and down the asphalt, forgetting to play defense. Only
the ball keeps them going, its electric orange power
instantly possessing anyone who holds it in his hands. He
waves at Jimmy and sits on the sidelines to watch them
run. On the bay the fog is creeping in as the tugboats
blow their two-tone chant: *Sam-son, Jim-me, De-bra,
next-game*, hi-low hi-low whatever the hell they're saying. They blow and he listens as he sits on their smooth
pavement on the hill. He is a rare spectator. There's a difference between watching the game and waiting for your
turn. He tries to clear his mind by following the bouncing ball. It's not easy. He's tried before. One afternoon,
still broken-footed, he snuck out here onto the hill above
the court. There's tall grass up there where you can settle
down to spy like a big savannah cat. From a distance, his

boys didn't look that good, unimpressive dots doing unimpressive things. The patterns meant nothing to him. He sat for only a few minutes before a longing in his muscles gave him cramps. Don't go back unless you're ready to play, ready to stride out onto the court to take your place. Your day will finally come. He closes his eyes and listens to the ball, remembering the feeling of stepping back on the court for the first time. The shouts that went up around him as he arrived.

"Damn, is that Shane?"

"Holy fuckin' shit."

"Back from the dead." Dragon was the first to reach him, putting one fist out. Up, down, knuckle to knuckle bump.

"What's up," Paul said, "Good to see you, man. Been a while."

"You healthy, Shane, or what?" Brian put out his hand for a simple shake. "You look pretty goddamn healthy."

"They hook you with a titanium replacement or something?" Rex pointed at his culprit foot, even getting the right one.

"Check out the kicks, man."

"Insurance pay for those?"

There were a million million things to say, the tiny possible responses to this homecoming, but for a moment he was struck mute with happiness.

"We been asking your brother when you're coming out. He's always like, Shane who?"

"Naw, he don't know nothing," Shane said, finally managing something. Jimmy was there already, grinning too, ripping away his sweats, the buttons popping like caps down the side of his legs.

"That's right," Paul said, "you broke your foot, huh?"

"Twice," Brian said. "Broke that bastard twice." Dragon shook his head and exhaled softly.

"*Three* times." Shane almost whispered.

"Three times." Dragon nodded. "Three times is better, that's the fairy tale, you know, it's over." He whisked his hand through the air, banishing the injury and all the months of misery like a conjurer.

"That's right."

"I don't know, we're just getting old," Rex said. "My knees hurt when I whack off."

"Your knees? Whatya, kneeling in front of the throne?"

"I like to keep it clean."

"You try arnica?"

"Glucosamine."

"My arm don't even straighten anymore, neither."

"Your arm don't need to straighten, ugly ass shot you got."

"Goes in."

"That is one of the great mysteries of the world."

"You should talk. That crazy Dragon shit."

"We are all a mystery," said Dragon. "That's exactly what I mean."

This, Shane thought, stepping out on the court, feeling the old chemicals coursing through his chest, this this this.

He hit his first shot of the game, losing his defender off a down pick and slipping to the shallow wing for a wide open ten-footer. The pick was Sam. The kid hadn't said a word to him but the minute Jimmy checked the ball, Sam stepped up quickly behind his man, planting himself down perfect to spring Shane free. Shane leaned left and cut right to brush off the kid's shoulder, popping out to find the pass from Jimmy waiting. It was like a play the three of them had been planning for months, planning their entire lives. It was three sets of instincts and shared expectations triggering one another—if you do this then he does that then I do *this.* He resisted the urge to dribble and simply jumped, just enough to put his legs into it. The ball left his hand and he watched the net sway like a hula skirt as the shot wiggled through. He glanced back at Sam and Sam nodded at him, sliding back on defense. They didn't say a word to one another until after the game.

Shane wanted to hug him. He wanted to hug every one of them but instead he nodded, put his hand out for a slap. "Hey, Sam my man, thanks for getting me going. Good to see you."

The kid nodded. "You been out, huh?" The way Sam spoke was almost despite himself, as if his mouth made one last ditch effort to snuff itself out. His voice still wanted to be high, a voice that had never really wanted to change, and he made an effort to bring it down low. He was twenty now and in some ways barely different from all those years ago when they first started playing together. His body had filled out, his huge shorts and shirt swinging loose around real muscles. But he still looked awkward. Still something in him like a kid.

"Yeah. My first real day back for almost a year."

"Feels good, huh?"

Shane gave him the biggest smile in his arsenal. "Hell yeah," he told him. "*Hell* yeah."

The kid shuffled in front of him, nodding, fighting his shyness, trying to continue the conversation. "A year," Sam said.

"You been coming out?"

Sam nodded, shrugged. "You know."

"Games been good?"

"They ai-ight."

"Bunch of old men up here, Sam. We're headed for the retirement homes, you gonna have to find a new game."

Sam smiled his smile, the mouth bunching up in the middle, almost turning down in a scowl. "I didn't know you was coming back," he said, finally.

"Shit, yeah. What else am I gonna do."

"I know, huh." He snuck a peek at Shane. "That last day you went down, though." Shane felt his throat contract, a sudden allergic reaction to the past. "Yeah," Sam said, "you said 'that's it, I'm finished.' I almost believed you. Way you said it."

Shane had forgotten that, had forced himself to bury that memory in clay. The moment rushed back to him:

the burning in his foot as the real jolt came from the center of his head. A moment when you remember: soon the flesh will rot. Soon it's time to die.

"I'm glad you're back," Sam mumbled, not looking at him, walking back out on the court to play.

What Shane felt as he watched him go was not that moment of death, but the feeling when you realized you were taking up a little space inside someone else's head. It meant that you really existed not only in your own imagination or in your family's but out there in the republic, because someone who owed you nothing remembered.

Now he is the one remembering. Now his mind is busy keeping Sam alive.

The guys finish, a game point no one seems to care about. They come slumping off the court.

"Bronze loquat," Dragon says by way of greeting. "We're thinking bronze loquat."

"What kind's that?"

"Tops out at about twenty feet, gets about half again as wide. Leaves a little shiny, little white flowers, needs a monthly deep watering. Tough little tree."

"Great name."

"How'd it go this morning?" Jimmy says.

Shane shrugs. "I dunno," he lies. "You win today?"

"Yeah. Good run, you know." He nods at Finesse and Rex, sitting on the sidelines, sharing a joint. "I was telling the guys about Sam."

"What about him."

"You know. Everything."

Shane feels a moment of panic, as if he's been caught at something. He feels a sudden urge to take the joint from them and suck himself out of this world. "Anyone hear something?" he says instead, trying to sound casual about it.

"Nothing," Rex says. "The whole thing don't sound right."

"What."

"I mean I bought pot from him before? but the hard stuff's a different genre."

"Sound like his friend to me," Bindo says. "If his friend's a real dealer, he's looking at Sam like a gold mine at that gym. Maybe Sam didn't have no choice."

"Yeah," Dragon says. "Maybe that guy's got a spell on him."

Shane glances at Jimmy. Tennessee and Sam. Sam and Tennessee.

"I hope he's okay."

"Let us know what we can do," Dragon says. "Anything you need."

"All right," Shane says. "Yeah, ask around, you know."

"Wait. He got a locker at that gym?" Rex says.

"I guess," Shane says, glancing at Jimmy.

"You check it?"

"Open it?"

"Yeah," Rex says. "Open that shit up. A kid living at home, you never know what you might find inside."

***

He sends Jimmy to the gym and goes to work a new job in the Haight. The appointment is near the Panhandle, home to the city's most psychotic basketball games, although the afternoon courts are empty as he loops past. Back on Haight Street, the commercial strip looks almost respectable, the narrow sidewalks swept and tidy, storefront windows unusually clean. Even the slovenly Haight Street kids, quintuple pierced and dreadlocked, seem not as slovenly as he remembers them. Healthier, tanner, less likely to drop dead of a strange blood sickness at any moment. On the corner of Haight and Ashbury, he sits at the stop sign for a moment between the Ben and Jerry's and the Gap across the street, a sight he simply can't get used to. The Gap's storefront window is plastered with images of teenage androgynes in multicolored down puffs staring offscreen, searching for something to steal or screw, with the tagline in big block letters below: "Everyone in Vests." The hell they do, Shane thinks.

He is stuck behind a parallel-parking car when one of the street kids comes tearing down the sidewalk with a cop behind him. The whole street freezes to watch, and the kids sitting on the sidewalk cheer their fellow delinquent on, pulling back their legs as he passes and then sticking them out again for the cop trailing behind. The cop trips but doesn't fall, staggering and turning on the kids while the whole block cheers for the fugitive. The cop is furious. He marches toward one of the kids who's tripped him, barks at him to get up, the kid stays seated, raises his arms in protest, I didn't do nothing, the street yells at the cop, leave him alone, the cop grabs the kid, puts him against the wall, calls on his radio, I need backup, the street yells police brutality, the store owners and restaurant owners come out to the curb to see what's up, shake their heads, go back inside. Shane smiles, rolling forward thinking hey I recognize this wacko city after all.

He works until the day's last light is all sucked out and his client kicks him out. It's the first day of a partial rebuild that looks like it might take weeks, but there he is on day one working into the night. Why not. Where else would he go right now? The guts of the chimney pour out onto his plastic tarp, the ruined brick and crumbling mortar spilling out like the house's spinal fluid, pooling around his dusty high-tops. He has his head in the chimney when the guy pops in to suggest it's time to call it a night. Shane usually knows better than that. Being sensitive to dinnertime and family time and the public-private lines of clients is important in his business. You have to know when to leave. You have to know when they want their house back. The guy's an ex-hippie lawyer, pretty laid-back, but still. The mistake bugs him as he hustles to clean up and get the hell out of there.

By the time he hits the street it's almost eight. He checks his messages: one from Jimmy, one from Lou. He calls Jimmy first.

"So?"

"I found his shoes," Jimmy says.

"The Jordans?"

"Yeah."

A bad sign. "What else."

"Some clothes and that's it."

No $10,000. No drugs. No suicide note. "That's really it?" he asks his brother. He is in the van now, letting the engine warm up.

"Yeah. But a lot of clothes. Like he's living out of there, you know? What about this?" Jimmy says. "He gets busted at the gym, right? And maybe he can't go back to Tennessee. Maybe he's in love with the shithead, who knows, but now he's lost his usefulness, he lost the drugs, he can't go back. So he tries to stay with some boyfriend. Not a boyfriend, just some guy he slept with once, some guy barely even remembers him, a one-night stand from the gym. Where else does he have to go? But the guy kicks him out, doesn't let him in, and Sam is fucked. He thought he had a way out. Then suddenly he doesn't." Jimmy's voice is quiet, he's speaking with more calm and quiet than Shane has ever heard.

"Why doesn't he ask us?"

"Because we don't want him to. We're like that guy. We have our thing we do together and that's all we care about. We don't give a shit about Sam."

Shane listens to the cell phone crackle, almost hoping it will die. "Go on."

"I don't know. I don't know what he does next."

He gets high, Shane thinks. He goes down to the train tracks and gets as high as he possibly can. He takes BART to Oakland. He buys a bus ticket for L.A. He wanders into that dark tunnel all alone as he can be. The van is running smooth now, gurgling 1977 six-cylinder delight. Shane sits there without speaking until his phone clicks softly, another call coming through. "I gotta run, Jimmy."

"We should go back to the hill," Jimmy says. "Call me later, okay?"

The new connection is chaos. In the background, Shane can hear the raucous rhubarb of a crowd. A bar, prize fight, bachelor party. A woman laughs soprano and insane while a low rumbling voice pounds home emphatic points somewhere nearby. He can hear Lou's voice but not the words until she moves away from Babel, burrowing into a quieter alcove.

"Are you at the circus?" he says.

"We are the circus."

"We who?"

"Sloan, Rich, David. Fat lady, strong man, tigers all."

"David. Fulton?"

"Yes. It's done. Done deal," she says, and he can hear that it's true, that it's a wonderful amazing thing. He sees six black briefcases filled with hard-packed bricks of hundred dollar bills. The brilliantine coast of Spain.

"You got it."

"The term sheet's signed. Everyone's on board. There's good faith flying all over the place. They're in. We're in." She's shouting the details in his ear but the sounds could be Outer Pigmy or Hindi-Urdu for all he understands.

"When did this happen?"

"Just now, right now, we just came from there. Marathon session. I can't believe it's night. Time flies when you're having money."

"And now where are you?"

"I'm not sure. Where are we?" she shouts out, and someone answers. She repeats the name, address.

"Hot damn. Congratulations." The word sounds stiff on his lips, too many syllables for feeling. "After all that, you did it. Made it."

"Yeah. Well, in some ways it's just beginning," she says, sounding like a wise and impish child. "Anyway, get your butt over here."

"I'm on my way." He is about to explain the state he's in—his clothes, his work-stained body—but she hangs up too soon. I just don't really care, he thinks. He drives across the city, headed toward success.

Success sits plump in the meat of SOMA. At the entrance, three valets hurry to make the proud line of brand new cars disappear as eager diners pour inside. No sign hangs out front, but this has to be the place, and now he spots the restaurant's name winking up at him in green glass etched into the sidewalk out front. A single word, uncapitalized, and he feels pretty sure that deep down it's not a word at all.

Hundreds of people fit in there. They sit upstairs and downstairs, at tables and booths. They perch on the edge of beautiful backless stools at the multiple bars, touching crystal glasses. They stand casually in between, assessing the terrain. In the center of the room, a three-story transparent wall of wine rises above them all, the proud bottles encased in glass like priceless insects or the preserved penises of famous men. The whole place makes him think about impending earthquakes, and not just any earthquake: the big one. Everyone's goblet leaping from their hands at once; the icy crack and avalanche of that great glass wall; grape blood running in rivulets through the crumbled brick. He can hear the screams as the earth shakes people from their stools, tossing them gently to the floor and folding the roof and walls around them like deathly tissue paper until those crushed and fancy bodies of once and future millionaires lie absolutely still, all shut up at last. Outside, the last elevated highways stumble and fall, rolling cars like craps dice through the streets and burying the tent and shopping-cart homeless in the underpass. The big one will go after everything and everyone as an equal opportunity destroyer. The differences come only later, when you realize what you've lost, what you're willing to lose, and what you're going to do now or next. Some will move back East, some will seek out former lives and homes, some will change their jobs and spouses, some will buy and most will sell, some will give up hope and some will decide to start for real this time, from scratch. Some will come out smiling into the rubble and get to work rebuilding, happy for profit, looking forward to the next one. It will be a day they all remember, at least, and an explanation for everything that follows.

He finds Lou and company near the back, at a big booth with too many bodies in it. His wife's green eyes meet his as he approaches. In the tasteful light, her eyes look dark and rich and clever, that ancient shade of cash. Her eyes run briefly up and down the clothes he salvaged from his van: the gray poly pants, the clean but wrinkled shirt, the ratty shoes. She smiles to herself. She leans over two men he doesn't know, her breasts suspended dangerously before their small open mouths. She gives him a winy kiss.

"Congratulations, baby," he says again. Lou smiles her biggest smile and rocks back into place. "Congratulations, everyone," he says, and they accept that with slight nods and inclined glasses, waiting for something smart to go with it but he can't think of anything. He looks around for a place to be. The waiter has found a chair for him and perches him at a corner, not quite at the table, in everybody's way.

"You missed the Harlan '97, I'm afraid," the stranger next to him explains, as the waiter reaches over to pour him a glass of wine.

"No thanks," Shane tells the waiter, halting him with his hand.

"I mean, the Ducru's no joke," the stranger says ironically, nodding at the waiter's bottle. "Excellent, excellent, excellent." The stranger's friend flashes a thumbs-up to confirm.

"No," Shane says, louder than he wants to, and they both look at him for the first time, a little startled. He glances at Lou but she hasn't noticed. "I'll have a beer," he tells the waiter. "Bud, if you have it. Something lager if you don't." The waiter disappears. His tablemates nod together, turn toward the conversation in progress, and delete him absolutely.

"That Russian duck," Fulton is saying, his arms spread wide against the booth back. He takes up too much room, his trained arms bulging out of rolled-up shirt sleeves, extravagantly holding court. "Maine blue crabs or something. It was pretty amazing stuff, this whole place gutted and empty and they're cooking on portable gas, you know. Spot lighting and impromptu tables, nice china, they had them in here like a movie set." He waves his hand at the room around them.

"How many were you?"

"About thirty, I'd say."

"But you weren't convinced."

"It wasn't that, you could see they were determined. But food and drink have never been my favorite pleasures." He winks at them all, catches Shane's eye across the table, smiles a wicked smile just for him. "Heavy on the taste and smell and sight. Light on sound and feel. You can have it all, you know." He stares at Shane.

"Sports," Shane says. They're all looking at him, now, wondering briefly what's going on. "Basketball."

"Taste?"

The salty sweat at the edge of lips, Shane thinks. He shrugs.

"I was thinking sex and drugs," Fulton says.

"Of course you were," someone says.

"Come on, you were telling a story. About how you decided not to invest in this place."

Fulton takes his eyes off Shane slowly, setting aside a puzzle he hasn't quite solved. "It's not that I didn't believe they'd make it," he says in a bright new voice. "They had an all-star team, the food was great, a thousand wines by the bottle, the drawings looked fantastic. But I dunno, a restaurant? Investing in a restaurant might seem sexy but doesn't have nearly the possibility of, say, oh, let's say a little tech company. How big can a restaurant really get?"

"Pretty big," Sloan says, looking around.

"All right, but let's be sappy and crass: how many restaurants stand a chance to fundamentally change the world? How many restaurants can make you twenty million overnight?" All their eyes rest eagerly upon him. "I dunno, it seems like something vain to do more when you're rich and bored and *done,* you know, invest in a big-deal restaurant. Like some stupid sports celeb or movie star. Nah. Give me a handful of people in a room somewhere, figuring it out every day, doing something that really drops your jaw, something holy shit you got to call somebody up now and tell them what you saw. Give me people who use their brains." He looks slowly from Sloan to Rich to Lou. "Give me you guys, any day."

"Damn. I told you we could have pushed up the pre," Sloan says, getting the laughs.

"Oh you did just fine." Fulton catches Lou's eye and winks her way.

Shane drinks his beer. He listens to their happy talk circle back to the deal's specifics. He can't or won't follow, and after a while he doesn't hear them at all. Their mouths are popping open and shut like fish, red mouths moving all around him, red mouths sucking down wine and wok-roasted lobster and crisp-crusted skate with picholine olives. How many nights a week can you do this? How many weeks? Table after table, men and women ordering without hesitation, spending hundreds, thousands of dollars here in the shadow of the great wall of wine. Will they remember this night for the rest of their lives? Will they remember it a month from now? He will. Lou will.

From the far side of the table, deep in conversation, Fulton finds him and raises his eyebrows lasciviously, can you believe this shit, can you believe all this, but Shane gives him nothing back. Fulton leans toward Lou and puts a friendly arm around her, pulls her in for a whisper, and they both look at him, smiling, agreeing about something that motivates Lou from her seat. The strangers rise and let her pass, and she comes to him. She scoots his butt over on the chair and sits down schoolgirl-close beside him.

"I'm glad you came," she says, whispering and kissing his jaw just below the ear.

He nods, turns his head, and kisses her cool forehead. "I think I'm going to go, though." He pulls her tight and awkward to him, shoulder to shoulder. He wants to say something else—something good, something right. "I don't know how you do it," he tries. "I don't know how you did it."

She smiles. "Yes you do."

"Not really. You amaze me."

"After all this time."

"All this time." 66.66 million dollars. He feels nothing.

"I guess I have to let you go," she says, a little sadly. "Or I'll come with you." It has just occurred to her.

Yes, he thinks. Come. "No, you stay."

"You sure?"

"Sure. You deserve this." He makes some small movement with his hand and she looks around at the restaurant, the people, her co-workers and new partners, consuming it slowly, pixel by pixel. He looks with her and finds Debra sitting at a table nearby, her back to him, long gold earrings swinging as she throws her head back and laughs too hard. On the second floor, above her head, Jimmy is sullenly waiting tables, while downstairs in the basement Samson scrubs the duck-stained dishes. And Shane is leaving. Without realizing it, he's risen now and the table halts the conversation briefly as they say well dones, good nights. Lou walks him towards the door.

"Are you okay?" she says.

"I'm good," he tells her. "Don't worry about me, I'm just tired. I'm happy for you, Lou."

"For us."

"Yeah. Wow. I." He waits for her to say something else, but she's waiting for him too and all he has are questions he's afraid to ask. He doesn't ask.

Outside in the cool evening air his head feels clear again, or clear maybe for the first time all night. He finds his van in the alley where he's parked it, pulls out and takes the right and then the left and then the right. Left. Potrero Hill is right there and has always been there, close.

19

A WHITE ACCORD sits in his parking spot in front of Debra's house. The thought of a boyfriend crosses his mind, a brother, some angry man called in for comfort on a crappy night. On the other hand, he thinks, sometimes a white Accord is just a white Accord. He parks on the far side of the lot, locks up the van and crosses to Debra's door. He's poised to knock when he hears something behind him, and turns to see a guy slipping out of the shadows near his van.

Shane's never seen him before but the guy nods, as if they've scheduled this appointment. From inside the project building in front of him, he can hear music, television, and children in progress. He feels his heart go double-time, pounding at the walls of his body as if it would like to get out. Instead of knocking he finds himself pushing off the door with one hand and walking toward the stranger in the lot. The guy watches him come, standing still and passive beside his van, and nods at him again. Then Shane feels the change in pressure behind him and plants hard off his right foot, that quick first step that serves him so well on the court. He ducks his head and cuts backdoor, away from whatever is coming his way.

The first guy behind him misses him almost completely, hand glancing off his sinking shoulder as momentum carries the man by, but the second connects hard with a kick to his right knee as Shane slips out of the way. It doesn't hurt very much, just a ringing there, like banging knees with someone on the court. His body spins, and for an instant it seems possible for him to dig in and run, down the hill into the dark pupil of the projects where maybe he will get away or maybe things will get a whole lot worse. He doesn't run. Kicks is leaning over him to kick again, thinking Shane is going down, but Shane is still spinning and then plants and straightens and punches Kicks in the neck. The man drops his chin at the last possible moment and they crack bone to bone, Kicks' head snapping back, feet stumbling away from him and then miraculously, to Shane's immense gratification, falling to the ground. His hand has gone numb, immediately. He is so surprised and happy he feels like laughing. He hasn't punched anyone for years.

The other two come in to tackle him in tandem and he loses his cool. They've all been strangely quiet to that point but Shane starts bellowing now, yelling obscenities as loud as he can, and they start swearing too. He's not sure exactly what is happening but he jams an elbow into something hard, sending the electric shiver up his arm. Then his head yanks back, someone has him by the hair and jerks him to the ground, pulling his skull inside out. The pain blinds him, he can't see a thing as he flails one arm back. Something smashes against his ankle and he loses his feet. He twists sideways as he falls, reaching out to pull someone with him, hitting the ground shoulder-first.

Man is he down. The little pebbles of the asphalt dig into his temple, but his main sensation is of strangulation as a large foot presses down on his neck. "You move I kill you, motherfucker," the foot explains. The foot sounds like it means every word but it's not Shane's choice, he can't stop moving, his body keeps trying to wiggle and jerk out of that deadly position. He feels hands in his pockets. A robbery, he thinks, surprised. Then the weight leaves him and he manages to push off and roll away, is halfway up when someone kicks him in the chest, he grabs onto the foot and pulls the man down and jumps on top of him to bite his cheek off but another kick hits him just above the crotch and another on the hip, and he has to let go and roll again and cover up as best he can. He hears a voice that sounds like Tennessee but he can't understand the words. Someone kicks him in the back and smashes his hands curled over his head and then it stops. The numb pressure expanding into heat, throb, deep ache. He hears them running and lifts up his head to watch the shapes drop off his horizon into the dark valley of the projects below. They run miraculously and finally he hears the reason, a police car burping sound and light on the projects road nearby. Amazing: somebody's called the cops. He feels his face with his battered hands. His nose, his eyes, his teeth. Everything seems to be in place, facewise. The rest of his body who knows. He sits up in the middle of the parking lot, watching the police lights whiz by. They don't stop, bound for bigger stuff than the likes of him. He smiles and half laughs and feels a jolt somewhere in his ribs. I don't remember that one, he thinks. Fuck. He listens to the sirens Doppler out of sight. Get up, he thinks. Get up now and it doesn't matter where they're going. They saved your ass anyway. Get up before Tennessee comes back to top things off.

He stands in slow motion and turns to face Debra's building. His legs wobble as he takes the required steps, carefully, steps are an accomplishment right now. He doesn't feel too bad for a five-hundred-year-old man. At the door he goes to knock and sees that his right-hand knuckles have ripped and split and are leaking liberally all over the place. He can't remember how to knock left-handed as he listens to the television yelling inside. Maybe he's okay. He almost turns around but then pounds righty with his wrist against her door until it opens.

Over her shoulder he can see her three kids whooping it up, rioting around the living room, full-contact TV night is what it looks like. The television set to stun and a stereo playing somewhere, the kids yelling at the top of their lungs. Life is boisterous and loud in there.

He says, "I'm sorry."

"Goddamn." She looks him over lightning-fast from head to toe and quickly checks over his shoulder. She reaches out and grabs his shirt, pulls him roughly inside, and slams the door behind him.

His hand is a big hit with the kids. They are in the kitchen at a little red Formica table under a bare lightbulb that hangs by wires from the ceiling, casting good hard light on his wounds as she cleans him up. She lets them watch the peroxide bubble up along his knuckles, their eyes skipping from the bloody foam to his face. The pain isn't too bad but he opens his mouth and pretends he's going to scream, and all three kids inhale with him before he smiles and winks at them and watches them release their breath. He laughs and feels the real hurt down below: his rib, his knee, his ankle. Thank god for Nike he thinks, if they'd been wearing anything but sneakers he'd be in a hundred pieces now.

"It was a fight, huh," says the younger boy, seven or eight, examining the asphalt scrape across his face. Kaleb with a K, Shane remembers. Samson, Demetrius, Kaleb, Sharina. What a crew, Shane thinks.

"He was robbed," little Sharina says, like she's the only one who understands.

"Well," Shane tells Kaleb, "there were four or five of them." Debra shoots him a look to tell him true or false this is bullshit but she'll humor him if he wants. He wants. "You see that hand?" It's looking better now, raw but clean. "That was right on his chin, and he went *down.*"

"Dang," Kaleb says, nodding serious and happy. He rubs a hand against his own chin experimentally.

"Always go for the neck if you can," Shane tells him. "But be ready to hit the chin instead."

"Like that," Kaleb says, trying to hit his brother in the neck. Demetrius smacks his hand away.

"But they got you," Demetrius says, determined to keep Shane in his place.

"Yeah they did. They won I lost, you're right about that." She's doing his jaw, now, not gently, holding his chin firm with one hand and brushing the rocks out with the other, and that hurts like shit. The kids can see his pain and now finally the two boys smile, nodding their heads with satisfaction.

"But you got him good, huh," Kaleb says. "You popped him."

"Oh I popped him," he says.

"Enough," Debra says, and they all go quiet. "Meetri, get the man a beer out the fridge, all right. K get me the phonebook and phone. Sharina honey come over here and sit with momma." The boys disperse and the little girl hops up on her mother's lap. "Open it for him," Debra's saying to Demetrius, "get the man a glass."

"I don't need a glass. I appreciate it."

"You a lucky man," she says. "Musta been just kids. Up here, they serious? they bust your head with a piece a pipe, don't even waste a bullet on you. They bust you, boy, they take you out."

"They got me pretty good."

"Shit. This like a kiss goodnight," Debra says. "You should be dead."

"Maybe."

Demetrius returns with a tall golden can and Shane pops it with his good hand and takes a big sip. The best beer he's ever tasted in his life. Then he notices the other can on the table, open. She watches him see it and she picks it up, takes a sip.

"What," she says. The kids aren't paying any extra attention to her as she drinks, and he thinks well shit, she lied to me about that too, didn't she. "What," she says again.

"Nothing. Thank you, that's all."

They all move into the living room and watch Debra call up his bank. She tells them he's been robbed while he lies there with ice on his hand. The cold distracts his body from its other problems. The bank is giving her some trouble.

"Yeah, well this his wife," she says, not looking at him, "we in the hospital okay so he can't exactly talk to you right now. That's right. My husband, Shane McCarthy." They ask her his mother's maiden name and social security number and other things his real wife doesn't know by heart. She repeats the questions aloud, sounding outraged—his mother's maiden name?!?—waits as he murmurs back the answer and then passes it along. It takes a while but in the end everything sounds straightened out.

"Now don't be waiting three weeks or something before you send out that replacement, all right?" She laughs. "You know I will. All right. All right. You too." She hangs up and grins. There's something about this she's enjoying, although he doesn't know what. If Lou could see her now.

"Credit cards?" she says.

"I can do that," he tells her. "You don't have to bother."

"You sure? I don't mind."

"No, I'm fine."

She shrugs. "All right. I'll be right back." She passes him the phone and the phonebook. "If you'll be all right."

"I'm all right."

He listens to her lead her kids upstairs. He can hear her arguing with Demetrius about something. "You promised," the boy is saying, but he loses that argument, a door closing to dissolve them into silence. Shane calls his cell phone company. Had to ditch that phone anyway. He lies back on the couch and closes his eyes. He hears the front door open and shut and lock. He sits up and the pain pushes a big blast of air from his lungs into the room. Debra is standing in the doorway with a paper bag in her hands.

"You sleeping?"

"No," he says. He has no idea how much time has passed. He knows he never heard her leave. He doesn't remember lying on his side.

"I get you a blanket," she said. She looks huge right now, standing over him in a puffy jacket with a heavy bag in her hands.

He shakes his head: no. But he doesn't get up. His

muscles feel like they've been stripped of fiber, drained of blood. It reminds him of being a little kid ready to put a pillow over his head and sleep through everything. "You go get something for your son?" he manages.

"Nah, I got us some beer, what you talking about."

"I heard him whining up there."

"They always whining about something. You want a beer?"

"No," he says. "You got any aspirin?"

She shrugs. "You don't want a beer?"

"No," he repeats. "I should go."

"You came over here, didn't you?"

"Yeah. But I'm scared to ask you," he says.

"What," she says. She squats down on her haunches so that they are eye level.

"The interview."

She stands up again, sharply. "Oh, you don't know already."

"No I don't. She didn't tell me."

"You didn't ask her, neither."

"No. I was scared to ask her too."

She thinks about that for a moment, calculating an obscure sum. "You scared all sorts a shit, ain't you?"

"Just tell me, will you? I. I know it didn't go too well."

"Oh yeah. It was like that," she says, pointing at his bruised hand, "'cept at least you popped him." She gives excellent sarcasm, under the circumstances. She pulls two beers out of the bag and clicks them open, placing them side by side on the little table. Slides one over in front of him and waits until he takes it. "I'll tell you," she says, "but you already know, don't you."

"I guess I do." He doesn't bother explaining.

"I fucked up. It's almost funny." She leans back and smiles. "I guess that happen enough it don't seem funny anymore. I guess it's not funny when you really are a fuck-up."

She stands up before he can say anything and disappears into the kitchen with the other beers. When she comes back she brings the big boom box with her, plugs it into the wall, and lets the radio sing for them in the background. It sounds like an oldies station, hopeful and harmonic.

"I'm sorry," he tells her. "Maybe I can talk to her about it."

She shakes her head. "That shit ain't gonna go, you know. That world? Come on, now. Look at me."

He looks. "You might be right. But there some things going on you don't know about, so let me talk to her anyway."

"Okay. Talk whatever you want." She smiles, then laughs softly to herself. "You a mess. You should see yourself. Sitting there like you gonna arrange all this and that. What happened out there?"

"I don't know. Some kids. Why'd you lie to me."

"To you? I don't lie to you. You got to know someone to lie to them. I don't even know what you are."

"Drugs," Shane says. The word sits there between them like a bloody glove. "Samson was selling drugs for

Tennessee. Down at the gym. You knew."

Debra rocks slightly in her chair, rubbing her nose gently with her hand as if soothing a slow itch. "Come on now," she says finally, "you know he wasn't no real dealer. You still don't get it, you don't know shit." He doesn't move. "What, he sell a bag or two to keep that punk up off him that make him some b-boy?" she says. "He do a little this that to make some money. What am I gonna tell you?"

"Just the truth."

"Fuck the truth. What truth?" She raises her hand like she's about to dash a delicate and invisible object to the ground. She lets it go. "His whole life, what I tell him? You got to get out of here. You got to stay in school, stay out of trouble, stay alive. And he do. Stay alive up here means stay away. And he do. But you gotta come home sometime. That punk got him clocking down there, you know, selling to the white boys, what's he gonna do? He hate that shit. He playing basketball with y'all, he down at the gym, bringing home some money, being my man of the house at home, sleeping with some faggot cross town. What world is that? How do you explain that when he can't even explain it himself? The truth." She tips back her beer, drains it. "Yeah and I drink. And my shit stink too. The truth. You wouldn't get it you had a thousand years."

"That what you tell Tennessee?" Shane doesn't know where the anger comes from but it's there, rippling through his wounds, throbbing in his hands. "When he says he killed your boy. When he says where the fuck's my money."

"I don't say nothing to him." She looks away, though.

"He just talking. He just looking for a play. He think you the daddy. Yeah. He think he following the money. Samson and his rich white dudes. He like every other nigga up here, just trying to get paid."

"Me."

"I *told* him. But he got these ideas about you and your friend and the rest of y'all at that gym. Y'all got money. I don't know," she says. "I don't know what to do. I'm desperate enough to go down to the Silly Valley, you know I'm desperate. That's the truth."

"What friend. My brother?"

"Naw. That richie rich you come up here with. That black Beemer. Heard about that bling-bling, too, none these niggas ever seen a Rolly like that before. I thought you were with him."

"He's not my friend," Shane says. "And I don't go to that gym."

"See I don't know about that. Talk about drugs, though, you a straight hypocrite. You up here that night. Who buys the drugs? Somebody selling, somebody buying."

"Who do you think I am," Shane says.

"What about your friend? All you all, just use them up and spit them out. All you all."

"Who do you think I am," Shane says again.

She stares at him and then at the carpet, looking for a lost something. "Some guy," she says, finally, in a sad voice. "I don't know." She peeks up at him. "I don't know, I guess you a good man but I just don't know. I don't know you. Maybe you are, maybe you are a good man."

"No," he says. "Look at me. You're right. I'm a fuck-up too. But that's all I am. Just a fuck-up who cleans chimneys and wishes he really knew your Sam and you and everything. But I don't."

"No you don't." She smiles. "I believe you." She watches him as he shakes his empty can, a golden flash of light to distract them both. The last thing he wants to do right now is think.

"Did you take those beers away?" he says.

"Yeah. I shouldn't have done that." She pops out of her seat and disappears, returning with the brown bag. She opens two more beers and they lean together to clink cans, the dull tinny sound making the room seem smaller than it is.

They've been drinking for an hour or so, one tall can after the other. "Were you ever married?" he's asking her. The music keeps on coming, JJ Soul Sounds of the Sixties announcing one hit after another, serving up blasts from the past.

"Nope."

"Do you ever think about it?"

"You proposing? I accept." She grins, smacks the table with her hand a bit too hard, then leans back on the couch, rocking her shoulders to the music. "I'm not opposed to it. But shit, these niggas out here? Getting married ain't any kind of answer. I got to depend on myself before I depend on someone else. And then. And then you got to find one that's worth a damn. The kind that even knows what married means."

"What kind's that?"

"I already told you I accept. Naw, all right, I like 'em a little darker than you, regularly. Let's see, you want the whole list, okay make it tall, dark, good job, don't tell me no all the time, don't tell me yes all the time, be a man, you know. Up here, come on now, man mean in jail or headed there or strung out, you know what I'm saying. Shit. I had me a man until just recent but there's always something. These girls up here they smell one coming around they all around my front door. Batting their eyes and laughing at the spit coming out of his mouth. And he right there grinning and squeezing on them like I ain't even there. No, you go get your own man, know what I'm saying. Finally I just be like uhn-uh, y'all have a good time and good night for real." She smiles. "He try to have it both ways, boy know what he missing but no no no. You don't treat me right, you out." She shakes her head. "Samson didn't like him either."

"No?"

Another can hisses open. "Wooo, Samson don't like any of them. You know, same old story, who gonna be the man of the house. I get a man in here, maybe I don't see my boy for days. But what I gonna do, I can't be waiting for no golden stamp of approval. Shit. You just supposed to be a momma, that's it, right? Well I *am* a momma, but you can't take care of them up here, you can't, you can't." Her voice is riding up thin and high. "You be at it 24/7 and they still disappear on you, still something happens to them. They still clocking or faggots or killed. You don't have no kids, right?"

"Not yet."

"You should have some. You make a good daddy."

"That's what I say."

"But watch out they come back on you. Samson don't like me drinking, don't like anything, he thinks he's my daddy. You gonna be my daddy you better take care of me not the other way around. I go down there to the Monte Carlo to drink some beers, it's fun down there, shooting pool and dancing to the jukebox. And leave him to take care of the kids, he's grown you know, and I come home late? He's waiting up for me, bitch me out, like damn. After that I don't go out no more. But see what happens."

"Where do your kids go?"

"I got a girlfriend she watch them, I do the same for her."

"You got some community up here, then."

"Here? We watch out for each other, there always someone home watching the house but you know, not that you could call close friends. One day they come over and ask for that cup a sugar and then they asking to use your phone and borrow twenty dollars and unh-uh. Best to just be polite you know but mind your own business. This here's just a stop, you know? but I'm getting back on the bus and getting out."

"And they're not?"

"No. That's a different mentality. These girls around here be sitting around gossiping stuff, all day she said she said. That shit's straight-up boring, what it is, like you don't got nothing better to do? I don't play that, best to stay away. Once you get in that shit, uhn-uh. They out there like chicken pecking at every crumb come their way. They don't miss nothing. What, you think it like a country club up here or something, all of us be singing 'We Are the World' and holding hands? Nah, ain't like that. Like that we wouldn't be up here. That's it, you know, people up here I respect they take care their own business and move to the next thing. There was one girl lived here a year ago, JB, she was all right, I liked her, she talk all day but she was a lot of fun, you know, she always dancing and joking around. She just a shit starter, she was a lot of fun. She got out, though. These other ones, they ain't going nowhere, they be out here 'til they tear down these projects and move all these niggas to the next one. And they start the same thing up there. Uhn-uh," she says again, "I don't really be hanging out with anyone around here. I don't got no one, really, when it comes right down to it."

"So you're the only decent shit starter around here now."

"That's right," she says, sliding him another beer.

"I doubt that."

"Who else I got? Oh, I got you, right?" She smiles at him. "You on my team, huh?"

"Yeah. I guess I am."

"Yeah and look at you." she says. "No, I'm playing, that's nice. That's a nice feeling. I mean, when you knocked on the door tonight, I felt bad for you getting jumped you know? I mean you got no business coming around here at night. And under the circumstances. But I was glad to see you anyway." She takes a big long pull on a fresh beer. "You a good one."

"I don't know what I am."

"I see you, you a man but you a good one. No one helped me out with nothing for a long time. You just, you got to be careful. You looked like shit, boy."

"I bet."

"I knew it was you. That's a nice feeling. I forgot. Have someone coming for you, taking care of you."

"I haven't done anything."

"You look all right now. That jaw make you look better, I think. Like you got you some character."

"You're better than all this."

"Shit you talking, you don't think I know that?"

"I just don't know how to."

"You know that you wouldn't be cleaning chimneys would you?"

"Don't know what I'd be doing."

"How old you think I am?"

"You're thirty-four."

"You ain't supposed to get it right."

"Sorry. I did the math."

"Don't look at me like that."

"Like what."

"Like I'm doing something wrong. We all adults here, ain't we?"

"I sure hope so." Lou could be home by now, she could be drunk beneath the great wall of wine. Adults.

"Yeah, you got your ass kicked, I fucked up my best shot for a job in how long, we having some cold ones and chopping it up. Well we almost outta beer and I'm tired of talking and what we do now? You could listen to me talk all night, huh? Or I'm boring you."

"You've never bored me yet."

"I'm boring me. Oooh," she says, pointing into the air. "I like this song. You like this song?"

"Yeah. I like all songs."

That sounds suspicious to her. "You don't like the OJs? Come on now, you don't like the OJs you just don't like music."

"I like them. Sound like the Temptations or something."

"They better than Temptations. Come on now. I grew *up* with this. You ain't too dead you can't dance with me. Now'd you got some character." She turns up the music and drags the coffee table out of the way. He gets his can off it just in time but their empties tumble onto the floor, leaking their last neglected drops into the carpet. They don't seem to care. She dances. She bends her knees and twists and turns in front of him, rolling her shoulders and neck. She stumbles a little to one side and puts out her hand for support and pushes over a cheap standing lamp. The light pops off in a death flash as it hits the ground and they both laugh. It's dark now except for the light from the kitchen and hall, throwing her long shadow against the beat-up wall. She turns her back to him and dances with her own shadow while he watches her thighs and ass and then she whirls around and catches him looking. She laughs and puts her hands on either side of her breasts, runs her own hands down her body.

"I want to see *you* dance," she says, laughing as if that might be about the funniest thing in the world. She reaches down and takes his hands, pulls him to his feet. If his body hurts he can't feel it anymore. She keeps dancing. He stands there, watching her, still touching hands while she moves and waits.

"Oh so you don't dance, huh," she says. Her mouth is close to him and serious as she moves his hands to her hips where his thumbs slip under her shirt to meet soft skin as she leans in and presses her breasts against his chest and keeps dancing. She can feel him hard against her and maybe his heartbeat too as she keeps her eyes on his. "Can't dance, got nothing to say."

"I want this." He can barely hear his own voice.

"I know it, I know, I want this too." She takes his good hand and moves it down between her legs. Her mouth hisses in the air next to his ear. "I need this, I need to feel this."

"Jesus."

"Yeah."

"I need to fuck you."

"Oh yeah," she says, "definitely."

***

He's thought about that sex long before it happens: Debra and him half-drunk and desperate on the worn rug of her living room. But even though he's already fucked her about twenty times in his head, twenty times in all the ways he could think of as he's stood in the shower at home, it still surprises him. All those times, in all the ways he could think of, but there are details he hasn't thought of. How she smells when she sweats, something fruit fermenting in the sun. How long and strong her fingers are. How it would hurt. He can't imagine what it would be like to fuck like this all the time, absolutely without shame. They break things. They lose their minds—lose them, two bodies flopping around without a working mind between them. He doesn't believe you can live like that. He guesses people don't.

They say nothing that whole time, except for once when he is sitting on the edge of the coffee table while she sits on top of him. It's muscular, this configuration, he holds her absolutely in with his arms looped under her thighs and her hands linked loosely behind his neck, she lets him have her weight as he moves her up and down. She slumps on him like a body you had to carry from a fire except for her hips which never stop moving. Maybe she thinks he is getting tired, or is going too fast, but suddenly she says in a sort of sad voice: "Don't."

"No," he says, and it doesn't matter if they know what they are talking about or not. Whatever it is, he won't do it, there is nothing more important than that. His body is his body. She knows it, and he knows it too: their bodies are the one thing that can't, won't let them down.

Eventually they go to bed. She is sleeping, soon. The whole thing is so peaceful. If you paint the walls in there, replace the dresser, put in a couple lamps beside the bed, hang a picture or two on the wall, some new curtains, it could be just another bedroom anywhere at all. Outside is quiet, an occasional car going by but not much more than that. He thinks about Tennessee, this kid who grew up calling her auntie and flashes his gun sometimes and teases her because she isn't buying. Auntie, auntie, what you need. You sell drugs and save up enough money to build a house for your parents back in the homeland, back in mythic Tennessee, and your parents leave while you stay in San Francisco in the projects doing what you do best. What a crazy story—Tennessee. He'll be dead soon, Shane thinks. I can just drive away tomorrow and never come back but he stays until someone kills him. It's quiet out there right now, Shane thinks, maybe he's closed up shop for the night, maybe he's sleeping too. Shane wonders if the kid's surprised every time he walks out there through the broken glass and gloom to take his rightful place: holy shit, check it out, another day.

Maybe an hour passes, or maybe twenty minutes of brief blackout death, and then he's awake again, sitting on the edge of her bed, listening to the quiet of the house and the world outside. He feels wide awake, like he's slept in his own bed for eight hours with his own wife in his own life and just now popped up before the alarm to face another day out there in the world. But instead he lives here with his three children and his missing son and robber punks and dope dealers and his woman lying still behind him with one long leg thrown over the top of the covers. There's blood on the sheets, his blood. Her foot is there beside him and he watches that still foot with the long toes and the dark creases of the knuckles and the light white brown of the bottoms of her feet. He reaches out and takes her foot in his good hand, feels its weight and substance, and then runs his hand up over the bony ankle, her long calf, the soft back of her knee, her back and then the inside of her thigh and then he takes his hands off her and watches the rest of the way up her body to her head buried in a tumble toss of pillow and sheet. What's it like inside that head? What happens in there that's different from what happens in his head or Ma's or Lou's or Jimmy's or Samson's? He wants to go in there and gather up everything he can find, all at once, spill her thoughts and memories at his feet and go through them one by one. And he wants to do it right here and now because he wants to know what will happen if he stays.

This is where he could belong, after all.

Instead he fishes around the dark floor until he finds his clothes. Everything aches, muscles and bones and hair and eyes, and his knee especially feels too big to be right. By the time he gets dressed and turns back to Debra she's expanded to fill that space he's left, stretched out luxuriously across the full acreage of the bed just like Lou does. Just as Lou is maybe doing now as he slips out of Debra's room and walks downstairs. The place is a mess. He straightens out the living room, opens the windows a crack to let the place air out, moves the coffee table back where it belongs. He goes into the kitchen with the beer cans and puts them in a trash bag to take them with him and throw them out. Samson watches him from his picture on the fridge, following his movements around the room. The kid doesn't look happy to see him. He isn't happy to see Samson either, to tell the truth.

"I don't know Sam," he tells him. "I don't really know."

Then he's limping out into the lightening lot where it's too early or late even for muggers, dealers, druggies, con artists, respectable citizens, or the walking dead. He is the only one out there as the sun comes up, and he drives off that hill to find the strongest cup of coffee in the universe and a *Chronicle* and a tall glass of fresh-squeezed orange juice and maybe a toasted sesame bagel with whipped cream cheese. If he can find all that and sit down for a minute in some place where other people are doing the same, it seems possible that he might be just another citizen out there going to work, starting his day. There is a cleaning to do in the morning and then he has to go the hardware store for some supplies and the rest of the day he'll stay busy on the rebuild. It's Friday, he thinks, as he drives off the hill and back into the city just waking up around him. He smiles, catching a glimpse of his dark scraped-up face in the rear view mirror. Friday, a basketball day.

20

AT HIGH NOON big Rex stands at center court with the ball on his hip, grinning at him in the straight-down sunshine as the other team goes scuffling off the court, mumbling mild murder to one another. They are killing today, Shane is killing, he's having one of those days. Ten, twelve, twenty days in his life like that. He shouldn't even be on the court, he can barely run, he looks terrible, he hasn't slept, he hurts, but there he is hitting ridiculous shots fading right and left and away, with guys hanging all over him. Brett holding his shirt and Brian clobbering his shoulder caveman style and Dragon belly bumping him in the lane. It doesn't matter. His knee doesn't work right. It doesn't matter. Even D-One can't stop him today.

Shane stands near the sideline breathing hard, his face slack, his muscles loose at rest. Jimmy comes up alongside him, reaches out like he's going to whack him amiably on the butt but halts mid-blow. He looks *that* fragile, like one little push might knock him down. His knee is definitely swollen and there are bruises on his thighs, a skinned elbow and of course the knuckles. His jaw looks like someone ran him over with a pair of baseball spikes. But what a game.

"You gonna tell me?" his brother asks. No one else out there has got an answer out of him. "What the hell happened to you?"

He begins his lie and then just stops, shrugs his shoulders. "Hard living," he tells him.

Jimmy cracks up. It's all about the skins and scrapes, Jimmy hasn't noticed his knee, none of them have, for some reason it functions fine with adrenaline on the court. "I should see the other guy, right?"

"Can I play ball or what. Goddamn I'm good sometimes."

"You're gonna suck tomorrow."

"Yeah."

"That baseline spin? That was too sweet. You never spin right. Where the hell did that come from?"

"It's true. I'm amazing."

"Oh right. I forget."

Nearby, the guys are howling and slapping Dragon on the back. They point at Shane and Jimmy to summon them over.

"We gonna plant that tree for real, now," Rex tells them. "Dragon's gonna be a daddy."

They stare at Dragon. "The cycle of life," he says,

nodding. "I'm all knocked up and shit." He passes a celebratory marijuana pipe, sending blue smoke floating through the air.

Shane steps to him and shakes his hand, a proper shake. "A daddy."

"That's right."

"Daddy Dragon."

"When's baby Dragon?"

"Six months."

"That's six months you better get your ball in," says Rex, taking a generous pull on Dragon's pipe. "You're gonna straight-out disappear for a while. Lock you in the kiddy crypt." Rex has juniors, two of them, he knows.

"What about J? He brings his little kids up here." It's true—J's an occasional, but he brings his kids in tow, two small boys and a world of toys to keep them occupied. Bikes and skateboards and whiffle balls and remote control motorcycles, whatever.

"Yeah" Rex says, "but you got to get 'em to that age first. It's all good, but for fact, for a while, the game has got to suffer."

"That's what I hear. However, I have made sure to work basketball in my prepaternal contract."

"Oh yeah, you'll see about that."

"I imagine I may disappear for a little while to tend my litter. But I will be back." The Dragon shakes his fist at the sky. "Oh yes. I will return in all my daddy glory."

"You gonna return all saggy-eyed and blood-drained, brother. You gonna return a broken man. But you will rise again." Rex is laughing now, smiling. "It's the best damn thing in the world, man, get yourself a couple beautiful babies, 'bout the only thing worth missing a game or two." He reaches out a big hand, the two of them slap, hold, release.

"It's my kid," Dragon says. "A boy."

"A boy."

Dragon nods. "I was down in Daly City yesterday, they got this plant nursery? So that's it, enough tree talk. I bought us a live oak."

"Live oak? Aw man, that thing get so big? Shadow the whole court."

"What about the bronze loquat?" Jimmy says.

"Fuck loquat. Live oak's the original."

"Yeah," Dragon says. "Plus I'm buying, so we're gonna plant that sonofabitch."

"When?"

"Tuesday."

"I don't know, is this a good time for planting trees?"

"Why not? Rain's coming."

"Gives a shit. We're up here three times a week, we'll just water that bitch. It's all about water, right?"

"My kid," Dragon says, "he'll be griping about this big-ass tree next to the court, throwing shade, messing with his game. I'm talking a big live oak, get all gnarled, gnarled and crafty. Nasty ants crawling all over it. I can't wait. Why you plant that stupid tree there, dad? All us over here sitting under the branches scratching our balls and yelling at our kids to shut yer damn piehole, play some ball! This here's your daddies' court, you should have a little goddamned respect!"

"Respect? Shit, we'll still be kicking their ass."

"Who got winners?"

"We do, always."

"That's what I'm saying."

"What about the park guys? They let us plant a tree?"

"I'll know a guy in Park and Rec," D-One says. "I'll talk to him."

"After all these years, they should know who we are."

"I bet they do."

"We're probably in the official record."

"Pictures of sexy Rexy in some file down at City Hall."

"And we gonna have a tree now."

"'Bout time."

They give Dragon another round of congratulations and then begin to leave, fading off the court back to wherever it is they go. Somewhere Lou is tucking her hair back behind her ears with a thin black pen. Somewhere Samson is dead or hiding or just plain gone.

"Pick me up tomorrow," his brother yells, as if nothing's changed.

"Okay." Shane realizes he's the last one standing there, the one with nowhere else to go.

Jimmy pauses. "Really, man, you look like shit."

"I'm all right."

"Okay. Well. Try not to fall off the roof."

Shane crosses himself, the force of habit. Only habit will get him through this day. "See you tomorrow," he says.

***

He does the work. He goes back to the guy's house and puts his hands into the guts of the house and does the work. The old lawyer doesn't ask him why he looks like he does. The lawyer doesn't know him and must figure that whoever he is these are the kinds of things that happen to him on a Thursday night. For the first time, Shane wishes the guy would ask. Right about now, Shane feels ready to sit in a client's kitchen after work, drinking a cold beer, talking about his fight last night and the dude's first wife and prostate trouble and whatever it is people talk about. He checks the time often as the day wears on, making sure to leave before any possible dinner time.

She isn't home yet and he goes down to the store and gets stuff to make that Thai soup with shrimp that never comes out as good as the one you can buy right down the street for $7.95. The house starts smelling good, though, especially when he sautées the shrimp shells pink to start the broth. And then in go the little hard disks of lemongrass, too. While it simmers he limps around the apartment a little bit and is surprised that it doesn't look any different to him. He looks it over piece by piece, remembering the day they decided to rent it together, the thousand things wrong with the place. I'm game, he said. Ain't no thing but a chicken wing, she said. But it was. Three days, long weekend, he sanded floors, she painted. An argument over stains and colors. They worked hard, they both know how to work hard. Encrusted in sawdust, he'd turn off the machine and brush the yellow out of his hair and slip into the next room to watch her rolling paint. Would we do that now, he wonders, work on a rented house together? Would we suspend our disbelief?

He takes a shower and stands out on the little front porch, watching the city. He sees all the little squares of light that mean people working, there are the cars locked in traffic as they try to cross the bridge, there's the Mission filling up with weekend fun, there's Potrero Hill. He wonders what he's going to say. He doesn't know. To the south, the airplanes launch steadily west into the sun, gliding over the trembling line of hills that rip an uneven edge across the sky. Down below the fog moves in a thin low column, slipping through the hilly gaps like Pharaoh's deadly curse. He can't see it but he knows above his head the fog is also pouring over Twin Peaks, gathering in a wave about to break over their place. It *is* beautiful here, he thinks, even now. You can always see something—you can see the end of the world.

He's back in the kitchen draining the broth and putting it back to simmer when he hears the front door open and slam shut and the clip clip clip of heels on the stairs that slow as they get closer. Clip. Clip. She hesitates and then turns before she hits the kitchen, her steps turning silent on the soft carpet of their bedroom. He watches the discarded solids steaming in the colander, dripping to the sink. He seasons the broth. She stands in the kitchen doorway, examining him.

"And there you are," she says. She's taken off her shoes and socks.

"I'm sorry." They seem like the only words he knows.

"Are you hurt?"

"Not really. I'm sorry," he says again.

She keeps looking at him, eyes to mouth and back again. He can't look at her but he can't look away from her either.

"What the fuck, Shane?" she says, finally. "What the fuck?"

"I got robbed. They took my cell phone. My wallet."

"Where were you?"

"They beat me up."

"Where?"

"The projects. I went to the projects."

Eyes. Mouth. Eyes. "I don't understand what you're saying." It's true, he can see it, his words mean nothing. "What the hell are you saying? Look at me."

He looks at her. "I went to see Debra Marks. That's where I went."

"You went. Ah. Okay."

He wonders why they don't have a pet. They could have a pet right now and it could trot up loving innocent between them, their hands dropping to its sleek fur flank. They could stroke its head and butt and watch it wiggle hedonistically oblivious, taking all the love it could get. It'd start purring now. It'd start barking hard when things go wrong.

"Why couldn't you just." He wants to hit her and hit himself, he wants to hit. "The woman. You interviewed."

"I know who Debra Marks is."

"No," he says. "You don't. You have no idea." He tastes the broth. He has to put something in his mouth. It's his best one that he can remember, with enough sweet and sour and spice and salt.

She takes the two steps across the room and knocks the spoon out of his hand and grabs the pot with both hands. He sees it in her eyes: the reflexive panic of dousing a fire, the boiling caldron splashing over him, bubbling his flesh up in welts. Do it, he thinks. Just do it. She hesitates, she's almost going to do it and then in one sudden movement she dumps it into the sink. The hot broth spills up over the sink, sprinkling his arm and splattering onto the floor. She jumps back with her bare feet, yelping twice. He watches her through the sudden cloud of steam, not moving to change anything at all.

She runs. She runs down the hall with a wordless high-pitched whine and slips into the bathroom and slams the door behind her. The faucet of the bathtub comes on. He stands outside the door and listens to the water and her crying. It's a deep sound, deeper than he remembers, air groaning out of the chest and stomach. He goes back to the kitchen and gets some ice out of the freezer and wraps it up in a plastic bag. There's no way for her to lock the door.

She's sitting on the edge of the bathtub, her feet in the tub under the running water. Her back to him. She doesn't turn around.

"Are you all right?"

"Get out."

"There's some ice."

"Get out."

"I'm going to. I brought you some ice." He drops it into the tub and it clangs loudly, sliding down the incline toward her feet.

"Don't you dare," she says, "don't you dare take care of me." She spins around to face him, her feet dripping water onto the white tile floor. Her feet are splotchy red in places. He feels relief. They don't look too badly burned. "Ever again," she says.

"I have to."

"Bullshit. Get out of here. Out!"

He takes a step back. He's getting out. He doesn't want to go but he doesn't know how to stay either.

"Say something," she says, "for chrissake open that fucking mouth of yours and say something! What's wrong with you?"

He shakes his head. He wants to ask her the same thing. "You don't need me," he says instead.

"That's what's wrong with you? That's what you came back to tell me? To tell me what I need?"

He hasn't come back to tell her that. He's come back to tell her all the other things, about how he's missed her, how he's lost her, how he's been longing for the present to end and for the future or past to begin or return. He's come back to lie about where he's been and what he's done and felt. He's come back to tell her what he needs.

And instead he says, "No. But you don't."

***

He is playing basketball in the dark, alone, at the Fire-house court. Never been there at night. There are no lights except for the ones from the street and a little something from the undulating city all around. The city is one sexy little critter from here, with the white and yellow lights in all its hilly directions, and the fireflies of the cars on the 101 cutting north and south through town. If they'd known about this court in high school, they would have come up here, he and his buddies, to get high and drink beer and huddle up to girls who'd want to go somewhere warm inside. Maybe on the weekends, maybe if he came up Saturday night there'd be some troubled teens doing just that.

He's working on his jump shot. It's a decent jumper, but one of the things he realized during his recovery was that his mechanics aren't all they could be. He's learned that when he jumps his body contracts and then expands but forgets to contract again when he hits the ground, so he hits the ground too straight, an iron pole absorbing the full force of weight and gravity through his feet and knees and back. This is probably why he got hurt, eventually. So he works on that. Crouches down and jumps, expands his body all the way, reaches for the rim and lets the ball go, and then begins contracting even before he touches down. His feet hit toe to heel and his knees bend and his hips sink down a little and then he's ready to jump again. His knee hurts plenty when he does this, but as he gets warm the pain starts to blend in and fade away.

It's hard work in the dark, although with the moon

and the city behind him he can faintly see the rim against the dark shape of the cliff behind and that's all he needs to see. His body knows the distances and what to do but then he starts concentrating on his body and the sudden awareness does him in. Now the ball goes long or short or wild left or right. He shoots terribly like that for more than an hour until he smells his own sweat again and feels his hands black with the night court dust. He stops and rests, holding his hands out away from him as if they're covered in blood. Then he goes back down to the van where he spits on his hands, rubs them clean together, and wipes them on a cloth before driving across the city to the nearest point of no return.

21

IT'S ALMOST MIDNIGHT when he parks the van in front of Fulton's house and sits there watching the dark front windows. Maybe no one is home but from being in there before he knows there might be a big ol' party out back and from the street you wouldn't know. A formal house, in that way, to conceal the private goings-on inside.

He takes out his new cell phone and makes the call and listens to the phone ring out, imagining the atoms that go up into the universe and then down again to land in the house across the street from where he sits. It rings a few times and then Fulton's voice is low and kind, asking him to leave a message. He doesn't. He disconnects and the phone winks off into darkness as he sits there listening to the late-night sports radio and thinking.

Fulton might be out of town. The man might stay out all night, he might be over at a girlfriend's or boyfriend's, he might be in a swank or sordid hotel room somewhere. Sex and drugs and rock 'n' roll. He might be gliding up the street any minute in his big black BMW, slipping into the auto-open gates of the garage that will swallow up the car and close to resume the compound's dark impassive front. Might be inside with the music cranked up or taking a crap or fast asleep.

Shane tries calling the house again and then gets out of the van and sticks his flashlight and prybar in his belt. He waits for a car to pass and then walks up to the front of Fulton's house and climbs up quickly onto the garage roof, moving from hold to hold: gas meter, window, gutter, ledge. It takes about ten seconds to go up one side and then he jumps down the other. Everything hurts as he lands, and he sits down for a moment, waiting for the pain to pass. He helps himself up and walks into the backyard slowly. The back is dark, a lone light squinting somewhere from the middle of the house. The kitchen, perhaps. He watches for a while but there's no one moving inside. He fishes the painter's ladder out of the bushes, extends it out to it fullest height. Then he climbs onto the roof and pulls the ladder up behind him.

Standing on the roof crest, he looks out over the city. It looks big tonight, big and cohesive, like a single organism with a million winking moving parts. The hip bone's connected to the eye bone. He has seen this city for thirty years, he can name every hill and neighborhood, most of the streets. Lou is over there; Ma is over there; Debra's over there. He knows the city's parts but the sum is no longer known to him. The sum is up for grabs. The sum is what all of them are trying to figure out.

You can do almost anything on a roof. You can stay there as long as you want because up is the direction of disappearance. No one remembers to look up. He puts his ear to Fulton's back chimney, listening for life. The chimney roars with the memory of a thousand fires, like an ocean in a seashell. He tightropes to the front chimney and listens there. He bends over and puts his whole head inside. Lou thought he should dress up in a Santa suit around Christmas one year, give everyone a kick—a rooftop Santa peering down the mouths of chimneys. Santa must be a tiny little person. Sweeps used to send little boys to crawl inside once, but no one can fit in chimneys these days.

He squats beside the single attic window. It won't be alarmed, he thinks, all the way up here and hidden almost completely from view. The wood and metal is old and after five minutes of patient work with the prybar he's snug inside.

The attic has a trapdoor with a retracting ladder that opens with a loud crack, dumping dust into the hallway below. He doesn't climb down right away, dangling his head down through the hole like an inverse periscope. *Hello hello*, he says in a funny voice, but no one's there to answer. No one's there to laugh at his little joke. He climbs down into the hallway and stands there holding the prybar in one hand like a bloody knife. You could sink the single metal tooth deep into someone's skull and that would probably do. That would probably take care of things. He heads toward the bedroom, catching a glimpse of himself in a mirror as he passes. Oooh, tough guy, he thinks. What are you up to, tough guy.

He finds what he thinks he's looking for immediately. There on the dresser, side by side, rests the gold and blue lapis watch and another one in platinum with diamonds crowded all around the bezel rim. Lord knows what Fulton's wearing tonight. What else he has around. He starts sifting through the drawers. Clothes are folded in that expert way of people who fold clothes for a living. In one of the drawers he finds some diamond cuff links and a ring. There's a stupid-looking pen that looks like it might be worth something too. Bling-bling. That's enough. He'd prefer to find a large stack of hundred dollar bills, but for now this is probably enough.

He stands at the foot of the bed and pictures the two of them in there, bumping and grinding or maybe just at rest. Later they arrange themselves impeccably side by side, preparing for a party. The man has a new watch, bigger and brighter than ever before and the woman wears an emerald pendant at her neck to match her happy eyes.

He rests on the bed for a while, leaning back against the pillows, propping his dusty boots one on top of the other on the pale green spread. The details of the room itself are a mix of past and present: the high wood molding, the classy baseboards, the small Neo-Logic lights, the seamless closet door leading off to yards of fine Italian fabric. The old world and the new world have been thoughtfully combined, but there is nothing Fulton about this room. Take away his personal ornaments, stuff your pockets with his watches, cuff links, pen, and ring. There's nothing left. The bedside table has no pictures, no knickknacks, not even a clock. The blown-up, framed satellite photos of San Francisco and New York and London are clever and edgy to a tee. Shane sits up and opens the little drawer, looking for something decadent and base: condoms, lubricant, molded plastic. A notebook, loose change, receipts. Instead he reaches in and picks up a thin gold chain. He holds it glinting up to the muted tasteful overhead lights, then pulls out the drawer and dumps everything on the bed. He throws the drawer across the room, watching it bounce off the wall. It leaves a gash in the plaster.

On the bedspread beside him, among the other trophies—a woman's wedding band, surfer boy beads, some trashy plastic earrings—lies the cheap watch, looking small and shriveled in its worn leather strap. He runs his thumb along the leather. All those years we told Sam not to wear it, Shane thinks, but he never hurt anyone, never grazed the metal across your face or caught the buckle against your shorts or skin. He was right. He shouldn't ever take it off. He holds the gold chain in one hand and the watch in the other. That poor motherfucker, he thinks. Did he think he might find refuge here?

Shane walks into the master bathroom and washes his face. He stares at his damp features in the mirror. It reminds him of being fifteen years old, drunk and stoned, trying to pull your shit together before you dared go home. That feeling of not knowing who you were but looking for yourself anyway in the center of your own pupils, trying to peer into your own head. He stares. Soon, in a week or two, he will be in the van again rising up and up the steep tilted slope, keeping the pedal steady as the once and future cons hop off their hoods and stoops and come running for him, what you need what you need, cursing him because he doesn't need anything except one last safe passage in and out of this place he's never once belonged. He will park the van near her door and watch out for Tennessee and hurry in with his big toolbox filled with money. Maybe there won't be much to say. She will be happy or mad to see him or maybe she won't care one way or another. They will sit on different couches, watching television with the kids until she puts them up to bed.

"I don't have anywhere else to go," he'll say.

"Well you can't stay here." She will wait for him to budge and when he doesn't she will shrug as if she knew this all might happen. "Just tonight. I'll get you a blanket," she will say, shaking her head as if he's one more kid she has to put to bed. He will settle into the ratty couch, listening to her door click shut behind her.

Sometime in the early lightless morning someone will come into the living room. Shane will not hear him or see him or smell him but he will know that he's there. His gaze will be a cool smooth metal ball resting on Shane's temple, and even as sense and power begin to trickle back into his muscles, the weight of this look will pin his head back against the sofa cushions. He will hear the footsteps fading, crossing the linoleum of the kitchen, but by the time Shane gets there that room will be empty too. Then Shane will step down the hall and open the door to Debra's room.

The kid will be wearing what he always wears: the sweatpants with the stripe down the side, the matching lightweight jacket, the white long-sleeved shirt beneath. The thin gold chain looking loose around his neck, the cheap watch with the leather band clinging to his wrist. His face will bunch up in the middle, all frown and forehead and tight jaw wrinkles. His hair cut millimeter-short. His shoulders will slump down and his arms will hang long at his side. The kid will not look at Shane at all. He will look down at his mom, sprawled out there in the sheets, her thigh and haunch exposed. The son will reach down as if to cover her, his hand stopping short of the bed and retreating at the last minute. His face will relax. He'll look so young, he'll look like his ten-year-old brother upstairs just blown up a bit for size. He's a funny-looking kid but with his face relaxed and in that dark room light he'll look almost handsome. Shane will watch him watch her sleep, and then Samson's head will turn quickly as if he's heard a sound. His eyes will travel around the room from the wall to the dresser, to the clothes stacked on the chair beside the bed, until finally they will come back to the doorway and settle upon Shane. The kid will stare at him and then shake his head. Come on, Sam's head will say. Come on outside, come with me. He will nod come on again and then look at his mom and turn around and brush past him out of the room.

Shane will lie there on that ratty sofa and open his eyes and close them and open them again. He will get up slowly, carefully, fishing around on the floor to find his clothes. Put on his pants, his shirt, his dirty socks, his stained work boots. He will go to the front door and unlock it and step forward and look around. There will be no one there. The van will sit waiting, nervous for its windows, like a horse tied up outside the trouble saloon.

"I'm coming," Shane will say. "Okay? You hear that, I'm going. I'm gone."

He will search around the kitchen for a piece of paper and write Debra a note. He will not write that he'll miss her or think about her or remember her or anything like that. Instead he will write:

> *I'm sorry about everything, and I'm sorry Samson's dead. Please take this and take care and go as fast and far away as you can. Please don't look back or come back. I won't follow or come or call again. I know it's not this simple, but I hope you make it. I think you will.*

He will not sign it. He will pull the money from the toolbox, $10,000, the most he could get for Fulton's things. He will pull out the thin gold chain and the watch. Then he will place everything neatly on the kitchen table and walk outside and never see any of them again.

His knuckles are turning white from gripping the bathroom sink, and he relaxes, runs one hand through his short hair. A car honks noisily outside, and he freezes again, caught in the headlights of someone coming home. But the honk fades away as the car passes. Not this time. He thinks about it: I could wait here for him. I could make him tell the story: when he picked him up, what they did, how he spit him out again. How many he toyed with, these years, how many white ones, brown ones, boys, girls, how many wives, how many poor ones, rich ones. The story of Fulton's pleasures. And then I can tell him a story too. I can fight or flee or burn the house down. If I wasn't such a coward, he thinks, I would kill him just because someone else should have to die. But that would be simply damage, wouldn't it. That might feel great but it wouldn't do a single person any good. Still, he thinks. Still.

He opens Fulton's medicine cabinet, the door gliding open on expensive hinges. It's a minor pharmaceutical treasure trove in there. Did Samson take some too, that night? Did he think he might find refuge here? Sure: the rich pleasure-seeking savior probably doesn't even remember his name. A fuck, a toke, a snort, another night gone by, while Sam slinks off stoned to wander into that tunnel, sick of this shit, heartbroke, head broke. Shane grabs a couple bottles for good measure, without any particular reason. Although he hurts. He does hurt, he takes a pill and cups his hands with water to wash it down. Maybe tomorrow, maybe tomorrow I'll need something to take an edge off the pain. Or maybe seven months from now, when business is slow, and Lou does not exist anymore except as a distant voice on the phone. He'll be sitting in his childhood home at sunset, the phone tucked under his chin, talking to his wife. They will call each other. They'll have to. Every couple weeks or so, a brief or medium-length conversation, avoiding both the future and the past. Maybe she'll never know why Fulton quits her board or what her husband did that night. Maybe she'll never know the full extent of Shane or Fulton's sins. She won't care. She'll have other things to worry about. Her business world, the whole world, will be a very different place then, crowded with failing falling stars, companies winking out one by one, their Web sites going dark. Her own company will change its suffix from Dot-Com to Technologies and step up layoffs as they count their ten months left of money. The city will slowly shrink again as the people leave, as the jobs disappear. Lou will explain these things on the phone and a mystery pill and an Anchor Steam will taste good right about then. They will agree they miss each other although they'll both know some things haven't changed. In their different ways, neither of them will trust the other, and at that moment this will be all they need to know. Nothing is final. You can always do something about it, or go down trying.

He's trying. He is sitting on the stairway now, gazing out over Fulton's house as if it were his own. Maybe he won't ever want her back. Maybe that's his not-so-secret secret. Maybe he will live a simple life, move back in with Ma for a while, play ball, clean chimneys. Maybe he will hire a couple guys to help him. Yeah. He will hire a kid from the projects, take some fucked kid with nothing going for him up on the roof and show him how the spines of houses work. The kid will be like a son to him, they'll go up to the court together at noon to play some ball, the kid will fuck him over one day and steal his tools, beat him, kill him, rob him blind. He doesn't know. Look at him, here and now. He obviously doesn't know.

A car engine lingers close outside again, a satisfied purr of coming home. Shane stands up sharply, floats down the stairs, jogs down the hallway to the front of the house. He peeks out the windows there but he can't see what's going on. This might be Fulton pulling in right now, there might be one last chance to get out the door and gone. Walk briskly down the sidewalk as the man climbs the steps to his own front door. A car door slams shut, an alarm does its two-tone beep. Maybe he's walking toward the door right now where there will be no choice but to meet Shane face to face. Shane grabs the door handle, putting his weight against it, holding it tight. They can meet there on the stairs and just destroy each other. It's easy. You can break your foot, you can rip down a chimney just like that but to rebuild the goddamn thing? You don't have to be a chimney sweep, you don't have to play basketball, you don't have to be a husband, you don't have to be anything. Those are the choices, but you have to choose. You must.

When *is* the best time for planting trees? he wonders. He opens the door.

ACKNOWLEDGMENTS

This book would be dead pulp and ink without my main man Ethan Remmel, friend since fifth grade whom I trust and love and count on, off and on the court. And the rest of my boys from States and Grattan—you know who you are.

I also want to thank the friends who have made my San Francisco—Sarah Malarkey and Jonathan Kaplan, Lindsay and Wally Sablosky, Michael Terrien and Hannah Henry, Larry Shadt and Claudine Friedberg, Jon Burke and Tami Lipsey, Catherine Generackos and Nick Denton and many many others. You are all the world to me, and don't let nobody tell you different.

Finally, I am deeply grateful to Jay Mandel, David Poindexter, Anika Streitfeld, Evelyn Somers, Steve Elliott, Jeff Friedman, William H., Bridget W., and everyone else who helped bring this book to life and keep me going—especially my parents, my sister, and my one true love, Meredith McMonigle.